Finding Home

ANGELA HARTLEY

Angela Hartley

This book is a work of fiction. Names, places, characters and events are all based on the author's imagination or are used fictitiously. Any resemblance to actual persons, living or dead, or actual events is purely coincidental.

Edition 3: October 2022

ISBN: 9798830339506

Cover design by Aubrey Labitigan Jai Design

Finding Home

I want to thank my family and friends for all the support they have provided me throughout the process of writing this book.

Being there to read, comment, edit or just bringing me the occasional cup of tea has been invaluable and has kept me going. Also, without their encouragement I would never have had the confidence to self-publish this book, which for me started as just a hobby during lockdown.

I hope you enjoy reading Finding Home as much as I have enjoyed writing it.

Finally, I want to dedicate this book to my mum. She inspired me to be a reader, and without that love of reading, I would never have discovered the joy of writing.

Angela Hartley

Chapter 1
Spring 2018

It was one of those cold, miserable early spring days when even the sun had not had the decency to make an appearance. The kind of day when you just want to hunker down and cosy up on the sofa in front of the fire, with a hot chocolate and a good book for company. As Amanda Reynolds stared at herself in the dressing table mirror, the woman staring back at her was not someone she recognised. Gone was her usual rosy glow and carefree smile, replaced by a drawn complexion with a sad and faraway expression. Her long blonde curly hair, normally worn loose to half-way down her back, had been neatly arranged in a tight knot under a small pillbox-style hat with a cropped black veil, shielding eyes that normally had a glint in them bright enough to light up the national grid, but today had lost their sparkle.

'Are you nearly ready? The car will be here in a minute,' she heard her husband Damian calling from the hallway downstairs.

Amanda, realising what time it was, quickly pulled back from her thoughts and concentrated on the day ahead. She applied her lip-gloss, picked up her bag and slowly raised herself from the dressing-table stool; steadying herself as she took a final glance in the full-length mirror, before making her way out of the bedroom door. Her legs felt like jelly; the act of putting one foot in-front of the other suddenly feeling like too much of an effort.

Her husband Damian Reynolds was waiting for her at the bottom of the stairs with his coat already on and Amanda's long black coat casually held out in his arms ready for her to step into. Damian went to work dressed smartly most days, with the exception of dress down Fridays, so did not look at all out of place in his dark tailored suit, but today there just seemed to be a little more polish than normal to his appearance, recognising the importance of the occasion.   At just shy of six-foot tall, with an athletic body and broad shoulders, Damian was a confident, good-looking man, comfortable in his own skin. With his dark hair and deep blue eyes, he had the natural ability to turn heads without really putting his mind to it.

Amanda carefully came down the stairs, allowing Damian to help her into her cashmere overcoat, giving him an encouraging smile and a gentle hug in the process.   Damian thought Amanda looked beautiful in her black calf length dress, fitted perfectly to accentuate her figure with the high-heeled pumps making her legs look much longer than her five-foot, five inches would suggest. Gone was her normal casual look of jeans and sloppy jumpers, essential daywear when coping with two small daughters and teaching Art to sixth form students; replaced by a glamour and sophistication that he had not seen in a long while.

Damian was proud of how Amanda had dealt with all the challenges of the recent weeks, how she had kept herself strong and focused, balancing the demands of a career, husband and two young daughters alongside dealing with the anxieties of her parents as they went through such a difficult time. Today was going to be especially difficult emotionally for her, and he recognised he needed to be there to provide the support she would undoubtably require, not just today but over the weeks and months to come.

'I'm here, don't worry, we'll get through this,' Damian smiled. 'Everything's going to be fine. You're a lot stronger than you think,' he added in his most reassuring tone, taking his wife's hand in his, gently leading her to the waiting car for the short drive to the church. Amanda allowed her husband to guide her, thankful that she had him to lean on and to trust, to be on her side no matter what. They had been married for just under seven years and had fallen into a comfortable relationship over that time, the early flushes of youthful romance swapped for the joys and demands of parenting.

As the limousine drove the short distance to the Catholic Church of St Anthony's where Amanda and her family had regularly worshipped, and where she and Damian had been married, she tried hard to conjure up happy memories to keep herself focused and keep the tears at bay. She recalled the pride on her dad's face as he had walked her down the aisle, the many games she had played with friends in the playground at the Junior school adjoining the church where she had gone from aged four to eleven, and the baptisms of both their daughters, the most recent only last year, at which her parents and grandad had almost self-combusted, so proud were they to be grand-parents and great-grandparents again.

Both her mum and dad were stalwarts of the Parish, so it was not surprising to see so many people congregating outside the church as the limousine approached, quietly pulling up outside the church gates. Many of the faces she recognised, but now was not the time to be tested on any of their names. It all felt a bit of a blur. Friends she had known from growing up in the village had gathered, along with neighbours and other parishioners who had been close to her parents, all wrapped up against the cold of the day in their sombre clothes, just glad the rain had not arrived.

Her mum who lived at the opposite end of the village from Amanda had opted to travel separately to the church with Grandad Tom – her dad's father, who himself lived so close to the church that a car was not really necessary, but had wanted to be included anyway.

They were just getting out of their car as Amanda's car pulled in. Amanda was pleased to see that her mum's sister Aunt Jane and her daughter, Amanda's cousin Clara were getting out of the car too. They had only flown over from America the previous evening to attend the funeral. Amanda had not had chance to speak to Clara yet, but hoped they were staying over for a few days to give them time to catch up. The two cousins were close, well as close as you can be with an ocean between you. There was no doubting they were related and could easily be mistaken for sisters themselves; both looked similar, blonde, tall and attractive.

The two sisters looked thoughtful and composed as they stood by the car surveying the scene, comfortable in each other's company, but equally unsure what to do next. Amanda knew how pleased her mum was that Aunt Jane had flown over to be with her to offer support, but having not seen each other for a few years, they no doubt wished the circumstances had been different for their reunion.

Clara took Grandad Tom's arm to guide him into the church; Amanda noticing her grandad was completely lost in his own thoughts, appearing detached from the rest of the group, was grateful for Clara's support. Tom Moreton was a spritely man in his early eighties; a proper old school British gent, with a stiff upper lip that he was trying desperately hard to prevent from quivering. Burying your son was not the right order of things and something he was struggling to comprehend.

Amanda approached her mum, Monica, and reaching out to embrace her was surprised at how slight her body had become under the thick blue winter's coat she had opted to wear in favour of the usual black normally reserved for funerals. Monica Moreton knew that the blue coat had been one of Ken's favourites, so had worn it, along with the pretty silk scarf with a design of spring flowers he had bought her for Christmas only a few short months earlier, in his honour. Amanda knew she herself had lost weight since her dad's death, but it felt nothing compared to her mum's apparent weight loss, who despite the extra make-up, looked gaunt and drawn under the dull spring sky.

Monica melted into her daughter's comfortable embrace, looking both lost and confused, as if she had left an important part of herself somewhere and could not quite remember what it was or where to look. A few friends and neighbours came up to offer their condolences and it was all the two women could do to hold themselves together before they slowly made their way into the nineteenth century Catholic Church of St Anthony's for the solemnity of the requiem mass that was to follow.

Father Michael Tate greeted the family at the church door. He had been the parish priest at St Anthony's for around fifteen years, coming originally from a busy inner-city church in the north of England, where the challenges he faced and the congregation he attracted were much different to those he faced today. He was truly settled in the quiet rural idyll and village life, praying on a daily basis the bishop would not move him away from his parish.

Father Michael had known Ken Moreton from day one, as Ken had been part of his welcoming committee when he first arrived. He counted him among his friends, the two men being of similar age and having early on identified a shared passion for gardening and growing vegetables in the church's grounds, some of the produce from which had been regular entries into the Church's annual Garden Party's prized vegetable competition. As such, leading the mass was an honour for him and his sermon was personal and heart felt, a true celebration of Ken's life, interjected with a few funny anecdotes of Ken helping out in the parish and some of the lengths they had gone to ensure their vegetables always won first prize. Monica and Amanda even managed a small smile at some of the recollections.

Once the church service was over, the congregation lead by Monica and Amanda moved quietly and respectfully to the graveyard at the side of the church, to a family burial plot Tom had bought some years earlier following his wife, Josie's death, but thankfully had not had the need to use himself yet. As he stood there, waiting for his son's coffin to be lowered into the hole he remembered his wife fondly, recalling the day they had buried her, never thinking his son would need it before him.

The sun had tried to redeem itself by making a brief appearance, but it was only half-heartedly shining; doing little, if anything, to lift the mood. Father Michael said a few more words of comfort in concluding his service, which floated over Amanda's head, lost as she was in her own thoughts. Finally, the coffin was lowered into the grave and after a respectful period people started to move away, muttering condolences as they walked past Monica, Amanda and Tom, leaving them to quietly contemplate their future. Eventually they walked arm-in-arm the short distance to the King's Head, joining the rest of their close friends and family for the wake, the local pub seeming the most appropriate place to celebrate Ken's life with a swift pint or two among the regulars.

Chapter 2
Three months earlier

It was late Thursday afternoon, the last week before Christmas, another cold and dark day with the promise of frost later that evening. Amanda was just finishing clearing up her art room of all the clutter accumulated over the preceding few weeks by her students as they had prepared for their Art exhibition in the town's library on the theme of 'Impact on Fashion of Climate change'. It had been a great success, with some really creative ideas on display. Amanda had felt great pride in her students' work, particularly from those in the lower sixth form who had only had a short term to get into the course, but were already showing great potential. At this rate if their course work continued to impress, they were on for some great grades by the summer.

Amanda had lectured in Art and Fashion Design at the local sixth form college for the last five years, being definitely one of the younger and more dynamic teachers on the faculty. The students loved and respected her in equal measure. Her trendy style and easy-going attitude made her an all-round great favourite. She displayed and received a high level of mutual respect; treating students both as friends and equals, but with the authority and control that clearly said 'no messing'. She brought a perspective that was both refreshing and challenging for the students and staff alike, which recognising most of the other staff were many years her senior Amanda found both encouraging and rewarding. Teaching was something she felt came naturally to her and not something she had to try too hard to do.

After graduating with a first in History of Art at Bristol University, Amanda had originally intended teaching Art at GCSE level to eleven to fifteen years. She soon got a job at the local comprehensive, initially as a supply teacher, being awarded a permanent position when a vacancy came up, but after a couple of years she felt that was not actually her calling. The strict syllabus and the relative immaturity of her students limited her creativity somewhat, so when an opportunity for a lecturer came up at the newly opened college a couple of miles out of town, she brushed up her CV and applied, being rewarded with the plum role of heading up the Art Department.

Amanda loved her job and was well respected, if a little unconventional in her approach and appearance. She immersed herself completely in the classroom, to the extent that should anyone enter the room unannounced, they would have been hard pushed to identify who was the student and who was the lecturer. But her style got results and annually her students' pass rate was well above the national average.

Today was the penultimate day of the Autumn term and tomorrow the Christmas holidays began. Yippee. Tomorrow the students would only be coming in for the morning to take home any course work or projects they needed to develop over the break, but in reality, Amanda did not envisage much work being done during the holidays, and in fact would prefer that the students had a clean break and came back refreshed. She definitely intended to.

It had felt like a long term, with students and teachers alike desperate to get a couple of weeks break, with nothing too demanding to think about or timetables to adhere to. In fact, if the atmosphere in the staff room was anything to go by, there would be a lot of eating and drinking taking place, with she suspected a few hangovers and comatose teachers over the coming weeks. Amanda particularly felt for those members of staff with adolescent children, who would probably in reality soon be counting down the days to returning to college for a rest, some normality and the start of the Spring term. Christmas was not a season everyone looked forward to.

Amanda though was looking forward to spending quality time with Damian and their two daughters Maisie and Alice, who at four and two were just starting to appreciate Christmas and to them everything was both magical and exciting. Maisie had gone to see Santa at the garden centre the previous weekend, reaming off a wish list so long Santa nearly fell asleep, whilst Alice, not quite ready for sitting on a stranger's lap, but at the same time not wanting to miss out, had clung excitedly to her daddy, and was delighted when Santa smiled over at her and offered her a little present.

They had then gone to choose the perfect tree, debating long and hard over the right one to pick, with the girls eventually choosing a Norwegian spruce that looked wonderful, but was far too big for their house. Damian, realising it was an argument he was not going to win simply smiled as he paid the cashier. He then securely tied it to the roof of their black Volkswagen estate car to avoid it taking off in the high winds, before carefully driving home through the Christmas traffic. At seven feet the tree proved a challenge to negotiate, but following lots of laughter from Amanda and the girls, and a few choice words from Damian, it eventually took pride of place in their lounge ready for the fairy lights and decorations to adorn it. It might have been a few inches shorter than the one they bought, but thankfully the girls did not notice the sawn-off bits by the recycle bin.

Amanda was just locking up the classroom when she felt her phone buzzing in her parka jacket pocket. The phone had been on silent all day and looking at the display she now realised she had missed a few calls and messages that would need to be returned when she got home. Teaching was not a nine-to-five job as there was always someone who needed something attending to, or question answered no matter what the time of day or night it was.

She recognised the incoming call was from her mum, so quickly pressed to accept before the ringing stopped.

'Hi Mum, is everything okay? I'm just leaving college so should be home in about twenty minutes – is there anything you need or should I phone you when I get in?'

'Hi Dear' replied her mum. 'Your dad and I were hoping to come round and have a quick chat with you tonight if it's convenient. We won't stay too long.'

'Yes, that's fine. Damian should be home with the girls by now so I'll message him to let him know you're on your way round and he can put the kettle on or better still open a bottle if you're in the mood for a glass of wine. You and Dad can always help with bath time too if you've got time.'

Amanda had a great relationship with her parents and as an only child who had not flown too far from the nest when she got married, she was still very close to them and they regularly popped around for meals or to see their granddaughters who they idolised. Having them on the doorstep also meant there was never a problem if babysitters were required at short notice.

'Okay see you soon then, but …… don't worry, we'll talk later,' her mum said hesitantly before hanging up the phone.

Amanda quickly messaged Damian to let him know her parents were on their way. She then switched her phone off, putting it back in her pocket, never giving a second thought to her mum's hesitation – she was regularly changing her mind and could get quite 'scatty' at times. She always seemed to have so many things going on in her life and so many pulls on her time, but that was one of the things she loved about her mum, she was never boring!

Her mum and dad had always been there for her, supporting her in whatever decisions and life choices she made, be those emotional, physical or practical things. As an only child this could have been quite suffocating with all their attention heaped on her, all their hopes and dreams focused on her achievements, but she was never made to feel that way. She always felt secure in their love and supported, and never felt pressured into doing anything she felt uncomfortable with.

Although Amanda had several close friends mainly from university days, not many of them lived locally, so without brothers and sisters to turn to her mum's was usually the ear she chose whenever any sensitive or personal dilemmas presented themselves. Her mum was a vivacious and sociable person always on the go, organising or supporting some event or other through the various charities and voluntary groups she busied herself with now she was retired, but she could always be relied upon to make time for Amanda. She valued her mum's opinion and her no-nonsense approach, renowned for never making a drama out of anything that a sensible and pragmatic approach could resolve. Amanda often felt her mum should have worked for the Foreign Office her diplomacy skills were so honed and she trusted her mum's judgement implicitly.

Her dad by comparison was a quiet and thoughtful man, most comfortable enjoying a pint at his local, or in his garden or greenhouse talking to his plants, or even in his shed oiling or repairing anything that had fallen on hard times. He was the most practical person Amanda knew, able to turn his hand to tackling any DIY project or home emergency. Nothing seemed to faze him and he could generally be relied upon to have a handy tool or gadget in his shed to save the day. Amanda liked to think of her parents collectively as the fourth emergency service and had them on speed dial whenever the need arose.

Since being married, Amanda had tried to turn to Damian for support around the house, but over the years she had quickly realised the futility of that. Her dad had equally tried to teach him some basics skills whenever an opportunity presented itself, but given he still struggled to correctly identify the pointy-end of the screwdriver, and the concept that he might one day own his own electric drill was laughable, she knew she was onto a loser here. She accepted his skills lay in other, less practical areas, but to be fair he was great with the children and was quite handy around the kitchen, happy to prepare meals and experiment with new ingredients and recipes whenever he could. They had been married for just under seven years, and whilst there were no longer any fireworks in their relationship, they were comfortable in their day- to-day life bringing up their family together.

Tonight was one of those occasions when Damian, arriving home early and seeing nothing obvious left out for dinner, decided to prepare something and make himself useful in the kitchen. He had read a new recipe in last weekend's Sunday supplement that he fancied having a go at, and by the looks of it most of the ingredients could be located in the fridge or cupboards, so he thought he would give it a go. Damian was an experimental chef who enjoyed the art of cooking, so what he did not have to hand he felt relatively comfortable with either using substitute ingredients or simply leaving things out.

When Amanda had messaged earlier to say her parents were on their way round, Damian had thought nothing of quickly adapting his recipe to ensure there was enough to go around. Amanda's parents were regular guests, who appeared to enjoy Damian's cooking and trying out his culinary experiments, so he just assumed they would be staying for dinner and be willing guinea pigs for whatever he created.

From the aromas Amanda smelt as she entered the house, shrugging her coat off and throwing it on the hall chair as she made her way to the kitchen, it was something Indian, she would guess. After a long day whatever it was would be welcome, particularly if it was accompanied by something preferably chilled to drink! Amanda was not a big drinker, but a glass of wine with a meal was something she really looked forward to in the evening and an easy way to chill out after the challenges of the day.

'Hi there, what we having – it smells great?' Amanda said as she lifted the lid off one of the pans to see what was cooking, managing to give Damian a quick peck on the cheek at the same time.

'It's an Indian curry I found in the paper at the weekend that I thought I'd try out – it's taken a bit of work, but hopefully it will be worth it. I think you'll like it' he said, 'I've put pizza and chips in the oven for the kids though, as I'm not sure it's quite to their taste and we can feed them before we have ours' he laughed imagining Maisie's face if a plate of curry was placed in front of her.

The girls had rather less-sophisticated taste buds, so were much happier with plainer foods preferably anything involving pasta or fishfingers. Whilst they usually sat and ate dinner with their parents, as Amanda believed eating as a family helped develop good table manners and allowed the girls to feel included, tonight it was going to be too late for them so it was a quick tea, an early bath and straight to bed for them, with a bit of spoiling from their grandparents and a bedtime story thrown in if they were lucky.

Amanda was just helping herself to a glass of chilled Pinot Grigio when the doorbell rang, followed by her parents entering the hallway and the girls running towards them shrieking with excitement. Although her parents had a door key, they always insisted on ringing the bell first to announce their arrival.

'Great timing, I'm just pouring the wine…. Dad, do you want a glass or would you prefer a beer?' asked Amanda automatically handing a glass of wine to her mum as she entered the kitchen. Monica took it from her daughter, before placing it on the worktop untouched. The normal smile or kiss she would offer in return was not there. Amanda also noticed a slight shaking in her mum's hand as she took the glass that she had never seen before.

'Thanks love, but a cup of tea would be just fine ……… we can't stop too long and I'm driving anyway,' replied her dad in a nervous voice, nowhere near his usual chirpy self.

While the girls jigged excitedly waiting for their grandparents to give them a cuddle and to come into the lounge to play with them, or to take them upstairs for their bath, Damian and Amanda exchanged a glance sensing something was not quite right. Amanda asked her daughters to go and watch the television for a few minutes. Something was obviously wrong, but neither Amanda nor Damian could put their finger on what it was, or if they had upset her parents in any way.

'Is everything okay Mum, Dad, you don't seem yourselves? Damian's made dinner and we'd assumed you'd be staying. The girls are looking forward to bath time too and have got some new bath toys to show you.'

'Sit down love….', said her mum, 'Dad and I have something to tell you both and unfortunately, it's not good news.'

Monica hesitated as she tried to organise her thoughts in an attempt to soften the blow, but Amanda's dad, sensing what she was trying to do, reached over to take Monica's hand and gave it an encouraging squeeze. He was a direct man and, in his mind, what needed to be said could not this time be sweetened with diplomacy or fancy words.

'What your mum is trying to say, is that I've been diagnosed with a form of stomach cancer that unfortunately isn't operable. I've known for a couple of months and have been having treatment at the hospital, but the Consultant informed me earlier today that the results from the latest tests aren't too promising. He said there isn't a lot left that they can do by way of tablets or medicines. He said I'd probably have around three to five years left, but ultimately it is terminal. We were hoping to delay telling you until after the new year and not spoil Christmas for you and the girls, but sadly your mum and I aren't good enough actors to pull that one off unfortunately,' her dad said with a wry smile.

Amanda looked stunned and was unsure what to say, or do, or feel. The way her dad had summed up the situation so directly and without room for doubt left her absolutely numb. Amanda was not at all medically minded, so could not even articulate the questions to allow her to put more substance onto the bare bones of her dad's prognosis. She had noticed him looking a bit down and acting more subdued than usual over the last few weeks, but as neither him nor her mum had mentioned any illness or even any 'old age' niggles, she had just written it off as tiredness. She had never suspected anything as earthshattering as this, suddenly feeling guilty for not noticing or being more caring towards her parents.

Her immediate response was to pull her dad into her arms and hug him tightly, praying that the strength of her love would permutate his skin and cure any ills. After a couple of minutes, she pulled away and questions started to form in her mind, but she soon sensed that tonight was not the right moment for an interrogation. Her parents obviously needing time to themselves to digest the situation. It was good that they had come to tell her, but it was clear that now they had done so, they were anxious to leave and return home. Further discussions would have to wait until the time was right.

Damian showed Amanda's parents out, giving them both a gentle hug as he opened the door, unable to offer any words of support of his own either. Nothing seemed right or appropriate for the circumstances, which was so unlike Damian who was seldom short for words and could usually be relied upon to say the right thing at the right time. But this had stumped even him, so out of the blue the revelation had come. There had not been any signs or indications as far as he had noticed, and nothing had prepared him for such shocking news, particularly so near Christmas.

After they had left, he walked back into the kitchen and took his wife into his arms, helpless to stem her tears as she quietly sobbed into his shoulder.

Chapter 3

When the alarm went off at 6.45am the following morning Amanda felt awful; she had tossed and turned all night, leaving her feeling like she had not slept a wink. Her mind had been going over and over the events of recent weeks and the things her parents had said or done, feeling guilty that she might have missed some signs, or more importantly if she had and had acted sooner, whether she could have done anything that could have changed this particular course of events. Had she been too tied up in her own world, too self-absorbed with her own pressures, concentrating on her own work life balance, that she had been unable to seen the obvious?

Damian, lying next to her had not slept too well himself either, conscious of how close Amanda was to her parents, therefore knowing how devastated and helpless she would feel at the moment. His wife was one of life's problem solvers, so feeling unable to solve what was being presented to her would be especially difficult for her to deal with.

'Do you want to use the shower first, or should I?' Damian asked, trying to sense the mood and wondering what Amanda would be planning on doing this morning.

College still had a day to go before the end of term, and knowing how professional Amanda was, he presumed she would still want to go in to finish off and ensure everything was in order before the break. He also had to consider his own plans. Ordinarily he would be heading for the 8.05 train for his thirty-minutes commute into Cheltenham, but was considering whether he should just phone in and work from home today. Thankfully his diary was not too full, and being Friday, when most people either left early or took the day off, he did not feel too pressured to go into the office.

A quick call to his secretary was all that would be needed. It would also allow him some time to spend with Maisie and Alice, who had been very disappointed the previous evening when bath time had not mapped out as planned. They had both been looking forward to giving grandad his usual bath-time soaking, so felt a little put out when Damian had put them straight to bed without even a bedtime story.

'I suppose I should get up and shower, it might brighten me up a bit,' replied Amanda in a tone that suggested it would take a lot more than a hot shower to brighten her up.

'Okay, I'll go and check the girls and put the coffee on whilst you get ready,' said Damian adding, 'and I'll make a quick call to the office to let them know I'm working from home today.'

He pulled on his dressing gown and slipped his bare feet into his slippers. The central heating had kicked in about thirty minutes earlier, but the room still felt chilly and downstairs was unlikely to be any warmer. He quickly checked on the girls, who thankfully were still sound asleep. They were both tucked up snugly in their own beds, but shared the same bedroom. Amanda had wanted them to have their own rooms, but Maisie and Alice had other ideas, so when Alice had moved out of her cot a few weeks ago, Maisie insisted that Alice's new bed be placed in her room. She even boxed up some of her cherished dolls to make room, so determined was she that they would share.

The girls would be waking up in the next half hour or so, and after munching their way through their usual breakfast of coco pops and toast, would be expecting Amanda to take them to their childminder's house a short walk away, but Damian would ring Susie and let her know there was a change of plan today. Susie was quite relaxed so would not have a problem with the short notice and thankfully was not the sort of person who would need any detailed explanation for the change in plan. The girls usually went there three days a week during term times on Wednesdays, Thursdays and Fridays, with Amanda's parents looking after them Mondays and Tuesdays. After last night's bombshell, any continuation, or more likely change to that arrangement would need to be parked for another day.

Once downstairs, Damian was soon reminded the kitchen had been abandoned the previous evening, with the Indian meal simply boxed-up and put in the fridge for another day, along with the barely touched bottle of wine. After her parents had left, neither Amanda nor Damian had any appetite for dinner and after a brief chat had gone to bed without feeling hungry. Dirty saucepans, half-drunk glasses of wine, utensils and all nature of small electrical kitchen appliances littered the worktops exactly where they had been left. Damian was not the tidiest of chefs on a good day, but a quick tidy around before filling the coffee machine with water and pressing the on-button soon made the room more presentable and removed any evidence from the night before.

By the time Damian returned upstairs with a cup of coffee, Amanda was showered and dressed in her customary college wear - jeans and sweat-top. She could not see the point of dressing up when she was essentially dealing with paints and glues all day. Her hair had been scooped back into a ponytail and whilst she had not aimed for the glamorous look, she was at least clean and presentable, and as ready as she could be to face the day.

'If you're okay looking after the girls, I think I'll pop round to Mum and Dad's after college for a chat. I should be home for teatime,' Amanda said, thanking Damian as he handed her a cup of coffee. She liked her coffee white with just a little sugar, but as she tasted it noticed he had put an extra spoonful in presumably to give her a bit of energy.

'Yes, no problem, take whatever time you need,' Damian replied adding, 'Just give me a call if I can do anything. I'll be at home all day with the girls anyway so no worries.' He had already called the office and let his secretary know he would not be in today. Being the boss had its advantages, and calling in to take time off without having to offer an explanation was one of them.

Amanda left the house about twenty minutes later, after nibbling half-heartedly on a slice of jam on toast in lieu of a proper breakfast. She still did not feel in the slightest bit hungry, but Damian insisted she at least try to eat something before leaving the house. The girls had just woken so she had managed to get in a quick cuddle with them too, reassuring herself that they were happy staying at home with daddy, before heading out into the dark winter's morning, wrapped up in her trusty Parka with added hat, scarf and gloves as extra measures against the chilly weather.

The short days meant the sun did not come up until much later, but the sky looked relatively clear, so hopefully it would be a dry day at least. Amanda really did not like the cold winter months, preferring springtime out of all the seasons, but at least it was not snowing today or worst of all forecasting icy winds. The car windscreen was a little frosted up, but it soon warmed up once the heater was switched on and Amanda got on her way, driving towards college on automatic pilot.

On arriving at college and unlocking the classroom, Amanda reflected on how much her life has changed in just a few short hours. The simple carefree feelings she had experienced only yesterday afternoon, with the end of term holidays just starting, Christmas only a week away and two weeks of relaxed family time to look forward to, replaced by a feeling of dread and helplessness; this total lack of control over the unknown being one of Amanda's major fears.

Around 9.30am, as expected, a few of the more diligent students started to mill into the classroom, laughing and joking as they ambled in, unaware of Amanda's preoccupation. They gathered together anything and everything they would need over the holidays, before wishing each other a happy Christmas and bolting for the door. There were no official lectures today, so no reason to hang around.

Amanda was aware that a few of the lads had arranged to meet-up in the pub across the road from college for a pre-Christmas drink, as they had invited her to join them yesterday, and to make plans for further meet-ups over the holidays, but she had politely declined. Some of the girls seemed to be heading into town for a spot of lunch and last-minute present shopping, which was much more up Amanda's street, but she had not had an invite to that, but either way no-one really paid her too much attention as they got on with their lives, which suited her fine under the circumstances. She was not up for the usual chit-chat today, and above all did not want any of her students asking her if she was alright, as relying on keeping her emotions in-check would be a bridge too far she feared, and breaking down in front of her students was not her style.

As soon as she was happy everyone who was turning up had been and gone, Amanda got herself ready to leave, switching off the lights and headed out the door, locking up as she left. She walked past the staffroom on her way out, but thankfully no-one was around that she needed to be polite to, so she quickly headed for the carpark, climbed into her car and pointed it left, heading in the direction of her parent's house. She had considered phoning ahead, but did not want her parents to have the opportunity to suggest she leave it for another day.

Amanda knew it was going to be a difficult discussion, but she needed to talk to them today if she was to get any peace whatsoever.

Chapter 4

Amanda's parents lived in the heart of the village, about ten minutes' walk from the church and primary school she had attended, and only five minutes from the pub, local shops and post office, now incorporated into the small convenience store, as had happened to the majority of the more rural post offices in the country. Their house was an old imposing detached Georgian property, one of the more sought-after properties in the area, renowned for its abundance of beautiful summer-time climbers around the door and the accumulation of pots of impressive flowers and shrubs on display in the formally laid out garden at the front of the house. It was the type of property whose photo could easily have adorned the archetypal 'chocolate box'.

The garden was both impressive and established, with the house having been in her dad's family for around five generations and it was now Ken's pride and joy and where he spent as much of his leisure time as possible. It had originally been bought by her dad's great, great grandfather, who had been a successful tradesman in the area and who enjoyed a relatively wealthy lifestyle. Over the years the family had died off and Ken was now the only surviving son, so in time the property would no doubt pass to Amanda being the only child.

When her parents had first married, they had moved into the house with Ken's parents, initially only temporarily whilst they found their feet and a property of their own. Having only recently graduated from university, and finding they were expecting a baby so shortly after they married, living with her in-laws for the first few years whilst they brought up a baby and then a growing toddler was a godsend for Monica, and an arrangement that seemed to suit everyone. They both loved the area and the quiet countryside, and got on great with Ken's parents so had no desire to move.

Monica's own parents had split up several years before she had left home to go to university when she was in her early teens and her sister Jane had been nineteen. Her mum had got quite depressed when their father left them for another woman, so it had been largely Jane who had brought Monica up, looking after her through her teenage years.

When Jane met and married an American and emigrated to the States a couple of years later, Monica missed her sister desperately, but soon realised she did not want to be the one left at home to look after their mum, who was getting more embittered by the day and was not good company to be around.

As her relationship had in fact never been great with either of her parents whilst she had been growing up, once she left home and made the break to go to university, and met and eventually agreed to marry Ken, she was more than happy to move to a new part of the country and start her new life.

Monica's mum, Moira Beraton, had died a few years later when Amanda was around ten years old, never really recovering from her broken marriage, and although she occasionally kept in touch with her dad, Christmas cards mainly, he had long since remarried and now had a family and grandchildren of his own. As his new wife had never really encouraged close contact with Monica or Jane, their relationship with him soon withered.

Shortly before Amanda started school, her grandparents, Tom and Josie, elected to move to a smaller property within walking distance of their old family home, leaving their only son and his wife and their young child to enjoy the house. Their hope was that it would give them more room and privacy as their family would undoubtably grow. They bought a small cottage close by and lived there happily, until her grandmother's sudden death some years later when Amanda was in her first year away at university. Her grandad was invited back to the big house to live with Ken and Monica again, but he opted to stay in the cottage with his memories, soon settling into his own new routine around the village. As the only child of an only child, Amanda had been doted on by both her grandparents, so losing her grandmother in her late teens was devastating, but she continued to have a close and loving relationship with her Grandad Tom, who although now in his early-eighties still had a wicked sense of humour and continued to be great company to both her and his growing circle of friends and acquaintances.

Chapter 5

It was around 3pm later that day when she pulled up at the curb side in-front of her parents' house. It was starting to get dark but she could see the Christmas tree lights sparkling in the front window, which brought a small smile to her face. The tree was the same artificial one her parents had had for years; full of all the decorations they had accumulated over the years. Although her dad was a keen gardener, he did not hold with bringing real trees into the house, being a firm believer that they should remain planted where God had intended them to be. It was an annual argument between him and his wife, but one that Monica was yet to win.

Amanda walked up the path and rang the bell, deciding against using her key on this occasion.

'Hi Mum.' She said as her mum opened the door a couple of minutes later inviting her in 'Do you fancy putting the kettle on, I've just left college and thought I'd pop in for a quick cup of tea on the way home'.

'Come through, we're just sat in the back – the kettle has just boiled. I'll bring you a drink in. Do you fancy a biscuit too?' said her mum.

'Thanks that would be great' replied Amanda suddenly realising that she had not eaten anything all day apart from the small piece of toast Damian had forced on her at breakfast that morning.

'Hi Dear, what a lovely surprise. To what do we owe this honour?' her dad asked as she walked into the back room and gave him a kiss on the cheek and a gentle squeeze.

This was her parents' favourite room and the one they spent most of their time in, with its high ceiling and large fireplace, already set with a cosy fire blazing in the grate. Although it was a large room, its tasteful, if dated furnishings meant it felt comfortable and inviting, and the view from the picture window overlooking the garden never failed to impress, regardless of the season. The front garden had more of a formality in its lay-out, but nothing compared to the garden at the back of the house, where although the lawned areas were almost manicured and the flower beds tastefully laid out with an array of plants and shrubs to match the season, it had a carefree appearance that looked like it was all effortless.

Even though it was winter and very little was growing, the evergreen shrubs still looked pruned; everything neatly cut back and deadheaded in preparation for the spring. The bird table, as ever stacked with nuts and seeds to attract a wide selection of birds into the safe haven of the garden took centre stage, and neither Ken nor Monica ever tired of watching their feathered guests pecking away at the seeds.

Her dad was sitting in his favourite armchair in front of the window reading his copy of the Telegraph endeavouring to do his crossword, a half-drunk cup of tea going cold beside him. Her mum's chair was opposite, her knitting put to one side whilst she had gone to get the door. Amanda wondered what her mum was making this time – she was forever knitting something or other for one of her local charities; only last month it had been dozens of poppies for the annual memorial service held at the local church for the Poppy appeal, raising nearly £200.

Monica returned a couple of minutes later with a cup of tea and a slice of lemon cake, placing them on the small table for Amanda with a smile. Monica loved baking, and lemon cake was one of her specialties, and one of Amanda's favourites. Amanda shrugged off her coat and sat down wondering now that she was here how to start the conversation she had been dreading having since her parents' bombshell the previous evening, but knowing that it was not something she could put off any longer.

Chapter 6

A couple of hours later, Amanda sat in her kitchen with Damian opposite her and tried to condense for him what she had learnt of her dad's illness and his prognosis. It had taken some gentle coaxing of both her parents to get the full story, as although they were not exactly reluctant to speak, neither had much experience of serious illness and struggled to really articulate in any scientific way what the issue was. They were both relatively private individuals when it came to personal matters, known to never moan or groan about their health, always laughing it off or putting any minor complaint down to the weather, or the season or something they had eaten. Consequently, Amanda had never had cause to worry about her parents' health before. Now in their mid to late fifties, and both technically 'retired' – although to be fair her mum had never worked, they had always seemed to live a charmed life.

However, it transpired her dad had not been feeling too well throughout the late spring and early summer months, with initially mild but increasing more grumbling stomach pains and other symptoms that just would not go away. He was busy doing his usual gardening, both at the church and home, raising his vegetables, and generally planting and weeding as the seasons demanded, so was too preoccupied to give it much thought until one day he realised it needed looking at and he could not put it off any longer.

Eventually with coaxing from Monica he made an appointment to see Dr Greaves his local GP, who made a referral to the Consultant, and after a series of tests was diagnosed with a form of stomach cancer. The prognosis, given it had already advanced to Stage 4 was not great. The Consultant had explained that there were treatments available to help slow the growth and manage the symptoms, but the cancer itself had spread, and as such it was both incurable and inoperable. He went on to explain that a three to five years life expectancy was typical for this particular cancer at the stage of its development; and with the symptoms and the manner in which they had developed, a change of lifestyle would be required, with added care to avoid further complications.

Her parents admitted they had discussed not telling her, not wanting to worry her unnecessarily, but had concluded that on this occasion it was unavoidable recognising any change in lifestyle would have to involve her too, so she had a right to know. Amanda knew the timing sucked, but was it ever going to be a good time to receive news such as this?

Damian listened and prompted with the occasional question, but in truth he had little to offer to lighten the mood and definitely did not want to offer any platitudes or say everything would be okay because he knew that was clearly not the case. He could sense Amanda was putting on the same brave face as she normally does whenever challenges arise, but deep down recognised her heart would be breaking knowing how close she was to both her parents and how unexpected this all was.

Damian knew that 'acceptance' was going to be a difficult stage for Amanda to reach once the initial shock had worn off, and sensed that once Christmas was over and life started to return to normal, whatever the 'new normal' turned out to be, the next few months and years would be a challenge for them all. He was not afraid to admit to himself how worried he was about how they would all cope or what level of support he could ultimately provide. Illness was not something he had much experience to draw upon or not necessarily something he felt comfortable around.

Chapter 7

Christmas morning arrived and for the girls at least it brought all the usual excitement and mayhem. For Maisie the excitement had been growing since their visit to Santa the previous week, but from Alice, who was really only experiencing it for the first time, the wonder and awe in her face were new. Last year Alice had only just started walking by Christmas time, so Damian and Amanda had had the added challenge of keeping her away from the Christmas tree and attempting to pull herself up on its branches. She had not really taken in anything, but this year, at just over two she was starting to mumble a few words and Santa was one of them. It was amazing to see how much they had both developed in the last twelve months and how delightful they were becoming.

The presents had been neatly stacked around the tree, with their glittery wrappings and fancy bows that Amanda had spent ages creating, but within a few minutes of seeing them the lounge looked like a tsunami had hit, such was the devastation. The girls were enjoying themselves and happily going from toy to toy, squealing as each box was unwrapped and its surprise revealed, before eventually seeing the bicycle and the tricycle, both adorned with ribbons and bows standing to the side of the tree.

'Wow…. that's just what I asked Santa to bring me!' exclaimed Maisie as she realised the pink bike with the doll's basket on the handlebars and the shining stabilisers already fitted was for her. 'Look Alice, there's one for you too – and you didn't even ask Santa for a bike. Dad, can we get dressed and go for a ride please?' pleaded Maisie jumping up and down with her sister, both squealing in excitement and clapping their hands together.

Amanda and Damian smiled at the sheer pleasure on their daughters' face and marvelled at the delight of their innocence. Amanda believed Christmas was such a special family time and one for making memories, so had made a conscious decision that come what may, they were going to ensure nothing spoiled that for their daughters or for her parents, who would be arriving shortly in good time to go to Christmas Day Mass with them and then staying over for a traditional turkey lunch with all the trimmings. Lunch would undoubtably be followed by more present unwrapping as her parents were guaranteed to be bringing a sack full of gifts that Santa had left under their tree.

'Yes,' replied Damian bending down to give the girls a hug, 'we could go for a quick ride before Church, but not before you're dressed and have had some breakfast. We should probably wait until Grandad gets here though, as I'm sure he won't want to miss it…' suddenly remembering that they couldn't go before Ken and Monica got here, as they had bought the girls matching cycle helmets as part of their Christmas presents to them!

Amanda had spoken to her mum a couple of days before, agreeing with her that there would be no mention of her dad's illness in front of the children. At four years old, Maisie was at that enquiring stage of her development, where everything said to her resulted in an often repeated 'what' or 'why' question, and none of them wanted that, today of all days. They secretly, if naively, hoped with the predicted three to five years ahead of them, the girls would just deal with grandad being ill as the new normal, taking it in their stride and thereby avoiding Monica or Amanda ever having to have that discussion. They had plenty of time to think about how they would approach that nearer to when the time came.

No, today was about celebrating and creating new and happy memories for them all.

Chapter 8

Before long, the Christmas and New Year celebrations were over and life settled back into its usual routines. The cold dark mornings, wet with frequently icy roads that made driving down the country lanes precarious, and short days with little sunlight, all contributing to the normal post-holiday blues. Most people struggled to keep their spirits high at this time of year, without the added worries of poor health that now seemed to pervade all around.

The new term started early in January, with Amanda relieved she could find some distraction in her work and her students, throwing herself into supporting their preparations for their up-and-coming mock exams, concentrating on those projects that needed finishing and submitting for assessment and generally doing whatever she could to occupy her time.

The February half term came around all too soon, with the worst of the winter weather appearing to be over. The first signs of spring were on their way, with the snowdrops and daffodils daring to poke out of the comfort of their roadside beds. With the improved weather, moods seemed to lift a little too.

Leaving college, a little earlier than usual, and knowing the girls did not need to be collected from their childminder's for at least another hour, Amanda decided to call into her parents' house for a quick cup of tea and a catch-up. Since Christmas, whilst she had spoken to her parents regularly and still called in during the week, she had deliberately and consciously balanced her time more carefully between being around to support, without becoming too overbearing. She recognised they needed time to themselves to adjust and did not want to add to their worries by mollycoddling them or being over sensitive as a constant presence in their home.

'Hi Mum, Dad, it's only me. Is anyone at home? Is the kettle on?' Amanda announced as she let herself into her parents' home and walked towards the back room, knowing at this time of day they would likely be there watching their afternoon quiz shows and playing along, shouting their answers at the television screen.

Her dad was sitting in his usual chair, and although he smiled when she walked in, Amanda noticed he did not look at all well. The smile that normally lit up his eyes, today looked almost pained.

'Hi Dad, how are you feeling? You don't look too good today. Is everything okay?' she said in a concerned tone, without trying to sound overly worried.

'I'm not feeling too good to be honest, I think I've got a bit of cold coming on,' he replied, coughing and spluttering as he did so, obviously suffering and feeling miserable.

'I've told him I'll call the doctors, but you know what he's like,' said her mum. Neither parent in truth called out or visited the GP unless it was absolutely necessary, preferring to deal with any symptoms themselves with a bottle of over-the-counter medicine or tablets from the chemist. This approach had worked so far as both had enjoyed relatively good health, but Amanda was concerned that this time it may not be enough.

'Do you want me to ring for you now? The surgery should still be open and I'd feel a lot happier if Dr Greaves could see you and prescribe something,' asked Amanda, adding more anxiously 'There's a flu virus doing its rounds at the moment that's quite serious. A few of the lecturers at college have got it and it's laid them low.' She knew her parents had had their flu jabs in the autumn, but also knew that did not offer any guarantees.

'I'll phone in the morning if I'm not feeling any better and make an appointment,' her dad said, leaving Amanda a little more comfortable, but still with an uneasy feeling. Previous experience showed her that although she could coax, she could not force her parents into doing anything they did not want to do, so she reluctantly left it at that, moving the conversation onto brighter things, including bringing them up to date on what Maisie and Alice had been doing, knowing this would lighten their mood.

The following morning, Monica phoned the doctors as Ken had not had too good a night's sleep, and worried by what Amanda had said the previous evening about the virus, felt she should not put it off any longer. The receptionist advised Dr

Greaves was busy doing his morning appointments, but would call round later that morning. Being well aware of Ken's health concerns and knowing they would not be calling the doctor out unnecessarily, the medical team at the surgery was eager to help.

When he arrived at the house a couple of hours later, Dr Joe Greaves gave Ken a thorough examination. He had been the family's GP for over thirty years, and apart from being their doctor he considered himself a friend too. He and Ken were of a similar age and had both grown up in the village, going to the same primary and secondary schools before wending their separate ways to university; Ken going off to read Engineering and Joe, Medicine. Over the years they remained close, going out for the occasional beer when they were both home, with Ken even asking Joe to be his best-man when he married Monica.

After graduating with his medical degree, Dr Joe accepted an appointment at the local hospital as a junior doctor specialising in geriatrics, before returning ten years later to the village as a GP working alongside his father. He eventually took over the practice when his father, Dr James Greaves retired. Living in a country village with a largely aging population, geriatrics had been the ideal specialism for him. He often reflected how useful his training had been when consulting the majority of his patients, listening to their growing list of age-related ailments. Dr Greaves Junior, as he was lovingly referred to by the older patients, was soon accepted back into the community, and over the years had grown the practice his father had begun, eventually earning the same level of trust and respect Dr Greave Snr had spent years building.

'Ken, I'm not too happy about your breathing…. you seem to be struggling quite a bit,' Dr Greaves said after his examination was complete, 'and the fact that you've had this for several days is a little worrying. I'd like to refer you to the hospital for an X-ray and some blood tests to rule out a couple of things. I'll phone through so they're expecting you, if that's okay with you? They may keep you in overnight for observation,' he added in a manner that really gave Ken no option other than to agree.

Ken, who had never spent a night in a hospital in his life was initially reluctant, but trusting Dr Greaves' judgement, and sensing there was no other alternative, reluctantly agreed. Monica watched and listened as the conversation between her husband and the doctor took place, her concern growing when she saw the expression on the Doctor Joe's face and the speed at which he made the call to the hospital, asking them to expect him within the hour. It was decided that an ambulance was unnecessary as Monica could easily drive, so she quickly pulled together a bag of overnight essentials, including his new pyjamas that were still in their wrappings left unworn from Christmas, and got ready for the journey. She would be home in a couple of hours and would phone Amanda then with an update, not wanting to disturb her unnecessarily when she was at work.

As promised, the hospital was expecting them, meaning there was no hanging around in A&E for assessment once Monica had booked Ken in at reception. Dr Greaves was well respected in the area, so the hospital team had taken his referral seriously and had acted on it without delay, transferring Ken immediately to an assessment ward and carrying out the X-rays and blood tests as required. Monica waited nervously in the family waiting room for a doctor to come and tell her what was wrong and when she could expect to take Ken home. So far, she had only been there for a couple of hours, but thankfully there were no parking meters at this hospital so she did not need to worry about getting a ticket, but the longer it went on the more anxious she became.

The hospital Consultant, Mrs. Thomas, phoned Dr Greaves a couple of hours later with the results and, as he had suspected, it confirmed pneumonia. The X-rays showed Ken's lungs were severely inflamed and the Consultant confirmed his breathing had become more and more laboured following his admission, with oxygen now being administered to help ease his breathing.

Dr Greaves suspected Ken had probably caught the flu virus a week or so earlier without realising it, intent on trying to shake it off as normal with a hot lemon and an early night. However, with his immune system significantly weakened by the cancer treatments, this had not happened and the virus had been allowed to take hold, enabling the more serious condition of pneumonia to develop. Ken's body had struggled to fight back, but by the time Dr Greaves had been called to carry out his assessment, the seriousness of the situation was in no doubt. Mrs. Thomas confirmed a course of antibiotics would be administered, but was not hopeful of the outcome recognising Ken's underlying medical condition. Ken was currently mildly sedated to help him recover his strength and normalise his breathing, but the next 24-48 hours would be critical she advised.

After speaking with Dr Greaves, Mrs. Thomas went directly to the family waiting room to let Monica know what the results had shown. Mrs. Thomas was a tall, well-built woman in her late forties with the ability to look quite imposing, but she was known to be quite the opposite, and had a great manner with patients and colleagues alike. Over her career she had broken bad news to many patients and family members, and although she was more than confident in doing this, it was not something that came easy to her or a part of the job she relished, but equally it was not something she shied away from or delegated to more junior members of her team.

She gently knocked on the door and entered, to see Monica quietly sitting in one of the comfy armchairs in the corner of the room, so obviously lost in her own thoughts and visibly confused at the sudden turn of events. The family room had recently been refurbished with money donated by a generous benefactor, providing now a much more comfortable and relaxed space, but it was still a room no one would choose to be in if given a choice. Mrs. Thomas introduced herself, then closed the door to give them the privacy they needed for the discussion that would undoubtedly tear Monica apart.

Chapter 9

After briefly returning home to collect some essentials, Monica remained at the hospital, sitting by Ken's bed for as long as they would allow. Given he was in the high dependency ICU this was not as long as she would have liked as the nurses needed regular access to their patient. They tried to explain to Monica that having additional people in the room only increased the risks of infection and hampered their ability to react urgently should the need arise, but as she sat in the corridor waiting to be readmitted, that explanation went over her head.

Amanda had arrived at the hospital driving there directly as soon as she had received the telecon from her mum. The two of them sat quietly in the family room holding vigil, patiently waiting for news. They hardly ate anything and drank very little as neither was prepared to walk to the restaurant to fetch food for fear of leaving the other alone. They occasionally dozed off, but were constantly alert to the door opening and any changes.

Over the forty-eight hours since he had been admitted, Ken's condition had not stabilised or improved as the medical team had hoped; the antibiotics had not improved his breathing and if anything, his condition was worsening. The pneumonia had really taken hold and the signs were not good. The doctors were worried, but tried their best to shelter Amanda and Monica from their concerns whilst they continued their work.

Later that evening around 10pm, Ken finally lost his battle for breath, with the medical team having to accept that there was nothing else to be done for him. The combination of the weakened immune system, resulting from the cancer treatments and the pneumonia, brought on by the virus, was just too strong for his body and the antibiotics to fight. There was nothing left than to go and tell the relatives the tragic news. The duty doctor knew this was his role and after taking a moment to collect his thoughts, he approached the family room.

Monica and Amanda sensed as soon as the door to the family room opened and the doctor approached them that the news was not what they had hoped for. They both reached for the other's hand and sat immobilised as the doctor took a seat opposite them and started to talk, the gentle tone of his voice washing over them with his words not making any sense at all.

Chapter 10

As midnight arrived and after there was nothing more for them to do at the hospital, they walked out to the carpark arm-in-arm, neither saying anything, simply carrying the small plastic carrier bag the nurse had handed them with Ken's personal effects; his glasses, wristwatch, the St Christopher medal that he wore around his neck and his plain gold wedding band. Not much to show for a life well lived.

Amanda, deciding to leave her car in the hospital carpark for Damian to pick up at some later stage, drove her mum home. Her mum was in complete shock and in no fit state to drive, but added to that, and the fact it was dark and heavy rain had set in, her mum would not have felt safe to drive herself anyway. Monica was a fair-weather driver, happy enough to potter around the village or tootle into town, but less comfortable on motorways with their speeding lorries, or on narrow country roads where she could encounter a caravan being towed and feel pressured to overtake. Her dad normally did any long hauls or night-time driving, always happy to ferry Monica and her friends around whenever asked.

The hospital thankfully had allowed Amanda and Monica some time to spend with Ken privately to say their goodbyes, but neither woman knew what to say under the circumstances, neither being prepared for this to be the outcome to their trip to the hospital for what they assumed would simply be some tests. Only two days ago Ken had been sat at home, reading his paper and minding his own business with what appeared to be a bit of a cold, but nothing too serious and now he was gone. They had both accepted his time was limited and therefore precious, but had expected that to be around four to five years, not a matter of weeks. There were things that should have been said, feelings that should have been expressed; and they both prayed that Ken had known in his heart what those things were, recognising they had been left unsaid. It was a cruel world.

The last forty-eight hours had been difficult and stressful, with neither of them getting much sleep, but Amanda did not feel tired; in fact, she did not know what she felt, other than numb and completely helpless. She was usually the strong one with all the answers, but tonight she felt drained. She had suggested staying with her mum so that she would not be alone, but when her mum said no, she did not want to push, realising Monica needed time to herself to get her thoughts together. They had hardly spoken to each other since leaving the hospital, both lost in their own thoughts; neither knowing what to say to console the other.

After ensuring Monica was settled, Amanda left to drive the short distance back to her own home. It was the early hours of the morning and the dawn was just starting to break over the hills in the distance. The sky was clear, promising a nicer day than the one before when the rain had been unceasing. She drove her mum's car, thankful again that her dad had always had the forethought to keep her on the insurance 'just in case!' He had always liked to cover his bases and plan ahead, managing risks before they arose. Amanda smiled to herself as she recalled, how as a retired risk assessor working for an insurance company, she had always thought with his personality he had been destined for a job like that. Although she knew he had studied engineering at university and started his working life in an engineering company, in the end that was not the career for him.

The roads were generally quiet through the village, with traffic light, but at this time of the morning they were empty and it felt like a ghost town. It even looked too early for the milkman. Amanda could not recall ever being out this early – even in her partying days as a student, but she liked the peace and tranquillity. It suited her mood.

When pulling onto her drive a few minutes later, she initially wondered where her car was, before it all came flooding back to her, reminding her why it was still parked at the hospital. Hearing the car approach, Damian opened the door and went out to meet his wife, enveloping her into his arms and leading her into the house and the warmth. She had rung ahead to let him know she was on her way, and was thankful he was waiting for her, not wanting to go home to a cold dark house by herself.

Amanda and Damian lived at the opposite end of the village in a relatively new estate of twelve 'executive' three and four-bedroom detached homes, designed to tastefully blend in with the local architecture and environment. They had lived there since the houses were built, moving in shortly after they had married and moving out of Damian's bachelor flat in Cheltenham. Amanda had yearned for the quieter country lifestyle, knowing she wanted any children they would have to enjoy the same relaxed way of life she had enjoyed as a child.

She had never really embraced the 'hustle' and 'bustle' of city living, so when these homes came onto the market, so close to where she had been born and bred, and her family still lived, she had jumped at the chance to buy one. To her they were perfect, albeit not as big as she would have liked, but for Damian, who still worked in the city running an IT and Communications business, and still hankering after more of a 'social life', it was more of an adjustment. Although he soon recognised the advantages of living near Amanda's parents once the children arrived for the support they could provide.

Damian led Amanda to the kitchen, handing her a cup of sweet tea, believing it would be good for shock, and knowing that she had not eaten or drunk much over the last day or so, started to prepare her some breakfast. He could tell from her eyes that tears were not long gone, nor new ones far off, but sensed correctly that she had been holding it all back, trying to be strong in front of her mum. Now she was home, though he was sure the flood gates would soon open and no doubt would be relying on him to get her through this. He needed to be strong enough for the both of them.

Thankfully they had about an hour before the girls woke up, time to talk and decide what they would need to do over the coming hours, days and weeks; where the priorities lay. Then he would put his wife to bed to get some rest and take over, as best he could, with the girls. There were arrangements that would need to be made, people that would have to be told and practicalities that required to be sorted, but all that would have to wait for now. It was not an area Damian had any experienced with, but he knew it was not something he could avoid if he was to support Amanda and his mother-in-law as he needed to.

Chapter 11

A couple of weeks after the funeral, Grandad Tom arrived unannounced early one afternoon at Amanda's house, ringing the doorbell with its merry little charm that always made him smile.

'Hello Grandad, what a lovely surprise,' said Amanda as she opened the door. 'What brings you here?'

'I've just come to see my favourite grand-daughter if that's okay?' he joked, knowing Amanda was his only grand-daughter. 'If the kettle's on, I'll have a cup of tea if you're making.'

Whilst the visit was unexpected, it was not unusual and never unwelcomed. Amanda was close to her grandad, more so since she had returned home from university shortly after her grandmother's death. He had mellowed a great deal and was good company, and great with the girls, doting on being a great-granddad and proud to show them off whenever he got the opportunity. Today he looked tired and a little distracted, not quite his dapper self. It was not surprising given all he had had to deal with over the last few months.

'I see you've driven; did you not fancy the walk? It looks quite a nice day,' asked Amanda, noticing his trusty Volvo in her driveway. Tom had driven the same car for years, and it still looked new, with very few miles on the clock. These days he rarely went much further than the local supermarket, or the garage to fill up with petrol, and really could not justify keeping a car running, but he believed it was his independence. At eighty-three he was still sprightly with good eyesight, so for however long he could get away with driving, he had no intention of parting with the car.

'I would have walked, but I wasn't sure you'd be in, and my bladder wouldn't have lasted the walk home without a visit to your facilities,' he laughed, although not with the normal humour this comment was usually accompanied with. It was a family joke that he was unable to pass a toilet without making a visit.

Tom lived in one of the old farm worker's cottages in the village, about a thirty-minute walk away, just opposite the pub where he regularly enjoyed a couple of pints, socialising and playing dominoes with the locals. Today, although the weather was good, it was also still only early spring and could be changeable, so that and the risk no-one would be home made the decision to drive easier. He had gambled on Amanda being by herself, knowing she was not working at the moment and that today was a day the girls were usually at their childminder's. Damian did not usually get home much before 7pm, so he was banking on them having the house to themselves and a chance to talk.

His son's death had hit them badly, not least of all himself, but Tom recognised Amanda was struggling particularly hard with the suddenness of it all. She had told him that she felt guilty that in the last few weeks of her dad's life she had not spent enough time with him, busy as she was at work, believing they would have a few years left together to say everything that needed to be said. She had tried to be strong, particularly around her mum, but Tom knew deep down behind the armour, Amanda was a sensitive soul and took things very much to heart.

In her attempts to be strong and keep going, and not wanting to let her students down, Amanda had initially returned to college a couple of days after the funeral, very much against Damian and the wider family's advice. Tom knew she soon realised, in fact before the end of that first week that she was not ready to return. She felt exhausted by the end of each day; feeling unable to focus on her students and the demands of the curriculum. To be fair to herself and her students she requested a short career break whilst she got herself together.

Her principal had understood and agreed, knowing a break would allow Amanda more time to spend with her family and help her mum deal with both the practical tasks and emotional stresses that needed to be considered. There was always a myriad of things to do following a death, people to inform, practicalities to sort and nobody should have to deal with this alone, particularly when grieving themselves.

After they had taken their cups of tea, and a plate of Tom's favourite shortbread biscuits, into the conservatory at the back of the house, Tom sat down opposite Amanda. He gently took her hand saying 'There's something I'd like to talk to you about if you've got some time,' adding once he had got her attention, 'it's about your dad.'

Amanda did not know what to say, so sat and listened as Grandad Tom continued, taking a deep breath before he started, aware the next few minutes were going to be difficult for him too. He also needed to choose his words carefully, mindful of how Amanda could react.

'When your dad first found out he had cancer, he came and spoke to me about something that had been playing on his mind for a while, but something he needed to discuss before it was too late,' Tom started. 'What he told me was news to me, and something I had never suspected, so whilst I was initially surprised and perhaps a little in shock, I want you to know that I was immensely proud of my son and how he had handled the situation.'

Amanda had no idea what her Grandad was referring to, but was intrigued to know more.

'Go on...' she said encouragingly, sensing her grandad was perhaps having difficulty organising his thoughts. Tom reached into his jacket pocket and extracted an envelope that Amanda could see straightaway was addressed to her in her dad's handwriting.

'What's that Grandad?' she asked, suddenly feeling more nervous about what she was about to learn.

'It's a letter your dad wrote a few weeks ago, early February, just before he died. He asked me to hold onto it for safe keeping and give it to you after he'd gone, or leave it with my papers for the solicitor to give to you should I go first...' adding with a little smile as he handed the letter to his grand-daughter. 'I didn't know when was the right time, but I don't feel comfortable holding onto it any longer. Your dad asked me to sit with you whilst you read it, if that's okay?'

Amanda took the envelope, carefully removing the folded sheets of paper from it, smelling a faint aroma of her dad's soap as she put the envelope down and took the letter into her hands. Her dad was not one for writing, so she sensed it must be important if he had gone to all this trouble, and she also sensed from her grandad's face that it was not going to tell her something she already knew.

'*My darling Amanda,*

The fact that you're reading this means I'm no longer around, for which I'm deeply sorry. I hope your Grandad is there though, and that he's keeping his promise to sit with you whilst you read this. Please give him my love and tell him what a wonderful father he was. I probably didn't tell him often enough how much I loved him and how proud I was of him.

I hope you and your mum are well too, and that you're looking after each other. I know how tough it must be, but being a husband to Monica and a father to you made me the proudest man in the world and I am thankful every day of my life for your love.

You will never know how much I loved you; from that very first moment I held you in my arms you meant the whole world to me and I knew I would give my life to protect you and keep you safe. I feel privileged to have shared your life and be able to watch you grow into a beautiful and confident young woman, becoming a mother yourself to the two most gorgeous grand-daughters a man could ever hope for.

Please don't either of you feel sad for me, and please try to get on with your lives. Maisie and Alice need their happy smiling mum around them, and your mum hopefully has many years ahead of her and needs to spend them enjoying life. Please don't let her waste it pining for me. I'm hoping she can have a few new adventures. It's at times like these, you realise how precious life is and how nothing is guaranteed, so I don't want either of you to ever put your lives on hold. You must follow your heart and your dreams wherever they take you and live your best life.

I don't know when you'll read this letter, as I don't really know how long I've got left, but I'm writing it whilst I'm still able. I've no idea how my condition will deteriorate over the coming months and years, hence what I need to let you know needs to be said whilst my mind is still clear.'

So far, Amanda had read the letter with tears quietly running down her face, but without understanding the obvious pain her grandad was sensing as he sat and watched her. She continued to read…

'The reason for the letter, and at this stage I hope you're sitting down, is to let you know something that I've kept to myself for over 25 years. This is something I can't take to my grave, as I don't know what the consequences of not knowing would ever have on you, so please accept my apologies for not telling you sooner or having the courage to tell you face to face. Also, whatever you may think about

what I'm about to tell you, please don't hold this against your mum. I truly believe she will be as surprised, and perhaps as shocked, as you are likely to be.

Here goes.... Whilst I am your dad and have loved you every single day of your life, treasuring you as my beautiful and talented daughter, I discovered many years ago that I was not your biological father. This came as a complete shock to me, as your mum had never once indicated there was anyone else in her life either before or after we met and married, but the fact remains that at some stage there must have been.

I can't really shed any light on who your biological father is, and can only assume that your mum has blanked this episode out as I truly believe she has no idea I'm not your father. She regularly commented to anyone who listened that you had my eyes, and she believed most of your mannerisms came from me too. I always sensed her sincerity, whilst always keeping quiet; never wanting to disappoint or disillusion her, but also knowing that that would have consequences that I wasn't prepared to face.

We found out we were expecting you a matter of weeks after we were married and you were born just short of nine months after the wedding. Everyone, including your mum and me, believed you to be a honeymoon baby. No one gave a moment's thought to you not being my child, everyone seeing how happy and delighted we both were to be parents, even if it was so soon and unexpected.

You were the most precious and cherished girl on God's earth, with your golden curls and cheeky grin, doted on by everyone who came into contact with you. You were a delight, and we looked forward to the day we could have more children and start to fill all those bedrooms with laughter. Neither of us wanted you to be an only child knowing what pressure that would put on you particularly as we aged.

After four years of trying to get pregnant, we consulted a doctor and were referred for an IVF assessment, as this was a treatment that had recently become available and seemed to be getting good results for parents such as us, so something we considered. Although we were both a little apprehensive, we decided to go ahead anyway – nothing ventured, nothing gained was our approach.

Your mum was fine and perfectly healthy, but my tests showed that I had male infertility, a condition that meant I could never have fathered you. When Dr Greaves Snr. explained it to me in more detail, I was shocked and initially couldn't believe it, so had one of the new DNA tests that had recently been developed. This confirmed what the tests had indicated. I never told your mum the full extent of my results, fearing what that might mean, and how it could upset the relationship we had; I just let her know the problem lay with me, not her.

As far as I was concerned, I was your dad and didn't want anything said or done that would question that. Before this day other than Dr Greaves Snr., who's long since gone, and Dr Joe when he became my GP, only Grandad Tom knew, and even then, that knowledge has only been recent. He was as surprised as I was, but is supportive of what I am telling you, and provided he outlives me he will do whatever he can to support you whatever you decide.

Over the years I have often questioned, but never doubted, my actions and have never doubted your mother's love in any way whatsoever, so please be kind to her. We just got on with life, accepting there wouldn't be any more children and being thankful on so many levels for you. You made our life and our family complete.

As I reflect now, I know that I need to tell you this before I die. There will be consequences, but I pray they will be good ones and that nothing bad will come out of my decision. I believe you have a right to know, should you choose to find out, who your biological father is and I would support you in finding out. In a strange way I am grateful to whoever he is, because without him I would never have had you in my life, so if you ever do meet him, please shake his hand for me. I am weirdly forever in his debt.

Just so you know, I've written a separate letter to your mum that Grandad has too. I will leave it up to you to decide whether to share it with her, but if you do, then hopefully it will help her to open up to you in a way she was never able to do with me.

Be happy my darling, follow your heart and live your best life.

Your loving Dad xx'

Sensing Amanda had finished reading the letter, Tom rose from his chair and walked slowly towards her, fighting the tears in his eyes, arms outstretched ready to embrace her. He took the second letter from his pocket, clearly marked with Monica's name, handing this to Amanda.

'This is the letter for your mum,' Tom said, adding, 'Your dad thought it might be useful for you to read it before you gave it to her to help her understand, and perhaps make it less of a shock. But it's up to you how you handle it.'

As his son had written, Tom had been equally shocked when he'd confided in him only a matter of weeks earlier, never suspecting anything. His wife, Josie, had equally never hinted that anything was untoward, and had encouraged Monica on many an occasion when she had pointed out the similarities in Amanda to her dad, reflecting often on what Ken had done as a baby and how alike they both were. Consequently, he knew this would never have crossed Amanda's mind and had no idea how she would react, or in fact what Monica would think should Amanda choose to tell her, which he felt was a high probability knowing how close mother and daughter were, and sensing how Amanda would need to establish some substance around what her dad had written.

It was obviously her decision what to do next, and although he believed they both had a right to know, he was unsure what that knowledge would bring, and selfishly was concerned what it would mean to him and the rest of the family too. He was an old man and did not like change, but realised sometimes it was unavoidable.

Tom knew that having the strength to face the future and get on with your everyday life when you are already mourning a loved one is difficult in itself, but add a curved ball such as this into the mix, which throws everything you have ever known and trusted throughout your whole life up into the air, well, that requires something extraordinary. Frankly Tom did not know how he himself was going to deal with it, never-mind how Amanda or Monica would react.

All he and anyone else could do would be to wait and just be there to support and manage any fallout there may be.

Chapter 12

Several hours later, after her grandad had left and Maisie and Alice were tucked up snugly in bed, their bath and bedtime routine complete, Amanda went downstairs. The house was quiet and in semi-darkness. In the hour since she had been upstairs with the girls, although the days were lengthening, the night had really come in. She closed the curtains, put on the side lamps and after pouring herself a large glass of wine, got comfy on the sofa. Needing someone to speak to, she reached for the phone and rang her oldest friend, Lisa Meadows. It was a couple of weeks since they had last spoken so regardless of her latest news, a catch-up was in order.

Earlier in the evening, she had intended phoning Damian, but remembering he had planned on working late and was staying over at his flat in the city preparing for an early pitch in the morning, she did not feel he would appreciate the distraction. He was doing a presentation at a new start-up company on the outskirts of the city that was looking to place a service contract for IT support, and tonight him and his team were finessing the messaging and the numbers ahead of their meeting at 10am. Amanda knew how hard Damian had chased this opportunity and what a potentially great fit it was for his business; his team's whole raison d'etre for the last three months seemed to have been focused on this and she did not want to be the one to ruin it for him with her problems. She would speak to him tomorrow afternoon once it was all over, although if they were successful in securing the contract, she realised her chances of catching him at all over the next few weeks looked pretty slim. She might need to book an appointment she thought to herself, smiling.

The last few weeks had been difficult on both of them for completely different reasons, with time spent together limited. She had been caught up in dealing with the aftermath of her dad's death and with supporting her mum; he had been consumed by his business and the obvious demands that was bringing. But for whatever reason, she had sensed an atmosphere developing between them, and worryingly she could not quite put her finger on it, or figure out what she could do about it.

Lisa however was always good for a chat and a gossip, and mid-week could be relied upon to be at home normally any time after 7pm, unless she had a function or a business dinner to attend, which in her line of business was pretty often. Her social life was a lot more glamourous than Amanda's, whose social highlight was an occasional trip to the gym to keep fit, visits to the supermarket to get the groceries or a coffee with her mum. She knew she needed to get out more, but recognised with two young daughters, a career to balance, as well as a husband who was rarely at home it was currently a challenge too far!

Lisa had been Amanda's bridesmaid, was Godmother to both Maisie and Alice and they had been friends since primary school; both growing up in the village and both opting for places at Bristol University because they could not bear to be parted from each other for three years once they had completed sixth form. Their friendship was an interesting one as Amanda was Yang, to Lisa's Yin. They were both completely different in their mannerisms, looks and outlook on life, but at the same time completely complementary in their value sets, both positive and focused, and above all completely trustworthy and loyal.

Lisa had studied Law and after graduating had successfully secured an internship with a medium-sized but growing law firm in Bristol, opting to remain in the city having enjoyed the lifestyle and atmosphere so much during their student days there. The city had a great vibe. She was a bubbly brunette, five foot, five inches in heels, but with a vivacious character, who thrived on social interactions with her many friends, colleagues and extensive network her career demanded.

She was very driven from a career perspective and over the years had honed her art; slowly climbing the career ladder and deservedly making a partner about eighteen months ago. She had worked hard and now specialised in family law, making a good name for herself and building a strong reputation in legal circles. A larger firm had tried to poach her a couple of years ago, but she was loyal and staying where she was had paid off when she made partner. She enjoyed her work, although some of her caseload was quite harrowing given the nature of family law, but at the same time rewarding when she got it right.

Lisa had had several casual relationships over the years with some interesting characters, but was currently not in a 'close relationship', and had no intention of ever getting married or having children herself. She firmly believed motherhood, or fatherhood for that matter, was not for everyone; this feeling being reinforced daily when she considered some of the cases she dealt with. No, she would continue to live-out her maternal instincts vicariously through Amanda and her Godchildren, happy to be the doting aunt who could be relied upon to arrive with armfuls of presents and spoil them rotten; then leave just in time for someone else to tidy up the mess.

She maintained she enjoyed city life too much with all the socialising and schmoozing the Legal world entailed, but whenever she had the opportunity, she secretly enjoyed going 'back home' to the countryside for chill-weekends with Amanda and the girls, or to see her elderly parents who still lived in the area. She, like Amanda, was an only child so felt a certain responsibility and duty to visit her parents whenever she could.

'Hi there,' said Amanda after Lisa answered the phone on the first ring. She was not surprised as Lisa was known for never being too far from her handset, loving social media in whatever shape, form or dimension she could find. Lisa did not particularly tweet or post much herself, as in her profession she had to be mindful what she shared about herself, but found it a useful tool for keeping up with everyone else's exploits. 'Are you free for a chat and a catch-up …… there's something I want to run past you. I'm not sure what to do and could do with some advice.'

'Of course, I'm free, whatever you need just ask', she replied 'I was going to phone you at the weekend anyway to see how you were doing, so you've saved me the call. How's your mum coping?' Lisa had come back to the village for the funeral and had exchanged a few words with Monica at the church, but due to work commitments was not able to stay for the wake. Like everyone else Lisa had not really known what to say or do under the circumstances, so had left feeling helpless.

Lisa had been a frequent guest at Monica and Ken's home when she and Amanda were growing up. She was always treated as one of their family, feeling completely included, almost like another daughter, so she shared their grief and their shock at what had happened. Lisa's parents being a lot older than Amanda's and quite formal in their ways, meant that although she loved them, she never quite enjoyed the same closeness or feeling of fun that she got from being with Monica and Ken.

'It's just I've had a bit of a shock and I don't know what to do or to think' continued Amanda, suddenly realising she had no idea exactly how or where to start in articulating what her grandad had told her, or what she had read herself. It still felt raw and unreal, but knowing that even though she did not want to believe it, in her heart she knew it must be true for her dad to have gone to so much trouble. When she saw his gentle sloping handwriting, she knew straightaway it must be serious. Ken was not known for writing much, always leaving that to Monica – his daily crossword was normally the most exercise his pen ever got.

'Damian is away at the moment, staying over at the flat tonight preparing for some work thing or another tomorrow,' she added not really sure what Damian was up to but sensing he would not appreciate the interruption, 'I don't want to disturb him, but I really need to talk to someone.'

'Sounds serious, what's happened?' asked Lisa curiously. 'Do I need to pour myself a drink and sit down?'

'Yes, and make it a double! You're probably going to need it. Also find somewhere comfy as it may take a while,' she replied not sure whether to laugh or cry, but grateful nonetheless of Lisa's response.

Whilst it was not unusual for conversations such as these to take place between the two friends, the shoe was normally on the other foot, with Lisa the one normally experiencing the dilemma seeking Amanda's sage advice or patient understanding. Lisa, over the years had got herself into quite a few predicaments, so Amanda was well versed in the art of listening, occasionally guilty of trying to stifle her laughter at the other end of the phone when Lisa explained her latest escapades. Lisa had a capacity for getting herself into some interesting situations, often with hilarious and embarrassing outcomes.

Lisa listened, growing increasingly shocked and surprised at what she was being told; prompting Amanda occasionally when she sensed she was struggling to get her thoughts or words out. Amanda read Lisa extracts of the letter, adding her own commentary where it helped to clarify, based on the events her grandad had explained earlier in that day that had taken place between him and his son.

Her dad had apparently become increasingly worried, following his own cancer diagnosis, about genes and genetic diseases, linked to inherited family illnesses. This, according to Grandad, had provided the extra impetus for Ken to tell Amanda the truth; thereby giving her that knowledge should she or the girls ever need to know in their future. He wanted her to try to find her real father, not just to take the news and bury it as he had done. He wanted her to face the consequences in a way he had not been brave enough to do.

'And your mum really has no idea?' questioned Lisa. In her years of practicing family law, she had dealt with many paternity cases, or cases where family members were lost and her clients needed to understand the legalities around tracing people, but normally resulting from adoptions or family estrangements. She had never had a case similar to this to deal with personally or aware of similar cases being discussed by her colleagues. However, whilst she was struggling to believe Monica had no idea, if she reflected on some of the scenarios she had encountered, it was not impossible to comprehend.

'Not that I'm aware, but I haven't spoken to her yet,' she replied, 'but Grandad says there have never been any indications whatsoever, so that kind of supports what my dad has said.'

Amanda thought back to what her mum had told her over the years, about when her parents had first got together, recalling the memories of how her dad had 'courted her' during their time at university, with the occasional trips to the pub or cinema, shared bags of chips in preference to fancy meals out, even quiet walks or cycle rides along the river when the weather allowed. As students there was never a lot of money to go around, so simple pleasures and acts of kindness went a long way. It was a true fairy tale of 'young love' and 'happy-ever-after', always told in a way that left no reason to question or room for doubt.

Their only real sadness, during an otherwise unblemished marriage, had been the fact that they could not have more children. Amanda was aware they had tried for years; they had both spoken with such openness about the process they had gone through before accepting the inevitable. They stayed strong together as a couple throughout this difficult time; never failing to count the blessings they had, with Amanda truly believing that the fact that they were such a small unit made their family bonds even tighter.

'As far as mum ever mentioned,' she recalled for Lisa's benefit, 'she and dad met when they were both at Birmingham University; she was in her second year reading English and dad was in his third year doing Engineering. They both graduated around the same time though, as dad's degree was a four-year course and mum's only three. They were serious about each other, so decided to get married as soon as they could, as neither wanted a long-distance relationship, plus they had the offer of moving in with Grandma and Grandad, so rent free accommodation was the obvious clincher.'

'Mum's family had lived just outside Manchester, but I don't think mum was very close to her mum, and her dad wasn't around. I think he'd left the area and I'm not sure whatever happened to him; in fact, I don't think I ever met him but I can't be sure. Mum was close to her sister, Aunt Jane, but I seem to recall she'd only recently married an American who'd been working over in England. They'd emigrated to America - so in reality mum had nothing to go home for. With Dad still living at home with his parents it was quite a long distance between them, and in those days, Mum couldn't drive, so keeping in contact would have been very difficult. No Facebook or texting then!'

'Well, there must have been someone, somewhere…...' observed Lisa with a wry tone to her voice, 'because without wanting to be rude, I'm sure it wasn't an immaculate conception, was it?'

'I agree, but Mum always said Dad was her only boyfriend. They were married when she was only twenty-one, and to my knowledge there's never been anyone else for either of them.'

'How long after getting married were you born?' enquired Lisa trying to work out the maths.

Amanda explained what she knew of the timeline based on what she had been told over the years, admitting the more she thought about it that there must be something in the story that she had missed.

Her mum and dad had married in early September in a small church in Manchester close to where Monica had been brought up, just a couple of months after graduation. It was a quiet affair, with none of the fanfare of the big royal wedding that had taken place a couple of years previously, just close family and a couple of witnesses. They had gone to a local restaurant for a meal afterwards, but it was a very low-key celebration with the newlyweds leaving after a couple of hours to head to the airport and their flight to Dublin for their short honeymoon, a present from Ken's parents.

Amanda had been born just over eight months later in the following April, so was always known as the 'honeymoon baby', but never having any cause to question that until now.

'Well, I agree there's definitely something missing in the story,' reflected Lisa once Amanda's version of events had come to its end. 'You really need to fill in the gaps though, and you can only do that once you've spoken to your mum. She must be able to recall something, even if it's something she's blanked out all these years.'

But as she said this, Lisa became more concerned what the reasons could be why Monica may had blanked it out; she had some limited experience of clients that had blanked events out, either consciously or sub-consciously, and generally when they were forced to recall it, it was not good. Normally the event related to, or resulted from, a bad experience or an abuse situation, and as a shiver went down her spine. She said a quiet prayer that this was not the case here.

'If I can help in any way let me know,' offered Lisa, suspecting as well as a sympathetic and friendly ear, her knowledge of the legal system might come in useful at some stage. 'Keep me in the loop please, and tread carefully with your mum.'

Having talked everything through with Lisa, Amanda felt a little better in herself, but she knew she would still need to speak to her mum before she would get any real clarity, or have any idea what to do next. It was not a conversation she was looking forward to, more so after Lisa had cautioned her to tread carefully, recognising it was a delicate subject. But if her dad was correct about her mum knowing nothing about this, there was no doubt it was going to be very difficult and would need sensitive handling to get Monica to open up. Amanda knew that until that conversation had taken place she would be no further forward.

She also needed to speak to Damian, again wondering whether she should disturb him tonight. He had made it pretty clear he would be busy all night, so she decided to wait until he came home tomorrow. Her relationship with Damian over the last couple of months had become tetchy and more difficult than usual, but she put that down to her not being herself. She gave him the benefit of the doubt that he was probably just being very careful around her, not wanting to say the wrong thing and giving her more space.

It was late now, so whatever she decided about following up on today's news would have to wait another day, but she instinctively knew it was not just her life that could change.

Was she strong enough to open up Pandora's box, potentially not just turning her world upside down, but everyone's around her too? She was risking opening up memories for her mum that had buried for over thirty years, at what price and with what consequences? But equally was she brave enough to keep it closed, knowing what she did now, but also knowing how important it was to her dad such that he had made it his dying wish for her to find out the truth? It was a dilemma for sure.

Amanda finished off the last of her wine and reflected on how her life had changed in just a few short months. Everything she had believed, the things she had valued and held close and even the person she was, her own biology were all now in question. Those fundamental bricks her life had been built on had been removed, leaving her with a real sense of instability and uncertainty about the future. Amanda was someone who always liked to take control of a situation. She was ordered, organised and prepared, so these new feelings of confusion and uncertainty were completely alien to her.

As she returned the dirty wineglass to the kitchen, adding it to the rest of the pots and pans by the sink waiting to be cleaned away after dinner, she decided that it could all wait until the morning. Having a tidy kitchen suddenly did not seem so important in the overall scheme of things.

Amanda decided a hot, deep and extremely bubbly soak in the bath was in order, one of the true pleasures in life. This normally did the trick to help her relax before bedtime. Remembering Damian was away, leaving her the bed all to herself with no-one to cuddle, she knew she would need all the help she could muster in order to get a good night's sleep. Tomorrow, she anticipated, was going to be a difficult day, but she suspected rather than a peaceful night there was most likely a lot of 'tossing and turning' ahead of her irrespective of how hot or relaxing her bath was.

Chapter 13
Spring 1984

Monica Beraton lay relaxing on the small lawn, well patch of grass really, in the back garden of the small terraced house on the outskirts of Birmingham she shared with three other girls. She was staring up at the cloudless sky, with the late spring sunshine on her face daydreaming and contemplating her future with mixed emotions. Today had been her last exam, her last day of university. If all went well and all the hard work she had put in studying over the last three years paid off, she would graduate in the autumn with a degree in English Literature. She was hoping for a first, but realistically would be happy with a 2:1. It was time to celebrate she told herself, to be positive and enjoy the long summer ahead of her, before starting work and launching herself on whatever career she could find.

Monica loved reading, so English Literature had been the ideal subject for her to study, but in truth she had not really given much thought to where it might lead career wise, or what she would do once she had graduated and needed to return to the real world. She had thought about becoming a librarian, or a teacher, or a journalist but none of these had really sparked much enthusiasm. She knew when she returned home to Manchester there would be pressure to '*get yourself sorted and find a job*' – she could almost hear her mother saying it already, partly because she could not tolerate idleness, but mainly because she would need her income to support them both.

Moving back home, restarting her life in Manchester, living under her mother's watchful gaze again after so long away – none of these was a prospect she relished; particularly as it would be just the two of them now that her dad had remarried and her sister Jane had emigrated to America with her new husband Brad. Monica loved her mother and got on reasonably well with her, but at a safe-distance. Close-up she knew it would be hard, recognising more than ever they were completely different characters. The freedoms she had enjoyed away from home, coupled with the independence she had developed at university had opened Monica's eyes to the world outside, and the endless possibilities she had never appreciated before.

Her mother, Moira was very straightlaced and 'proper' in both her attitudes and general approach to life. Monica often thought her mum had sleepwalked through her teens, twenties and thirties, oblivious to the need to inject any fun into her youthful existence. Monica deduced from her occasional phone calls home that her mother's social life was now non-existent, with her wider life experiences appearing to be limited to the ten-mile radius of her home; the number of friends falling off after her divorce, fading away gradually as one-by-one they lost contact. By the time she reached her forties, Moira was old before her time, almost like an old maid ready to kick up daisies, any remaining life being sucked out of her on a daily basis, replaced by a cynicism of the world that Monica was uncomfortable with. Although she did not know exactly what she did want from life, the one certainty Monica did have was that she did not want to live like her mother.

Also, without her sister Jane there as her sparring partner and confidante, she would have no one to turn to in either the good or bad times. The two sisters were close, even though they were four years apart in age, Jane being the older, so Monica felt that loss even more. Living in a house with other students had been great fun, and whilst they had all had their moments, they had generally got on well. Adjusting back to life at home was going to be tough.

Monica would also miss Ken. They had been an item for the last couple of years, growing very fond of each other. Ken was her first real boyfriend, so she did not have any experience to compare her feelings to, but she felt a real fondness and affection for him, which probably amounted to love. She knew she loved being with him, loved the way he made her feel, making her laugh, but she was not sure if that was what being 'in-love' meant. He was kind, considerate and steady, someone she would miss when he was not around.

Ken had already secured a job at an engineering company on the outskirts of Bristol, not far from the picturesque Cotswold village of Castle Heighton, just outside Cirencester he had always called home. He planned to move back there, to parents he loved and had missed dearly, commuting to Bristol until he found suitable accommodation in the city. When they were at university, he had travelled home most half-terms and holidays, taking Monica with him on occasion to introduce her to his parents. She had loved it, had loved the feel of the village, the countryside and the way Ken's parents made her feel, both welcoming her and including her without effort. It was a far cry from Manchester and the homelife she had endured there. She had taken Ken up to Manchester the previous year as there was a music concert they had managed to get tickets to, but Monica's mum had not been anywhere as near as welcoming; suspicious of Ken and his intentions, so they had not hung around longer than they needed to, or been back since.

'Hi there, can I join you?' Monica had not heard Ken approaching, so was a bit startled when she opened her eyes to see him peering over her, smiling as she lay on the grass. 'Do you want me to bring you out a drink or something to eat?'

It was a lovely day to be out in the garden relaxing and enjoying the spring sunshine, appreciating the uplifting effect it had not just on her, but on everything around her. The flowers were coming into bud and the birds were cheerfully singing in the trees and bushes that enclosed the garden and gave it its privacy. The promise of summer was on the way.

Monica felt extremely lucky that their rental house had its own private oasis in the middle of what otherwise was such a busy and noisy city. She often sat there reading or just thinking when she had spare time. Birmingham was lively, but sometimes too lively for Monica, preferring the quieter things in life.

Ken was a regular visitor to the house, getting on well with Monica's other housemates and occasionally staying over if they were late getting back after a night out. He also enjoyed the garden and gardening, so was never discouraged if he wanted to cut the grass or do some weeding whilst he was visiting. Left to their own devices he suspected none of the girls would know which way to hold a trowel or how to use the lawn mower – let alone have the strength to push it given it was so old and cumbersome, but he kept his thoughts to himself for fear of being termed anti-feminist.

The four girls each had their own room so there was a degree of privacy, but with a constant traffic of visitors crashing on the floors whenever it suited, none of them ever felt alone. It was all very relaxed, but chaotic at the same time; four girls sharing one bathroom was challenge enough, without throwing more people into the mix, but no-one seemed to care. They had a rota for cleaning, cooking and doing the shopping which largely everyone adhered to, but other than that everyone just got on with it, accepting it as the norm.

Ken lived in a similar set-up nearby, but it was a much larger house shared with a group of eight students, all lads. It was more of a party house; regular drinking with loud music coming from one or more of the rooms at any one time, with no rota for cleaning and no one really having the inclination to prepare one. Ken kept his own space tidy, but the chaos and disorganisation in the communal areas made the girls' house by comparison quiet and palatial. He often crashed or studied at Monica's just to get some peace and would happily have moved in had it ever been suggested.

'Thanks, that would be great,' she replied, pleased to see him. 'There's some beer in the fridge if you feel like helping me celebrate. Help yourself to a bottle, and I think there may be some crisps in the cupboard, but there's not much food left as we've all been eating up leftovers or whatever we could get our hands on for what seems like ages!'

Ken had completed his course a few days earlier, so had already had his own subdued celebrations the previous week; he was not much of a socialiser or party animal, but a couple of pints with the lads in the local had been the order of the day, followed by a curry from the Raj, locally considered the best curry house in Birmingham, or more importantly from a students' perspective the cheapest.

No, he had stayed on to wait for Monica to finish her finals; to be there to support her and hopefully distract her from worrying not just about her exams, but what came next. Whilst he had been looking forward to going home, he knew it had been preying on Monica's mind; she was not at all keen to go back to Manchester, where there was no job awaiting her or family ready to welcome her. He knew that university had opened her eyes to the possibility of a different life, but what the life could hold was equally unclear to her.

Ken had grown increasingly fond of Monica over the last couple of years; the fact was he had grown to love her, but was not sure if she felt the same. Their relationship was close, and in recent months had grown physical, but neither had spoken about what would happen after university for them in any serious way, other than they knew they wanted to keep in touch. It was not a discussion they had consciously avoided, just one they had never had, but he knew he could not just abandon her.

'What's on your mind?' he asked as he handed Monica a cold beer, taking a swig of his own. The promised crisps were not in the cupboard, so lunch would have to wait.

She sighed; that one sigh speaking volumes and telling Ken all he needed to know. Their train tickets were booked for the following day, boxes and bags all packed up. Ken's train heading south back to Cheltenham, then connecting to Castle Heighton, Monica's north straight into Manchester Piccadilly. Ken had already managed to take most of his things home on his last visit, but Monica still had all of hers left to take, and lugging that on the train just added to the growing list of things she was not looking forward to.

'I've got a proposal' he said taking a deep breath, before carefully considering his next words. It was something he had thought of recently, but never put into words – not even practiced in front of a mirror, but now after seeing Monica's obvious distress knew he needed to take some decisive action. 'What do you think about us getting married?' He sat back, waiting for Monica's reaction and watching her body language, before deciding what to say next.

'Married? Where's that come from? We're not even engaged' replied Monica surprised, but not in a way that completely ruled out the idea.

Although she was very fond of Ken, she had never felt herself in love with him; but then again had never been in love with anyone, so had nothing to benchmark against. She was only twenty-one, so marriage was not on her agenda for some time.

'I'm in love with you' Ken continued, reaching for Monica's hand, 'and the more I think about it, the more I realise I don't want us to be apart; thinking of you going back to Manchester, knowing you don't want to is tearing me apart too.'

Ken kept staring at Monica, encouraged by the fact that she was now smiling, still not having ruled out his proposal, or worse started laughing at him.

'I know we're both young, but it feels right – for me at least. We could live at my parents' until we get our own house, and you could teach or do whatever you want once we've got settled. I know we've never discussed it, but it's definitely something that would make me happy – what do you say?'

He continued to hold Monica's hand, scared that if he let go it would break the moment, giving her the chance to run away or worse still ridicule his idea. The more he thought about it, the more it formed in his head, the more certain he became that this was what he really wanted; the challenge now was to convince Monica of his love and the seriousness of his proposal.

They sat quietly for a while finishing their beers, both lost in their own thoughts, mulling over the implications of what had just been said, neither sure of the next move. Monica, whilst really taken aback by Ken's proposal – it being the last thing on her mind when she had woken up this morning, was gradually warming to the idea, balancing off the positives and negatives in her mind. The practicalities were swimming around in her head, the possibilities, opportunities this could open up.

She tried to conjure up the negatives too, but struggled to find any that did not immediately turn into a positive. Ken's proposal gave her an opportunity for a new life, in a different part of the country, surrounded by people that cared for her, and who she cared for too. There would no longer be any reason to go back to Manchester and live the life she feared was waiting for her – other than to face her mother and tell her the good news.

'Yes,' she said, with a smile on her face as broad as the proverbial Cheshire cat, 'yes please. I'd love to marry you.'

Chapter 14

Once the decision was made, neither Ken nor Monica could see any reason for waiting or having a long engagement, both deciding to get married as soon as practically possible. Whilst Monica would have loved to be married at the village church in Castle Heighton and never return to Manchester, in reality it did not seem fair to her mother not to be married from her home, particularly given this was officially where Monica still lived, so arrangements would be easier to make.

Ken had changed his rail ticket to travel up to Manchester, escorting Monica and all her luggage home, but with the intention also of asking her dad for Monica's hand. He was old school; believing this to be the correct protocol, not wanting to get off on the wrong foot with either of her parents. He was aware that they had divorced some years earlier, with her dad no longer playing a major role in Monica's life, but nevertheless felt it only appropriate to ask him, giving him the opportunity to attend the wedding and even walk Monica down the aisle if that was what they wanted.

Ken had phoned his parents the previous evening with the news, pleased that they were both happy for them, but mildly surprised that they did not seem at all shocked by the decision or the suddenness of their plans. Tom and Josephine, or Josie as she was known, had suspected there was a growing closeness between them on the occasions they had met Monica, so were delighted to welcome her into the family. She seemed a lovely young lady who they believed would make Ken happy.

Monica's mum, Moira had been more surprised and less accommodating, taking Ken a lot longer to win her over or even bring her round to the idea. Having an unhappy marriage behind her, she was no longer a great advocate of the institution, wanting something more for Monica, but also wanting her daughter back home with her, not living one hundred and fifty miles down the motorway. Being divorced and with Jane in America, she was on her own now, with no prospect of anyone else on the horizon. Since her divorce she had become very introverted, and never encouraged another man into her life.

Moira eventually, but reluctantly, accepted that they would get married with or without her blessing, so went along with their plans, although it was not something she felt like celebrating.

The date was set for the second Friday in September; all the Saturdays had been booked up at such short notice. The local Catholic church was booked for the service, along with a small restaurant for a meal afterwards. It was a modest low-key gathering as Ken was an only child, so other than himself, his parents and Joe his best man, there was no-one else on the groom's side. Monica had her mum and dad, who thankfully decided to attend without his new wife, her old school friend Theresa, acting as chief and only bridesmaid and a couple of family friends on her mother's side. They totalled less than twenty people, so a very intimate affair to say the least.

The only real disappointment for Monica was that her sister Jane, and her husband Bradley Grayson, were not able to attend the wedding. The two sisters were close and wrote regularly, swapping stories and sharing their news. Jane and Brad were expecting their first baby within weeks, so travelling back to England was not really an option, especially with a baby in tow. Jane could have come by herself, but could not imagine wanting to leave her baby with Brad or even with her in-laws for any length of time. Monica was excited for them and understood, hoping that at some stage she would be able to visit and take Ken with her to meet her new niece or nephew once they were married and had got settled. She had not had the chance to visit Jane yet, but the photos she sent of her new home and lifestyle made everything look picture perfect.

Jane had been living in America for just over five years now, moving to the quirky town of Salem in Massachusetts where Brad's family lived, just under an hour's drive north of Boston. Brad worked in an investment bank, commuting into Boston daily, which left Jane free to run the house, along with a small hair salon she had recently bought in the town. Jane had worked for the previous owner, gaining her hairdressing qualifications by attending a local college, so when the owner announced she was retiring, giving Jane the option to buy it, it was an easy decision. It was a well-established business, a low-risk known commodity, and with Brad's business acumen thrown in for free how could she fail! She was loving being her own boss; developing the business further by introducing new beauty treatments, which in turn brought in a different clientele.

Jane was intending taking a few weeks off work on maternity leave after the baby had been born, leaving the salon in the safe hands of one of the other stylists, but knew she would not want to be away too long; in her mind she was already planning where in the salon she could put the crib once the baby was here, although she knew Brad was not too happy with that idea. His parents were also keen to be hands-on grandparents, especially as this was their first grandchild.

Jane had met Brad when his business had first sent him to England for a couple of months to look at a development opportunity the company was considering investing in. He was one of their up-and-coming young analysts. At the time Jane was working as a receptionist at the hotel in Manchester where Brad was staying. Over time Jane got to recognise Brad's routine, looking forward to any opportunity to waylay the handsome American for a chat. A few of the other receptionists had their eyes on him too, but Jane with her long brown hair, pretty smile and infectious laugh stood out and caught his attention.

Brad had not made many friends, or if truth be told much of an effort to go out since he had arrived in Manchester. He was not a natural socialiser, feeling a little awkward around people, so generally opted for room service for his evening meals. He knew there were many restaurants and bistros locally that he could have easily gone out to, but did not really relish the prospect of sitting there eating alone after a long day at the office.

So, when he eventually plucked up courage to ask Jane out for a coffee, he was pleased if not a little surprised that she had agreed. Coffees were followed by the occasional dinner date, or sometimes they would go to the cinema, or see a show or even a band Jane had wangled complimentary tickets to. Brad soon realised how much of a social life was available once you started looking for it and gradually relaxed into city living.

Their friendship developed over a period of weeks, both curious about the other's lifestyle, interests and cultures. Monica had met up with them on one occasion for a coffee, instantly sensing the feelings her sister had for him went further than friendship, and by the look in Brad's eyes those feelings were reciprocated.

Brad eventually returned home, but after a few weeks of writing and frequent telephone calls, he asked Jane to come over to Boston for a visit. Their relationship blossomed from there, and the rest they say is history. Jane loved the American way of life and was instantly adopted by Brad's family, who adored her and her English ways. She never once looked back on her old life.

They had married the following spring in a small civil ceremony in Manchester, neither wanting a fuss nor a religious ceremony, much to Moira's chagrin who had expected a full church service and nuptial mass for both her daughters. Jane and Brad held firm though, accepting that as their family and friends were split over the two continents, logistically anything else would be a nightmare that could only delay their plans.

Brad's parents, Kathryn and Richard Grayson, and his two brothers, Jacob and William, had flown over for the ceremony to join in the celebrations, exploring a little of Manchester and getting to know Jane's family, but whilst Jane's mum, Moira, made them all welcome, it was obvious their lifestyles were so different that no long-term friendships would be struck.

After the wedding Jane and Brad returned to the US, initially moving in with Brad's parents whilst their new house was being built. The house would be a wedding present from Brad's parents. Brad's family came from 'old money'; a long-established family from the Boston region, originally making its fortune several generations earlier from importing foods and other goods to the new world. They had built a thriving business that continued to grow under the current management of Brad's parents and his brother Jacob. Brad took an interest in the business, providing financial advice and support, but otherwise did not have any day-to-day involvement.

When the house was ready, Jane was like a kid in a sweetshop, choosing the furniture and all the fixtures and fittings, without having to have a constant eye on the cost of everything. Coming from her working-class background where money was forever tight, this was a luxury she had never enjoyed before. She had always been conscious of having to be sensible with her money, to save what she could and had been asked to contribute to the family budget as soon as she had received her first wage packet.

Brad by comparison had enjoyed a very privileged upbringing with his parents being unbelievably generous and supportive throughout his life. She and Brad had designed the house themselves; an imposing four bedroom detached property, full of all the mod cons, with a sweeping driveway and a garage for two cars, set in around an acre of land that would one day become a garden. It was ideally situated too, just fifteen minutes-walk to the coast and only a short drive into town. It was idyllic, the type of property any new bride would dream of living in.

Jane recognised she had landed well and truly on her feet when she met and fell in love with Brad; she could not believe her luck and never once regretted the day she had agreed to have coffee with the tall handsome American.

Chapter 15

It was a miserable afternoon as Monica lay on her single bed in the small bedroom at the back of the house she had once shared with her sister, noticing everything was largely unchanged since she had gone away to university three years earlier. She listening to the rain beating against the windows as they rattled in the frames and heard the constant drip-drip from the gutters which were either blocked or damaged. She could not remember the last time her room had been re-decorated, but presumed not since her father had left home some years earlier. Her mother was not one for DIY and paying for a decorator was something she would not want to do, or more likely probably could not afford to waste her money on.

Monica was surrounded by the childhood posters of her various teenage crushes; lovingly cut from the magazines and comics she had occasionally bought and pinned or taped to the walls above both her bed and Jane's bed that still occupied the small room, just in case they had visitors. The walls still had the shelving her dad had fitted, now over-ladened with books she had read over the years and the trinkets she had collected but could not bear to throw away. There was still a collection of soft toys sitting in the corner of the room, which had probably not been touched or played with for at least ten years. Books were her passion and she had loved reading the classics from an early age, Jane Austen being her particular favourite, preferring them to the more modern fiction and magazines her friends enjoyed. Give her an old romantic heroine any day, whisked away by her hero for her happy ever after.

As she sat there, surrounded by her past and almost frozen in time, her mind kept replaying all the things that had happened to her in the last couple of weeks. She could hardly believe that only last month she was a student cramming for final exams, unsure of what her future would hold. Today, a matter of three weeks later she had finished university, was engaged and planning her wedding. She would be married in less than six months, with the prospect of a new and exciting life ahead of her, living in a beautiful part of the country that would take her far away from the industrial north and the homelife she was so desperate to escape.

Whilst still a little apprehensive about how quickly everything had happened, also recognising there remained elements of the overall plan that needed to be fine-tuned, not least of all being what she would do for her career, on balance it felt right. On a practical level she believed that her and Ken could make a good life together and she was sure the feelings she had for him would deepen over time. He loved her and was taking her away from all this, and that for now was enough. He was her modern-day Mr. Darcy, she thought to herself smiling, rescuing her and taking her off to live happy ever after, just without the trusty steed to ride off on.

'Monica, are you still upstairs daydreaming?' her mum shouted from downstairs, harassed as usual that her daughter was not helping her to prepare their tea. 'Jane is on the phone and wants to talk to you. Hurry up it will be costing her a fortune.'

Moira was still not fully bought into the wedding plans, and had expressed as much to Jane herself earlier, but was going along with them for Monica's sake, secretly hoping that they would be cancelled before the big day arrived. She did not understand the need for the rush, being completely insensitive as she was to how unhappy Monica felt returning home, naively expecting her to pick up her old life, almost as if she had never been away.

The old adage 'marry in haste, repent at leisure' kept going through Moira's mind. She had suspected Monica might be pregnant and had questioned her daughter the previous weekend, feeling relieved with the answer, but then became more confused why there was a rush.

For Moira, Monica's return home was something she had looked forward to, if only for selfish reasons, lonely as she was in the house by herself. It never once dawned on her that it might not be what her daughter wanted, or that her daughter was not glad to be home.

'Hi Jane, lovely to hear from you again. Is everything okay? Nothing wrong with the baby I hope,' said Monica half out of breath after running down the stairs. She had already rung Jane with her news, and as disappointed as she was, accepted that Jane could not attend the wedding. She had toyed with the idea of delaying it for a few months until Jane could travel back home with the baby, but in reality, that meant the following spring at the earliest, and frankly she did not fancy the winter at home in Manchester kicking her heels waiting. No, it would have to go ahead without Jane.

'Yes, everything is fine,' Jane reassured her, 'it's just I was speaking with Brad the other evening about how disappointed we are about not getting home for the wedding, and Brad made a great suggestion. He wondered if you fancied coming over here instead for a few weeks during the summer. A bit of a break before the wedding. What do you think?'

'Wow, that would have been brilliant, but I don't think I can afford it with all the wedding stuff to sort and pay for....' replied Monica disappointedly.

She had never flown before, in fact she did not even own a passport, but the idea of going to America was exciting and something she definitely intended to do as soon as she was able, but for now what little savings she had were earmarked for the wedding. She was going to need to buy her outfit, having already decided to look for a lovely dress instead of an expensive wedding gown, but also assumed she would need to contribute towards some of the other costs. Her dad had kindly offered to pay for the meal, with Ken's parents' present being their honeymoon to Ireland, but there were bound to be other expenses she had not thought of – and her mum had definitely not offered to fund anything yet.

'Don't worry about that,' reassured Jane. 'Brad has already said he'll pay for your airfare as an early wedding present, and once you're here you'll stay with us so it won't cost you anything. Come on, it will be great to see you – and if you leave it a couple of months and come early July you can help me with the baby. You can stay as long as you want over the summer, and even if you leave at the end of August, you'll still be home in time for the wedding.'

Jane and Brad's baby was expected mid-June, just a few weeks away now, so whilst Jane was excited, she was also starting to get a little apprehensive, so having Monica around to support her in the early days would be good. Brad's mum was going to help too, but having her sister around would be even better.

Monica thought about it for a while, before replying 'Okay, let me have a think about it and see what Ken says. If I can get everything in place before I leave, and can get my passport sorted, I'd love to come,' suddenly feeling very excited at the prospect of a trip to the States and seeing her sister. Her life was definitely a bit of a rollercoaster at the moment, and this was an offer that had come completely out of the blue. The surprises kept on coming, and thankfully they are all positive, thought Monica to herself as she crossed her fingers for extra luck.

Moira overheard the conversation, excited for her daughter, but a little disappointed that the invite had not been extended to her too. Although they talked frequently on the telephone, it was a long time since she had seen her eldest daughter, and although they had never been particularly close, deep down she still missed her. Jane's life since she emigrated was so different from what it had been, with Moira recognising that she did not really play a role in it anymore. Their lives had diverged so much over recent years, that sometimes Moira did not know what to talk to Jane about, or understand what Jane told her about. She had seen photos Jane had sent, but had no real appreciation of the lifestyle she now enjoyed. She was also resigned to the fact that she would probably not be playing much of a role in her new grandchild's life once it arrived either.

Whilst this saddened Moira, she was not sufficiently motivated to do anything about it, so had to accept it as the inevitability it was. Her daughters had chosen to leave her, as had her husband and now she was all alone, left to wallow in her own despair.

Chapter 16

Early the following morning, Monica was anxiously waiting outside the post office at 9am willing the doors to open.   Thankfully the weather was dry after the downpour they had endured the previous day, as she joined the queue of pensioners who had all arrived even earlier than her to collect their pensions and share their moans and niggles with the others in the queue. Monica tried to keep her face straight as she overheard a couple of elderly women exchanging details of their recent trips to the doctors; each one trying to out-do the other on the nature of complaints and ailments they 'enjoyed'.

If she was serious about going over to see Jane, then getting her application for a passport submitted was her top priority. Monica had never needed a passport before, never having travelled further afield than Wales. Some of the students she had studied with had already been on package holidays to Spain and Majorca with their families, with others even planning gap years travelling to more exotic destinations on their own once they had graduated. Places like Australia, New Zealand and Thailand had even been mentioned. Travel was just one of those luxuries Monica had never experienced, and flying, well that was going to be a whole new ball game. It all seemed very glamorous to her, so far removed from what she was used to; she could not believe how excited she was and had to keep pinching herself to check it was all real.

Holidays when she and Jane were growing up had generally been limited to a road trip to a Butlin's holiday camp for a week, or a long-weekend camping trip to the Lakes; but thankfully nothing that required them travelling too far in her father's old blue Morris Minor. Monica remembered the time they had gone to Butlins's at Skegness when she was around seven; Jane and herself crammed into the back seat along with all their bags. It was so hot and uncomfortable, that by the time they got there her legs were so numb she thought she would never be able to walk again. There was a constant chorus from both her and Jane of *are we there yet?* Anything beyond an hour's drive was too much in that car, with even her father admitting it has taken much longer than the couple of hours drive he had thought.

The following year they stayed nearer home, booking a week at the Butlin's camp in Pwllheli, but the car struggled so much through the winding Welsh hills, with the impatient drivers creating a cacophony of beeping as they formed a convoy behind them, frustratingly unable to overtake round the tight bends.

Holidays dried up completely once her parents divorced, with the occasional trip to Blackpool on the bus to see the illuminations, or a short visit over to see an elderly aunt in Scarborough being generally as far as her mother felt comfortable venturing with two young children in tow. Their father had in time moved on and remarried, having a baby son just over a year later, leading Moira to begrudgingly point out to her daughters that there would be no chance of an invitation for them to spend their holidays with him now that he had got his new family.

No, America was going to be the second biggest adventure of Monica's lifetime, after university that is. They say travel broadens the mind, introducing you to a host of new experiences and opportunities; well after such a sheltered life, Monica was definitely ready for her mind to be broadened and anxious to embrace any new experiences she could get her hands on, and having the opportunity to share that with Jane was just the icing on the cake.

Monica was just a bit upset Ken would not be travelling with her, but knew that having time to herself before the wedding would be good for her confidence, allowing her to further develop that sense of independence she had recently started to gain. They had been together almost every day for the last couple of years, with Monica becoming increasingly reliant on Ken, so a month or so apart, where she could make her own decisions should not matter – after all, they had their whole lives ahead of them when she got home and became Mrs. Moreton.

Chapter 17
Present day

Damian had arrived home from work relatively early the following evening, bounding into the kitchen and heading straight to the fridge for a beer, excited about how the presentation had gone and optimistic that his company would secure the deal. His team had apparently 'pulled out all the stops', with the 'messaging being spot' on, 'hitting all the customer's hot buttons' with the 'financials looking sound'. As he spoke, Amanda tried to follow all the management jargon, assuming correctly from the look on his face it was good news, but in reality, she was just waiting for him to calm down and take a breath, so she could take the opportunity to talk to him.

Throughout the day, she had reflected on her discussion with Lisa the previous evening, replaying it over and over again in her mind, increasingly knowing that the 'do nothing' option was not one she could take. She was sure her dad had confided in her for a reason. He could have so easily gone to his grave without ever saying anything, with nobody being any the wiser. But he had not done that. He had taken a huge and presumably calculated risk, trusting principally in her love for him. She imagined he had written the letters with his fingers crossed, praying the bombshell would not backfire on him, and in so doing sullying Amanda's memories of him and the close relationship they had enjoyed.

He had also recognised there would be consequences, but the more Amanda re-read the letter, the more she got the sense that her dad was pushing her towards them, perhaps sensing that everything was not as it should be with her life.

Amanda knew there was the potential, with an unquantifiable risk, that whatever stones she upturned could significantly impact not just her life, but the lives of those around her. Her mind continued to spin with thoughts of her marriage, her daughters, her career choice, her relationships with her mum and her Grandad Tom – in fact everything she valued, to question what it was that her dad sensed was not quite right, but could not bring himself to say to her directly.

'Well done - that all sounds really promising, when will you find out if you've been successful?' Amanda enquired supportively.

She recognised that even though she wanted to blurt everything out that was whirling around her own head, she should probably bide her time. It was important she had his full attention once she started talking, so she decided to wait until he had let off steam and calmed down a bit. She needed him to concentrate and be focused, so resolved to be patient and wait until after Maisie and Alice had gone to bed, after which they could both relax and talk without interruption.

A couple of hours later, once dinner and bath time were complete and the girls tucked safely in bed, they eventually went into the lounge. Amanda noticed Damian was still looking at his phone, having taken several calls and text messages throughout the evening, so still was not sure if she had his full attention, but decided she would risk it. She had waited patiently all evening and if she waited much longer it would be time for bed.

'I had a visit from Grandad yesterday afternoon,' she started slowly, waiting until Damian looked at her before she continued. 'He brought me a letter Dad had written to me just before he died.'

Damian, sensing immediately from the tone of Amanda's voice that this was more than a casual comment, put down his phone and looked directly at her, trying to read her face for any tell-tale signs about what might be coming next. Although he knew Tom was a regular visitor, popping in for cake and coffee, or sometimes something a bit stronger whenever he got the opportunity, this did not sound like one of those occasions. Also, bringing a letter from Ken seemed unusual. In all the years they had been together, Damian could not recall a single occasion when Ken had written a letter. That was not his style.

'Oh, what was that about?' he asked, adding, 'is everything okay?'

'Well, yes and no…' Amanda began, her voice suddenly starting to quiver as she tried to speak. 'I'll let you read the letter for yourself, rather than me trying to explain, but the fact is Dad wasn't my dad - and he now wants me to find my real dad. Frankly, I don't know what to do or what to think' she added, as the tears she had been holding back all day suddenly started to flow uncontrollably.

Damian, completely taken aback by what he had just heard, reached over to Amanda, pulling his sobbing wife into his arms whilst she continued to cry. He did not know what to say to comfort her, or even where to begin in asking her what she meant, so just held her until she was ready to go on.

After she had calmed down a little, Amanda handed Damian the letter. She sat quietly as she watched him read it, trying to gauge from his expression what his reaction might be. In her own mind she already knew what she needed to do, but wanted Damian to reach the same conclusion, without any direction or prompting from herself. She just prayed that he would not dismiss it and tell her to forget all about it.

Amanda knew Damian was not the type of character that displayed his emotional side easily, or dealt with his personal feelings openly and had reluctantly accepted this as one of his traits. Early on in their relationship, she had recognised his default mode was to avoid sensitive issues whenever he got the opportunity, feeling much more comfortable to sweep whatever he could under the carpet and just move on, frequently leaving Amanda to tackle whatever could not be ignored. Generally speaking, this worked well for them, in a sort of good-cop, bad-cop type of way, but occasionally it was a sore point particularly when she really needed his support.

However, Amanda did recognise that Damian's strengths lay in other areas. He was great at decision making in any business scenario; good with managing their finances; could be relied upon when dealing with practical issues, provided these excluded DIY, but just not the best shoulder to cry on. Amanda realised, as she waited for him to finish reading, it was this more practical perspective she was relying on to help balance her emotional reaction. She needed him to help guide her through the minefield that potentially lay ahead.

Chapter 18

The following morning turned out to be bright, breezy and currently rain free, but if the weather forecasters were to be believed, there was the promise of showers in the afternoon. Damian had left on the early train, as usual, keen to get back to the office and debrief the wider team following the successful pitch the previous day. He needed everyone to be prepared and ready to roll should they be awarded the contract. He felt really positive and upbeat, more so than he had in a long time. Business had been okay recently, but without this contract, he might begin to worry.

Although he and Amanda had talked everything through the previous evening, with him agreeing with Lisa's views that Amanda needed to speak to her mum before she made any decisions or did anything else, he personally did not feel too impacted by what he had read, or feel that he could add anything by staying at home, so continued as if nothing significant had happened. Thankfully Amanda had not asked him for anything specific or any particular help, but he made a mental note to get his wife some flowers on the way home to help cheer her up. He would ask his secretary to remind him when he got into the office.

It was Wednesday, and even though Amanda was taking a short break from college on compassionate leave, she had decided to keep the girls in their routine as much as possible – so today was one of the days to drop them off at Susie's, their childminder. Maisie was due to start school in September, so only had a few months left at Susie's, but Alice would continue to go there for a couple of years until it was her own turn to go to school. They both loved Susie and enjoyed playing with her two children, one of whom was also pre-school and would start at St Anthony's reception class with Maisie in the autumn. Both Amanda and Susie knew how valuable it was to have friends and agreed that the transition for both of their children would be so much easier because of their established relationship

Amanda had decided that once she had dropped the girls off, she would call in at her mum's house for a coffee and a chat. She had mixed emotions about how the conversation would go; her mum had been quite withdrawn since her dad's death and not her usual self, which Amanda accepted as normal, but at the same time she found it upsetting and was determined not to let her mum wallow in her grief. She was only fifty-five and in Amanda's mind too young to be wearing widow's weeds. To quote her dad, life had to go on.

'Hi Amanda, hello Maisie and Alice, don't you both look beautiful today. I love your wellies!' said Susie in her usual bright manner, ushering the girls into the house, relieving them of their coats and bags on the way. 'Isla and Josh are already in the playroom, why don't you go through and join them?' Both girls hurried off as directed.

Amanda always sent them prepared for all seasons, with a bag containing a clean change of clothes should the need arise. But knowing that with the rain forecast for later today, they would be begging to play in the garden once it had stopped, today clean dry clothes would be a must. The lure of stomping in the puddles and splashing each other was something no child could avoid.

'Thanks Susie. Are you sure you're okay if I leave the girls for a couple of hours? I should be back early afternoon to pick them up. There're just a few things I need to sort out and doing it without them in tow will be so much easier.' Susie noticed that Amanda looked tired and drawn, not her usual bubbly self, but then that was only to be expected given the circumstances.

'No problem, they will be fine with me. Isla and Josh missed seeing them last week, so don't worry. Just come back when you're ready,' reassured Susie, adding, 'I imagine you and your mum have got a lot to sort out at the moment,' empathetic to what Amanda must be going through. Her own mother had died when Susie was a teenager, and whilst she had not had to do too much 'sorting out' of her mother's things, she remembered clearly her father being besides himself trying to get everything organised, whilst battling the feelings of being lost and helpless at the same time. It was one of those memories that had a bad habit of resurfacing every time someone she knew lost someone close, Susie thought to herself.

'Yes, lots to do. I'm just off to my mum's now in fact. I'll let her know you were asking after her,' smiled Amanda before turning and walking towards the gate, 'See you later then, I'll phone if anything changes.'

Amanda got back into the car and drove the mile or so to her mum's house. As she pulled up outside, it was lovely to see the creepers starting to bud around the door, with the tulips and daffodil bulbs bravely pushing their heads up after such a harsh winter, eagerly looking for the first rays of sunshine. Amanda smiled, remembering this was the time of year her dad had loved best. New life awakening from its winter hibernation, full of promise and anticipation for the summer ahead. Her dad loved to potter in the garden regardless of the season, but the spring was his favourite time of year and as such had become hers too.

As Amanda walked up the path, she wondered what would happen to the gardens now and who would manage their upkeep. Her mum loved the fruits of dad's labours in the garden, relaxing in her sunchair enjoying the scents and colours of the wide varieties of plants Ken planted, or hosting a ladies' coffee morning under the pagoda, but she was not known for putting on her wellies or gardening gloves and turning over the soil too much herself. Amanda imagined they would have to look for a gardener, mentally adding this to the list of things that needed to be sorted at some stage, but perhaps not a priority for today.

'Hi Mum, are you at home?' shouted Amanda as she let herself in through the front door and walked towards the back room. The front door had been locked, but she did not for one minute presume her mum would not be sitting in her normal chair at this time of the morning. In fact,

Monica had hardly left the house in the weeks since Ken's death, relying on a host of neighbours to kindly bring the occasional bag of groceries to the door if they were passing. It was not that she could not go out – she just did not feel up to it at the moment. In a small village like theirs, people were bound to stop and speak to her, offering their condolences and enquiring after her, and frankly whilst she knew it was all well intentioned, she did not feel like risking it at the moment. Perhaps in a few weeks she would feel ready, but not yet.

'Hello Darling, what brings you here?' smiled Monica, looking up when she heard Amanda approach. 'This is a nice surprise. Have you time for a drink? I'll put the kettle on,' immediately answering her own question.

The two women busied themselves in the kitchen, making cups of tea and slicing a fruit cake that one of the neighbours had dropped off the previous day, comfortable in each other's company, but at the same time neither needing to speak or even knowing what words to use to break the silence. Monica and Amanda normally had a chatty relationship, speaking on the phone each day if not in person, but recently they had struggled to find that easy rapport, both perhaps conscious of triggering a memory or saying the wrong thing.

Monica put everything onto a tray and carried it back into the sitting room, placing it on the low glass table as Amanda hovered, wondering where best to sit before she started the conversation that she could not put off any longer.

Her dad's favourite armchair, worn over many years and in need of reupholstering, looked empty and abandoned without its resident occupant.

Amanda toyed with sitting in it to be close to her mum, but decided against that, opting instead for the settee alongside her. From here she hoped she could read her mum's face better, but still be close enough to comfort her when she needed it, and having already read the letter written for Monica herself, she had the tissues at hand.

'Mum, there's something really important I need to discuss with you,' started Amanda once they had both got comfortable. 'I had a visit from Grandad the other day and he brought me some news.'

'Oh dear, he's okay, isn't he? I only saw him last week and he didn't mention anything', automatically assuming the news related to Tom's health. At eighty-three he did remarkably well for himself, but equally she knew things would eventually catch up with him – as they did with everyone she mused.

'Yes, he's fine, no need to worry there,' Amanda tried again, 'No, the news was about Dad.'

'Oh….' Monica looked surprised, completely clueless as to where this conversation was going, but sat back waiting for her daughter to continue.

'Dad wrote me a letter just before he died that he left with Grandad for safe keeping. He also wrote one for you, which he asked me to hand to you.'

'A letter? Your dad never wrote letters. Are you sure it's from him?' questioned Monica, surprised at what she was hearing.

'Yes Mum, it's here in his handwriting' reaching into her bag to pull the letters out, then handing one to Monica. 'I've read mine, and once you've read yours then we can perhaps have a little talk about it.'

Monica took the letter, gently touching the envelope where Ken's writing so obviously was, still at a loss to even guess what the contents of the letter might be, but realising from the way Amanda kept looking at her, it was not to be ignored.

My dearest Monica,

I have no idea where you'll be or, when you'll read this letter, so as I write it, I'm picturing you reading it in the garden, sitting in your deckchair with a cool G&T in your hand. Hopefully the sun is shining on you and all the flowers are looking at their best. But if it's the middle of winter, then I imagine that big fire blazing in the grate and you wrapped up all cosily, staring out into the garden watching the birds scrambling for their food.

Whatever the weather, I want to imagine you happy, and I pray that you are keeping well and that Amanda is with you as you read this letter. You two are the most precious people in my life and it's important to me that you are both strong supports for each other. I want you to get on with living your lives, and taking every new opportunity life throws your way.

What I am about to say, I have already said to Amanda, so please don't feel there is any need to keep this to yourself. The mere fact she has given you this letter is a reflection that she has taken what I told her seriously, and as such I ask you to please do everything in your power to help and support her, whatever she decides to do.'

As Monica finished the first page, she still had no inkling where this letter was going, or why Ken was reaching out to her in this way. Amanda looked at her, encouraging her to continue reading.

'Amanda has always been our shared joy, delighting us in everything she did; from that tiny baby that kept us awake at night, to the teenager that equally kept us awake at night, to the beautiful and confident young woman she has become, giving us those two gifts, our precious granddaughters we have been so privileged to share. Every stage of her life has positively mapped onto ours, and I for one wouldn't change a moment of it. I count myself so blessed.

I remember how disappointed we were when we didn't have more children, and the process we went through with IVF and all the tests and treatment to find out why. This period of our lives for both of us was emotionally very difficult for different reasons; but for me it revealed something that could have changed the course of all our futures if I had acted differently. It is for this reason that I'm writing now in case you're beginning to wonder where my ramblings are taking you. I was never known for my letter writing, was I?

Monica smiled to herself as she read on.

As you will recall, it was my test results, not yours, that determined we couldn't have more children. Whilst we were both disappointed, we decided to move on, counting the blessings we already had and accepting we didn't need another baby to make us happy; we were already a happy family with so much going for us.

At the time however, I wasn't as open as I should have been about what my test results were, but effectively they showed that I was impotent; but what the doctor went on to explain was that this was a condition I had always had, not something I had recently developed. What this meant was that I could never have fathered Amanda. A subsequent DNA test confirmed this.

I've selfishly lived with this knowledge ever since, knowing that if I questioned it, there was a real possibility that you could leave me and take Amanda too. I loved you both so much, I always have, and could never contemplate losing either of you. In my eyes, and more importantly in my heart, Amanda is my daughter. For keeping this from you I ask your forgiveness.

The question of who Amanda's biological father is has only recently concerned me; more so since my diagnosis and the growing research and insights around genetic diseases and inherited illnesses. As our grandchildren grow, I want them to have access to the best life they can, and if this helps protect theirs and Amanda's health in any way, then I am grateful whatever the consequences.

I wanted so much to talk to you about it, but never knew how to broach the subject, or the right words to choose. I suppose I've taken the coward's way out and hope that you don't think any less of me because of this.

I've long since accepted that there must have been somebody else in your life at some stage, but as you've never given me any cause to question your love for me, I never saw the need to open this up. I truly believe you've always seen Amanda to be the honeymoon baby everyone else believed her to be, and I hope that by forcing you to relive this now that it hasn't reopened any bad memories.

As such, if you can find it in your heart to help, assuming it's at all possible, I would like Amanda to find her father. I presume if he's still around he will probably be as shocked at the news as you are – suddenly acquiring a grown-up daughter he never knew about. I hope he doesn't bear me any ill feelings for not being more open. My selfishness has robbed him of so much of her life. As for my feelings towards him, I've explained to Amanda that the only feelings I hold towards him are of deepest gratitude for the gift he gave us.

Please forgive me, your ever-loving husband, Ken

As Monica had been reading the letter quietly to herself, Amanda had watched her mum's face closely, trying to gauge her changing expressions to determine what could possibly be going through her mind. Amanda had already read her mum's letter, therefore knew exactly what it contained, so the feelings she saw reflected in her mum's face of disbelief, followed by the shock her dad had predicted, but also a real warmth in some of the memories it was provoking were all expected. Eventually there came the more puzzled expression as her mum was obviously trying to work through what was being suggested, including the realities of the situation it depicted.

After a few moments, Monica raised her head and looked directly at Amanda, unsure what to say. The tears that Amanda had predicted had not arrived, in fact Monica was not giving much away, but Amanda was sure her mum was working something through in her head.

'Well, that is a shock, I don't know what to say,' said Monica, looking at Amanda, this time she was the one trying to gauge her daughter's reaction.

She could tell from the expression on Amanda's face that she had come today looking for answers, obviously already accepting what her dad had written to her, never questioning or thinking there could be any other alternative.

Monica reflected: Ken was right, she had never once questioned the fact that he had not been Amanda's father, always believing their baby was the product of a happy honeymoon. She even believed Amanda carried Ken's mannerisms, even having a look of him as a baby from the photos Josie had shared, which all reinforcing the certainty she had felt.

She also recalled the IVF process they had gone through, the tests, the waiting, the agony of finding month after month that she was not pregnant, and the eventual acceptance that she would never be a mother again. Monica had suffered with mild depression and anxiety at the time, but as the months passed had been content to accept at face value what Ken had told her about his results, never digging any deeper or questioning either him or the consultant on what she had been told.

She reflected now whether subconsciously she had known not to scratch too hard, happy just to accept what was being said and get on with their life, but not because she suspected anything about Ken, more the risk that it could drive a wedge between them. She was concerned if Ken wanted more children, he may leave her and find someone else; always in the back of her mind the fate that had befallen her mum when her dad left home, divorcing her mum and starting another family with another woman.

Ken was right, they had enjoyed a great life together, their small family unit. Monica was as keen as Ken not to upset the equilibrium in any way, not to risk putting their comfy life in jeopardy.

'Is it something you feel able to talk about mum or do you need some time?' asked Amanda, conscious of not wanting to be too pushy, before adding, 'I appreciate it's been a shock for you, it was for me too. But Dad's right, I do want to find out more, and would like your help.'

'I know darling, but do you mind if we pick it up another day, it has been quite a shock and I want to do some reflecting on what your dad has said, if that's okay?' replied Monica, clearly trying to buy herself some thinking time. 'Why don't you come around later in the week for lunch and we can have a longer chat. I'll give you a ring.'

And with that, she picked up the teacups and walked them back into the kitchen, drawing a clear line under the conversation for the time being.

Chapter 19
Summer 1984

When the official envelope had arrived on Monica's doormat a month later containing the passport, to say she was ecstatic was a bit of an understatement. The trip could now take place, she could finally start to get her arrangements in place.

'It's here. My passport has arrived!' she said excitedly when Jane answered the phone on the second ring '...how soon can Brad book my flight?'

'Brilliant, I could do with you here yesterday,' said her sister laughing, pleased to hear the excitement in Monica's voice, 'Clara is really taking it out of me and any help at all would be appreciated. I can't remember the last time I slept!'

Jane had delivered a healthy 9lbs baby girl three weeks earlier, and whilst everyone was delighted, Jane was shattered. When they came home from the hospital, Brad had taken a couple of days off work to help, but it was a busy time for him and getting a longer break at the current time was not really an option. His parents helped out where they could, but their time seemed to be spent cooing over the crib rather than attending to the more practical jobs, so Jane felt like she was entertaining them as well as nursing a new-born.

Brad had at least organised a lady to come in for a couple of hours each morning to do the housework and help with the cooking, but Jane still felt she was meeting herself coming backwards there seemed so much to do. Life was hectic, but when she looked at Clara's angelic little face she was not complaining in the least.

Monica did not know the first thing about babies, but that was not going to stop her helping out. She was so excited to be going to visit Jane, and meeting her new niece was just the icing on the cake as far as she was concerned. She would happily learn to change any number of dirty nappies if that was what it took.

'I'll get Brad to book you on the first direct flight over,' said Jane, conscious that she did not want an indirect route that could see Monica getting lost somewhere. 'I'll ring you later with the details. He can meet you at the airport too so that you don't get lost once you've landed.' Jane added, knowing how inexperienced a traveller Monica was, and regardless of how excited she was now, knew how anxious she would be on arriving at Boston's Logan International Airport not knowing where to go. Salem was only a forty-minute drive away, so in American terms, just around the corner.

'Well, I can be packed and ready to go by tomorrow morning - I've checked the bus times to the airport and they're pretty frequent. Mum has leant me an old suitcase, I've changed a bit of money into dollars, all the plans for the wedding are in hand, so I don't think there's anything else left for me to worry about over the next few weeks. I'm all yours, and I can't wait to see you and meet my new niece.'

'Okay then, leave it with me. I'll phone you when it's all sorted. I've got to go; I think I can hear Clara crying. She must have just woken up,' said Jane, suddenly registering what the noise in the background was. She had hoped to get herself a quick drink and a sandwich before Clara woke up, but obviously that was not going to happen now.

'Great. I'll wait for you to ring me back then' said Monica hanging up the phone, unable to contain her excitement. She could hear her mother in the background, quietly tutting to herself; unhappy that Monica was leaving her again after only returning from university a matter of weeks earlier. In her view, Moira felt the trip was unnecessary. She could not understand why she wanted to go to the other side of the world, especially with a wedding to plan – something else that she felt was totally unnecessary.

Jane phoned back the following day confirming the details of the one-way flight booked for the day after that. Monica just needed to pick the ticket up at the British Airways desk when she got to the airport. Jane also went through a list of instructions on what to bring, including dos and don'ts for the journey. She confirmed exactly where Brad would meet her at the airport, but gave Monica an emergency telephone number just in case.

Monica could hardly contain herself as she went to bed that evening.

Chapter 20

Her first experience of flying was all that Monica had dreamed of and more; the excitement of going through the airport; being shown to her seat by the glamourous stewardess; even the meal was better than she had expected, having stocked up on crisps and biscuits in the shop beforehand just in case. She watched the film – Educating Rita, which she had already seen at the cinema with Ken the previous year, but it still made her giggle to think of Jane as the inverse of Rita; Jane having just finished her college course to become a hair stylist, whereas Rita was using education to better herself to move away from hair styling.

Monica even tried to get a couple of hours sleep, so that when she landed in Boston, she would not be too tired. Jane had mentioned with the long flight and the five-hour time difference she could be jet lagged, but Monica really did not understand what she meant, having never gone through time zones before, other than putting the clocks forward in the spring or backwards in the autumn, but that was only an hour so surely did not really count.

Having finally navigated her way through the airport and survived the ordeal of Immigration and Customs, Monica feeling shellshocked was relieved to see Brad waiting for her, and even more delighted to see her sister by his side, looking tired, but with a smile on her face from ear to ear. Monica dumped her bags, leaving Brad to rescue them before they were trodden on by people rushing past, screamed and ran towards Jane, giving her the biggest cuddle she could manage, oblivious to the crowds around her, or the scene she might be creating. She was here, in America, and simply could not wait for the summer that lay ahead of her, or all the new and exciting adventures that she was going to have.

Chapter 21

The next couple of days were almost like a whirlwind for Monica, once she had got over her jetlag and settled in with Jane and Brad, and finally having a chance to cuddle her new niece, Clara. Monica was not particularly maternal, with little if any experience of children and even less with babies, but she soon got the hang of changing nappies and happily helped Jane with the feeds and pram-pushing whenever they went out for a walk. At only a few weeks old, Clara did not do much but sleep, eat, cry and need changing, but nevertheless she had the ability to make everyone coo all over her wherever she was. She was a delightful baby with a head of curly blonde wispy hair and the brightest blue eyes Monica had ever seen.

Monica was impressed with Jane and Brad's house; it was so spacious and modern, and very pretty into the bargain, with all the furnishings and fabrics Jane had chosen making the house feel cosy and lived in. She had her own room, with a big double bed to stretch out on, even an en-suite that was bigger than the bathroom at home, with its own bath. Monica had only ever had a single bed before, so this in itself was a luxury, but to have a bath to use whenever she wanted, without having to wait for the boiler to heat the water up, or ask her mother if it was alright to use the hot water, well this took it to a whole new level.

Monica, who had briefly met Brad's parents, Kathryn and Richard Grayson, and his two younger brothers, Jacob and William when they had all come over to Manchester for the wedding, was now getting to spend some quality time with them, getting to know them better and feeling very relaxed in their company. Jacob was just a year younger than Brad and looked very similar in appearance to him, both taking after their father in looks and mannerisms; quite shy and reserved, but exceptionally polite. William, or Will as he preferred to be called, was five years younger and resembled his mother in appearance and outlook, being much more relaxed in his manner, very open and chatty. Both brothers still lived at home with their parents, neither apparently declaring any current love interests, according to their mum, although looking at the twinkle in Will's eye when his mother mentioned this, Monica was not too sure.

Jacob worked in the family business, currently learning the ropes and helping out on the marketing side, while Will was still at university studying Economics; home for the summer and looking for a good time. He too planned on joining the business after his graduation the following year, although possibly taking another gap year before finally settling down. He had already had one year out before going to university, travelling around the States mainly, but thought another one going off to Europe would be a great idea, especially if his parents would fund it. He had met a group of guys who were planning something for the following summer and he was seriously thinking about joining them.

Monica noticed how well they all got on together, how relaxed the atmosphere was whenever they met up, and more importantly how much Jane was welcomed and accepted within their obviously close-knit family unit. There was an intimacy there that neither she nor Jane had ever experienced with their own family back in Manchester, a closeness that Monica hoped she could emulate with Ken's family when she moved down to live with them after the wedding.

The family was also welcoming to Monica, including her in whatever activities they could, happily introducing her around to their friends whenever the occasion allowed. Kathryn, or Kitty as she preferred to be called, took Monica into Salem for coffee shortly after her arrival to show her the sites and explain the quirky little town to her, along with its history of witches and the famous witch trials back in the late 17th Century. Being brought up and raised in the area, she was obviously very proud of her town and took great pleasure in showing it off.

Monica was fascinated as Kitty explained about the thirty people, mainly women who had been tried and found guilty of witchcraft, nineteen of whom were subsequently hanged. Kitty showed Monica the memorials around the town to the witches, explaining a little about how over the years some of those found guilty have been exonerated, but also how the town continued to celebrate the witches, with all its ghostly tours, supernatural events and haunted attractions that could be found all over the town and accounted for a lot of tourist interest and people's livelihoods.

Kitty also took Monica to the Peabody Museum in the centre of Salem, pointing out it was just a couple of minutes' walk from Jane's hair salon. Kitty loved the museum and was not only a regular visitor, but also one of its patrons, working with other local businessmen and volunteers in support of the museum's long-established tradition of displaying the world's best exhibits and collections.

Kitty gave Monica a potted history of her husband's family's background; noting that their importing business had its origins back in the late eighteenth century when their ancestors had arrived from England to seek their fame and fortune. The Grayson family had begun importing tea and spices from the far-east back in those early days. She pointed out that many of the traders had a habit of bringing antiquities and arts from the colonies back into America along with their cargos, and eventually the museum had been created to display them. The family's close connections with the museum, developed through their business being so intertwined with the maritime history from those early days, continued to this day.

'Hello stranger!' Jane smiled as Monica returned home from her most recent trip with Kitty to the town to collect some essentials for dinner. 'You must have been up and out early. Have you had breakfast?'

Kitty was cooking dinner for the whole family that evening and had invited Monica to go shopping with her to collect the fresh lobsters from the market; having never seen or eaten lobster before, Monica could not refuse.

'Yes, thanks,' Monica replied. 'I've been down to the market with Kitty to get lobsters for dinner and we picked up a coffee and a pastry in town at that little French café just opposite the harbour. It was fun, I've never seen a lobster close up before - they were still alive and Kitty had to choose which ones she wanted from a barrel!' she laughed, enjoying each new adventure this holiday was bringing.

'Well, I definitely think America suits you as much as it suits me' said Jane, sensing how much fun Monica had had over the last few weeks and how relaxed her sister had become. 'Perhaps it's time to rethink whether you go home, or whether I could tempt you into staying here longer – there's plenty of room,' added Jane, half joking, half testing her sister's plans for the future.

Jane had never met Ken, so whilst she had nothing against him in principle, the whole concept of them getting married had taken her by surprise, particularly learning from Monica that the proposal had come from nowhere. Jane sensed Monica's drive was associated with not wanting to stay at home with their mother, but was unsure this was the right motivation for making such a momentous decision. However, she was happy to go along with Monica's plans, respecting her decision, but still questioned to herself whether it was the right path for her to take, or whether her sister needed to live a little before she settled down.

'Oh, by the way', said Monica, reaching for a cup to pour herself some coffee from the pot that Jane seemed to constantly have on the stove, 'I was speaking to Will earlier, and him and a few mates are taking out a boat at the weekend and going up the coast. He asked if I wanted to join them. Apparently, it's Labor Day weekend, whatever that means. What do you think? Will I be okay going with them?'

'I think that's a brilliant idea' replied Jane, 'Brad and I did that a lot last summer, before the joys of motherhood descended. There are some really pretty coves up the coast where you can swim and go ashore for a picnic or a BBQ, so don't forget to pack your bikini and especially your sun-cream. You'll love it and it will do you good to mix with more people your own age.'

Jane recalled her first summer in New England a few years previously; remembering how draining she had found the soaring temperatures, particularly around July and August when not only the tourists arrived, but a lot of people returned from the cities to enjoy their summer homes. Everywhere got busy and claustrophobic and the town's dynamics changed considerably as everywhere swung into holiday mood with their spirits lightening.

Coming from Manchester, and having enjoyed many a damp and miserable British summer, Jane had not been prepared for any of this, with the heat and the humidity inland becoming almost unbearable in those early days. It did not take her long though to realise the best relief came from the breeze the closer you got to the coast, so the waterfront was the ideal place to be.

As this weekend's forecast was particularly hot being out at sea was a great idea and Jane, a little enviously, knew a day's sailing would be a lot of fun, especially if it involved Will and his friends who were never far from a party. Jane would need to make sure Monica was well protected as she did not relish the idea of sending her home in a week's time with sunstroke and first-degree burns; the lobster look was definitely not a good one for a bride-to-be she thought to herself.

Chapter 22

'Will's picking me up at 8.30am he says,' shouted Monica from the top of the stairs as she was busily getting her bag together, making sure she had everything she needed ready for a day at sea.

She was dressed in a strappy red T-Shirt and a pair of denim shorts over her bikini, with a pair of sensible sandals with a rubber sole so she would not slip on the deck. On Jane's advice, she had packed a broad brimmed hat plus the highest factor sun-cream she had ever seen, along with a change of clothes, some trendy sunglasses and a jacket for when it got cooler later on. Monica had borrowed most of her outfit from Jane, conscious that her own wardrobe was totally inadequate for today's outing. In fact, her sense of style and fashion had developed considerably in the few short weeks she had been in America, with most of the clothes she had brought with her for one reason or another no longer deemed appropriate or stylish enough. Also, her complexion had really improved in the fresh summer air, her hair had lightened and her cheeks were bronzed, and without noticing it she had obviously lost some weight, as what clothes she did still wear were feeling loose on her.

Thankfully she and Jane were similar sizes, so borrowing clothes had not been a problem.

Will and a couple of the other boys had organised the food, a few more were bringing the drinks and Will's friend Rob, who's parent's boat they were borrowing, had planned the route. They were heading to a quiet cove a couple of miles north of Salem, which was not marked on any of the popular tourist maps, so guaranteed only to attract the locals. Will had mentioned there would probably be at least a dozen of them, with a few of the boys bringing some girls along, which Monica was pleased about as other than Will she did not know anyone. It promised to be a good day, and another adventure for Monica to add to her ever-growing list.

'Will's here Monica, are you nearly ready?' called Jane, opening the front door to her brother-in-law with Clara in her arms as she heard him pull up into the drive. He was driving a battered-up Jeep that he had bought the previous summer and was planning on doing-up in his spare time, but Jane noticed he had not made much progress. He always had great ideas, but was not known for following-up on many of them.

Jane got on well with both of Brad's brothers, but she especially loved Will, finding his good-natured attitude to life and sense of fun contagious. But like most younger siblings it was not difficult to see that he got away with murder, capable of twisting everyone, especially his parents, around his little finger with minimal effort, other than a simple lopsided smile or a cheeky glance.

'What a bevy of beauties!' said Will as he leapt out of the car to greet Jane, Monica and Clara now waiting for him on the doorstep, 'A sight for sore eyes, oh, and how's my big brother today?', he added suddenly seeing Brad standing in the background with a cup of coffee in his hand, laughing at him.

'Do you fancy joining us too?' Will asked.

'Hi, we're fine thanks, and thanks for the invite, but after the week I've had, I feel like a lazy day with my feet up, being waited on!' joked Brad with a sideways glance at his wife, knowing that even though it had been a tough week at work for him, today he needed to help Jane with Clara. He knew how much Jane enjoyed motherhood and how easily she had taken to it, but equally he knew how draining it was on her and how much it was taking out of her both physically and mentally. Monica was being a massive help and he was loving having her to stay, but with her out of the house for the day, he knew that he needed to pull his weight and give his wife a bit of a break and some pampering into the bargain. Parenting was great, but exhausting in equal measure.

'Okay, then if I can't tempt you, we'll get off, and I promise to bring Monica back in one piece,' replied Will, giving Jane and Clara a kiss, and Brad a pat on the back before picking up Monica's bag and throwing it into the back of the Jeep alongside his own.

'Off we go, the ocean awaits,' Will said, smiling at Monica as they sped off in the Jeep headed towards the harbour, the wind in her hair and a growing sense of excitement in her stomach.

Chapter 23
Present day

Once Amanda had left, Monica returned to the back room and sank into her chair, feeling totally at a loss, hardly believing what she had just learnt or how this made her feel. Ken was right about one thing, it was a complete shock – but in reality, she was not sure which element surprised her most, the fact that Amanda was not Ken's daughter, or the fact that he had kept that information to himself for over twenty-five years, never wanting to risk discussing it with her for fear of what it would do to their family bonds. She felt deep sorrow that he had not trusted her, or more importantly trusted her feelings for him, and for him to now be apologising – when he suspected she was the one who had been unfaithful, added another dimension to an already confused state of affairs.   Monica   reflected back on her wedding day over thirty years ago, their brief honeymoon in Dublin, a present from Ken's parents, staying in the small guest house on the banks of the river Liffey, and then finding out about the pregnancy shortly following their return home. She recalled how happy they had both been, even though they were so young and it was completely unplanned.

Whilst Monica's mum was alarmed and concerned by the suddenness of the pregnancy, Ken's parents welcomed the news and were very supportive, both practically and financially to them both. Any plans Monica had to start a career, or train to become a teacher were simply shelved as they all prepared to welcome the new baby into the family. Once motherhood arrived Monica abandoned her career plans fully, being content to simply concentrate on being the best mother and wife she could be.

In Monica's mind there had been no fly in the ointment, but her mind started to drift back further than the wedding, to consider the unthinkable.

'Jane, can you talk?' she asked anxiously when Jane answered the phone. 'I've got a bit of a dilemma that I could do with discussing with you.'

'Of course, Brad's gone fishing for the day with Jacob. He won't be home until late, so I'm all yours,' replied Jane, curious to know what the problem was. 'What's happened, is everyone okay?'

Jane had rung Monica more frequently over the recent weeks since Ken's death, concerned about how her sister was coping, but never one to pry. She was well aware Monica could hide her feelings, preferring not to deal with anything that could usefully be put off, but knowing everyone dealt with grief differently, she had become more attuned to the nuances in Monica's voice.

'Yes, we're all fine. In fact, Amanda has just gone, but the thing is she's left me with a letter from Ken that he wrote shortly before he died. He said he's not Amanda's biological father and he wants Amanda to find out who he is.'

'Whoa, hold on a bit. Can you please re-wind - I've no idea what you're talking about – how can this be possible?' said Jane, completely puzzled by what she had just heard.

Monica took a deep breath trying to find the right words, knowing that without Jane's assistance she would not be able to move forward. She needed her to help fill in some of the blanks in the picture that was slowly forming in her mind. Memories were coming back that had long since been buried, and over time forgotten, assumed never to resurface under any circumstances, let alone the scenario she had just had presented to her.

Chapter 24
Summer 1984

When they arrived at the harbour a short while later, Will quickly parked up the Jeep in the sailing club's carpark, noticing that most of the friends they were meeting were already there, crowded around the far end of one of the jetties already laughing and seemingly in a mood to party. He leapt out of the car, grabbing their bags in the process, and quickly lead the way towards Rob's parent's boat where the others were already waiting. Monica did not know much about boats at all, but Will had explained on their drive down that it was a four berth, mid-sized Cabin cruiser, just under 30 feet long. That did not mean too much to her, but she liked the way it gleamed in the sunshine, brilliantly white with blue stripes and the metal work all polished and shiny.

Monica had never been sailing before, in fact she did not even know anyone who owned a boat, so was not at all sure what to expect, but once on board she was instantly impressed by everything around her. Although they were not the last to arrive, of those that were already there she did not recognised anyone, other than Rob, their captain for the day, who she had met a couple of weeks ago at

Will's house when Kitty had prepared dinner and invited a few people over.

Rob and Will had been friends for years and were roughly the same age, Rob being nine months older. They had a shared passion for sailing, having originally met when learning to sail as teenagers at the sailing club where their fathers were both members. Now, whilst still only twenty-two, they were both experienced 'captains' and regularly earned extra cash over the summer season skippering small crafts for tourists. Rob was a great laugh, fun to talk to, but also extremely pleasant on the eye, with his tanned athletic body and sun-bleached hair, so whatever happened Monica was not regretting coming along for the ride.

They sailed for about an hour north hugging the coastline before switching off the engines and dropping anchor in a small sheltered cove, where the sea was crystal clear, calm and very inviting. Before too long, everyone was diving into the water, splashing around and generally having a great time.

Monica, normally quite shy and reserved, decided to throw caution to the wind and stripped down to her bikini ready to join in. Thankfully she was a confident swimmer, so had no qualms about diving in, but most importantly she felt relaxed and not at all self-conscious among Will's friends who had made her welcome. In her new red bikini that Jane had helped her pick out, showing off her slender figure, toned and bronzed with all the recent exercise she had got from pram-pushing Clara around the town, there was no lack of admiring glances as she gracefully entered the water.

By mid-afternoon they had all been messing around in the water for some time, so Rob decided to take the boat ashore to give them time to set up the camp fire and start to prepare the BBQ for later that evening. Monica helped Rob carry the food and drinks off the boat, whilst the others set about clearing the area to create some room to sit and have fun. Everyone seemed to have their own roles; all very orchestrated like a well-oiled machine, implying to Monica this was a regular occurrence. One of the girls had even brought her guitar, so Monica presumed there would be music later on, with perhaps some dancing, looking at the effort that was going into clearing the area of all the drift wood.

Monica had noticed that Will had been occupied most of the day with a leggy brunette called Sonia; someone who he was obviously not meeting for the first time, which probably explained the twinkle in his eye whenever Kitty said he had no current love interest. She was very bubbly and had a really infectious laugh. She seemed a lovely girl, but Monica having spoken to her earlier presumed Will was not interested in her for her intelligence.

As the sun started to go down and the early evening began to draw in, Monica gradually realised that Rob was paying her an increasing amount of attention, and whilst she had not openly encouraged it, she was very flattered and did nothing to discourage it. Most people had coupled up by this stage, with just a few that had not happily chatting on the side-lines having a laugh and joke together.

Rob was gorgeous, funny and very attractive, but quite mature at the same time. He was also really considerate of the fact that Monica was not one of their usual group, so always went out of his way to include her. She was getting on great with him, and before long was finding herself flirting with him as much as he was flirting with her, becoming more and more relaxed as the evening progressed.

The mood quietened considerably after they had eaten, with the soothing melodic tones of the guitar having a relaxing effect on the group, so when Rob turned towards Monica and gently kissed her, she returned his kiss without hesitation, sighing almost in a hypnotic state at the pleasure it brought. Several of the couples were already snuggling around the fire, keeping warm as the night cooled, so Monica did not object as Rob put his arm around her, pulling her closer. She relaxed into his embrace. After a while he asked her if she fancied a little stroll before they started to pack up the boat and return back to shore. Monica saw no harm in his suggestion, and as she stood and took Rob's hand, allowing him to guide her, she felt completely at peace with the world. As they strolled off into the woods hand in hand, her mind was as far away from Manchester and Ken as you could possibly imagine.

Today was turning out to be one of the best days of the holiday so far, Monica thought to herself as she strolled through the trees with Rob and she was in no hurry for it to end. She was anxious to cram as much as possible in before her return flight home, just three short days away. The summer had passed so quickly, and with so many new experiences and opportunities having been opened up to her, Monica knew she was going home a completely different and more confident person that the young girl who had arrived just six weeks earlier.

This was a summer she would never forget.

Chapter 25
Present day

'So, hold on, what are you telling me?' asked Jane, startled at what Monica had said when reliving her last few days in New England all those years ago. 'Are you really saying that you slept with Rob and you've never mentioned it to me or anyone else before?'

'Well, yes, I suppose I did - but it was just a one-off – and completely spontaneous, it just happened. I don't think I've ever really thought about it since, and I've definitely never spoken to anyone about it, or been in contact with Rob ever again. In fact, it never dawned on me that there was even a possibility of getting pregnant. How naive must I have been!' replied Monica, for the first time feeling what a fool she had been 'It was just a bit of fun at the end of the most perfect day on the water. Just a couple of kids mucking about I suppose.'

Monica allowing herself to daydream, recalled to herself how she had felt when Rob had first kissed her, later making love to him under the stars, lost in the moment; how completely different to the way it had felt with Ken, who although she loved dearly, had never made her heart beat the same way. With Rob, it had been so dreamy, so romantic, so carefree, with the sound of the waves lapping against the beach as their only accompaniment. Life had been so relaxed that summer, and the way they had ended the night had provided the perfect crescendo to an idyllic holiday.

Reflecting now, Monica recognised that was the point at which her life was reborn. Her summer away had allowed her to shake off her somewhat dreary and dowdy self, enabling her to become a vibrant young woman, confident in her body, with that new found independence and her eyes opened to the opportunities around her.

'And you never questioned it when you got pregnant so soon after the wedding. Did you not check your dates?' she heard Jane ask, bringing her back down to earth and the reality of the situation they now found themselves in.

'No, I don't suppose I did. We were all just so tied up in the moment that it never dawned on me to check my dates. If you remember, the wedding was only a couple of weeks after I got home, and I just threw myself into that. Then when Ken and I got home from honeymoon and we found out I was pregnant, I just presumed like everyone else did that the baby was early, and none of the doctors ever suggested otherwise. Ken was so happy, and I was feeling so settled and contented in my new home with the baby that I never gave it a second thought. Looking back now, I probably just blanked the whole episode with Rob' *a bit like a dream* she thought to herself.

'And Ken had never hinted over the last twenty-five years or so that he had any inkling Amanda wasn't his, or asked if you'd had another relationship?' Jane questioned, suspecting that most husbands would have surely raised this if they had any doubts, let alone incontrovertible DNA evidence, wanting to know some answers.

'No, he did not, and in all the years we've been together there's never been any mention of Rob, or any other man for that matter, so nothing for him to question me about,' replied Monica, suddenly feeling that she needed to defend her actions and reputation against what might be coming next from her sister. 'We loved each other, and I believed that as far as each of us was concerned it was a faithful marriage. And by the sound of things, Ken kept the secret to himself for selfish reasons to protect the status quo, fearful of what he might unearth if he ever questioned me. Amanda was the light of his life and he would never want to do or say anything that would risk losing her or jeopardise what we had as a family.'

'Well then, what are you going to tell Amanda?' asked Jane curious to know how Monica planned to deal with this. 'By the sound of it, she is intent on finding out and following up on whatever you tell her; and knowing Amanda she won't rest until she's found out exactly what happened. I know what a determined young woman she can be when she puts her mind to it.' Jane loved Amanda dearly, and would not do anything to upset her, or want to see her upset, but she also knew how strong willed and tenacious she could be.

'I'm going to be honest with her, I think she deserves that, don't you?' said Monica, adding, 'In fact, Jane, I could probably do with your help. Do you have any idea if Will is still in contact with Rob or knows how to find him? It's just I never really knew anything about him, other than he was Will's friend and his parents owned the boat we sailed on. Also, when I do tell Amanda she's going to want to come over and meet him – and as I'm presuming this will be as much as a shock to him as it was to me, I might need you or Will to act as a go-between.'

'Thinking about it,' Monica continued, 'he probably won't even remember who I am, or was. I'm probably just another notch on the bedpost for him!' she laughed to herself, knowing full well that once she had flown home, he would never have given her a second thought. 'He'll have his own life now too, which I imagine this is going to disrupt, but I can't see an alternative – can you?' Monica sighed quite exasperated. 'Ken said there would be consequences, but he obviously had no idea what when he dropped this particular bombshell, and frankly neither do I.'

'Leave it with me and I'll make some discreet enquiries. I'll ring you back as soon as I find anything out,' replied Jane, agreeing with Monica that avoiding the truth was not a viable option, but equally navigating whatever stormy seas lay ahead was going to be a challenge. She and Will were still close, and she trusted him implicitly, so she would have to find a way of broaching the subject, without setting the cat among the pigeons too soon.

'And Monica, please try not to worry in the meantime, I'm sure everything will work out okay,' she added with a confidence she did not quite feel and her fingers tightly crossed as she spoke.

Chapter 26

Amanda had left it a couple of days, but by the Friday morning her mum had still not been in touch to arrange to have lunch and hopefully start to open up to her about who her biological father was. She did not want to be pushy, but at the same time was fidgety to know what was going on in her mum's mind. They were in the habit of speaking to each other every day, but Amanda had decided not to phone the previous day to give her mum some space, presuming her mum would be in touch when she was ready to talk.

Damian had been distracted the previous evening too when she had tried to speak to him about the conversation she had had with her mum, or more so her lack of response, but she could tell from his grunts and his monosyllabic answers that he was not in the mood to discuss anything with her either. He still had not heard anything about the big contract he was trying to secure, so knowing how anxious he was about that, so had not pushed him too hard.

They had been a bit like ships that passed in the night recently, with them both lost in their own thoughts. She had noticed that Damian was spending more nights than usual at his flat in Cheltenham, but had not really given it too much thought. She knew how much pressure he was currently under at work, how many hours he was putting in, so just assumed adding extra hours commuting was something he was looking to avoid.

Amanda had then messaged Lisa to see if she was around, but her friend replied saying she could not talk as she was at a swanky Legal function in Bristol, but would catch up over the weekend, so all in all she had no-one to turn to other than Grandad Tom, but as it was a Thursday evening, she knew he would be in the pub with a couple of his friends playing dominoes. Some habits were sacrosanct, and Amanda knew for her grandad that dominoes and a pint on Thursday with his cronies fell into that category.

Amanda was known to be quite driven and focused, so once she had set her mind to anything, she had to get on with it. Patience was a virtue she knew, but not one she excelled in, so waiting for her mum to get in touch was frustrating, and in her view not the best use of her time or energies. She decided to give her a ring, surely a little nudge could not hurt.

'Hi Mum, just wondering how you are? I was busy yesterday, but I didn't know whether you wanted to meet up today for lunch?' she asked, hoping to prompt a positive response, 'We could meet up at the Coffee Pot in the village if you fancy a trip out. My treat,' added Amanda, thinking a neutral venue might provide the perfect backdrop for what could be a sensitive discussion, rather than at home, in the house she had shared with Dad for all those years.

Monica, who had spent the previous day in a series of phone conversations with Jane was cautious in her response, but at the same time conscious that putting barriers up or trying to use delaying tactics would not work, particularly where Amanda was concerned. She knew her daughter, and knew that once she got the bit between her teeth she would not let go, so there was no point in avoiding it any longer than was necessary.

'Okay darling, that sounds lovely. And you're right, a change of scenery would do me good. I suppose I really should try to get out a bit more, I can't avoid people indefinitely, can I?' she laughed. 'I'll meet you there at 1.30pm. The walk to the village and a bit of fresh air is probably the exercise I need.'

Monica had not set her foot outside the house in the month or so since Ken had died, relying on Amanda to drop off any essentials, with neighbours also kindly offering to do little jobs for her when asked. She had not relished the thought of bumping into people, having to explain perhaps where Ken was, although in reality in a small village such as Castle Heighton news travelled fast. She knew she needed to start making more of an effort, and if what she was about to tell Amanda had any of the consequences she imagined it could have, staying at home and mourning much longer would not be an option. Losing Ken as she had so suddenly, had focused her mind somewhat. She would have to man-up, after all she was still a fit and healthy woman, only in her mid-fifties, so her priority now must surely be to heed what Ken had written and make the most of what life lay ahead of her.

Amanda was already sitting at one of the quiet corner tables when Monica entered the Café, chatting to the young waitress who she knew from the mother and toddler group the village ran in the church hall that they had both gone to at the time she had Alice. It looked suspiciously like the young lady was due a second baby in the not-too-distant future by the sight of the bump she was proudly displaying.

'Hi Mum, I've just ordered a coffee; shall I make it two?' asked Amanda, adding 'I'm having the lunch special too. It's one of my favourites!'

Monica glanced at the board, 'Yes, I'll have the same,' quickly thinking anything for an easy life, as she took her coat off, hung if over the back of the chair and sat down opposite her daughter, noticing the anticipation in Amanda's face for whatever it was her mum was about to tell her.

The quaint and cosy little café, with its pink polka dot curtains and mismatched cups and saucers, was a magnet for the village social life. It had a regular clientele, mainly consisting of mothers meeting up for a chat over coffees and pastries after dropping their children off at school across the road, or retired folk calling in for a cup of tea and scones mid-afternoon to pass the day, eager to pick up the local gossip. The café also did a good take-away service, with a brisk trade from the local businesses particularly around lunchtimes, but by this time any rush was over and Amanda and Monica knew that it should be reasonably quiet for a chat.

As Monica settled herself into her chair, she leaned towards her daughter and spoke in a quiet voice, Amanda noticing the way she clasped her hands tightly as she began, recognising instantly her mum's usual habit when she was nervous or anxious about anything.

'I just want to start by saying what a shock the news was to me the other day, so I can't begin to imagine what a shock it must have been to you too,' Monica started, unsure exactly what to say next, or how to continue, not knowing what could possibly be going round in her daughter's head at the moment. After speaking to Jane and understanding her options a bit more over the last forty-eight hours, she had played the conversation she needed to have with Amanda over in her head several times, but still the words did not come easily.

'Go on Mum,' encouraged Amanda smiling at her, then taking her hand by way of reassurance and demonstration of her continued love and support through what had so obviously come as a shock to both of them. 'Whatever you have to say, I love you. I'm here and I will support you no matter what. I just need to understand what Dad meant by what he'd written, and if it is true whether there's anything we can do about tracking down my biological father, as Dad wanted me to do'.

'Well, I think there is a possibility it is true, but it's a long story and something that I've never mentioned to anyone before. It goes back to the time just before your dad and I got married, just after we had finished university,' began Monica, trying to read her daughter's face to gauge her reaction, gradually building up her confidence to go on.

Over the next few minutes, Amanda listened carefully as her mum relived the time she had spent with her sister, Aunt Jane in America in the summer of 1984. Her mum pointed out it was the year before Amanda's birth. So, whilst Amanda had heard the story of her mum going over to help her aunt in the early days following Clara's birth many times before, she had never really questioned or considered the timing of it in any detail; she just knew it was before her parents had got married. It had never been discussed in any way that suggested or raised any questions in anyone's mind; just one of those happy memories of when the two sisters had spent quality time together, supporting the new baby and enjoying the American way of life.

Amanda had once visited Salem with her parents when she was a teenager and had spent some time touring around New England, so was familiar with what her mum was describing and had even met some of the people she spoke so fondly of. It had always been one of Monica's happy memories, the glorious summer of fun and freedom after all the hard work of university; her first, and last, hurrah before getting married.

As Monica's story progressed, Amanda became more mindful of what Lisa had said about not pushing her mother too hard, conscious that the memory could be a difficult one to relive. Lisa had warned Amanda that the circumstances surrounding whatever had happened could potentially be traumatic. So, whilst Amanda still could not see the link between this episode in her mum's life and the question of who her biological father was, she was keen for her to continue; waiting patiently, simply prompting and encouraging her mum to go on.

'What happened Mum, can you tell me what the link is between this trip and me? There's something I'm still missing.'

'Yes dear, I'm coming to that now,' replied Monica, sensing she could not pad the story out any longer, knowing she had reached the point at which she must open up about the memorable boat trip and finally introduce Rob, Amanda's biological father, into the picture.

She took a deep breath, a sip of her by now cold coffee and continued, both of their lunches remaining untouched.

'Wow, that's quite a story,' remarked Amanda once Monica had finished. The tale about the boat trip was something Monica had never discussed before, so Amanda heard for the first time about the day Monica had spent with Rob, how it had made her feel and their eventual kiss under the stars, leading to the point when they had made love, just two carefree youngsters, high on life, without a care in the world.

'I'm just so relieved that at least I was conceived as a happy accident, not some unpleasant encounter, which I have to admit has been worrying me,' added Amanda, reassuringly smiling at her mum, conscious of how she must be feeling having had to discuss that event with her daughter, and sensing how she must feel having to admit that she had let her dad down, being unfaithful just days before their wedding.

'It was just one of those moments, we just got carried away. I never for one moment thought about getting pregnant, or even considered the risks of it,' added Monica. 'Once I came home, and your dad and I got married, then he was all that mattered.

We were so happy when I found out I was pregnant, I just assumed you were his baby. I didn't think about Rob again. It never once crossed my mind you could be his. I honestly think I must have subconsciously blanked it from my mind.'

'So have you never seen or been in touch with him since – and Dad had no idea who he was either?' asked Amanda 'Do you know if he's still alive?'

'No, your dad didn't know him. In fact, I don't think I've ever mentioned his name to anyone. Yesterday when I spoke to Jane about it, it was the first time I've ever discussed that night, or had to face up to the consequences of what we did. It's all a bit of a mess, isn't it?' sighed Monica.

'So, where's Rob now?' asked Amanda 'If he was a friend of Will's, then are they still in contact, could you find out?' suddenly excited that this might not be the end of the story, but a way forward.

'I've already asked Jane to do some digging, and it would seem that yes, he is still alive and although he and Will haven't kept in close contact, Jane has managed to find out where he lives. She hasn't told Will why she wanted to know though; she just concocted some reason and apparently Will didn't question her. You know what men are like!'

Sensing that she needed to tread carefully, Amanda looked at her mum and asked 'How would you feel about me getting in touch, and possibly at some stage going over to meet him? Would you be okay with that?'

'If your dad wanted you to meet him, then I suppose I would have to be okay with it, provided that's what you really want?' she enquired, but looking into Amanda's eyes, Monica saw no doubt that this was what her daughter wanted. 'When Jane asked around, she found out that Rob's not too well at the moment. She doesn't know what the issue is, but I think it's reasonably serious from the sense she got, so if you did want to talk to him, then I would suggest you go over in person and not break this news to him by phone or email. Jane has already offered to help you and said you can stay at her house whilst you're there if you want.'

Amanda got up from her chair and put her arms around her mum, showing her not only how much she loved her and didn't judge her, both also to thank her for being so open and honest about what was obviously a subject she never imagined they would ever need to discuss.

The depth of emotion displayed between the two women as they spoke that afternoon above all demonstrated how much they were obviously still grieving, how raw their feelings were. Both knew however that ignoring this bombshell was not an option, and regardless of how it played out it had the potential to change the dynamic of their lives forever. But they recognised theirs was a strong bond that could not easily be broken, so whatever lay ahead they vowed they would face it together. They would seek out the truth Ken had so obviously wanted them to discover and face the consequences he foretold, whatever these might be.

Chapter 27

After Damian had listened to Amanda talking him through the latest developments, he simply said, 'So when are you going?', knowing full well that nothing he said or did would change what Amanda was planning on doing. He generally admired her determination and her ability to focus, knowing that once her mind was made up little would change it, but occasionally where emotional issues were concerned, he acknowledged her tendency to be a little impulsive, invariably without too much appreciation of the wider issues.

'I spoke to Aunt Jane a couple of hours ago and she has said I can go whenever I want to, but like Mum, she suggested I don't leave it too long as Rob is apparently not too well. She thinks it might be something or nothing but isn't sure,' said Amanda adding, 'I've checked online and flights into Boston are almost daily, so I'll go as soon as I can get things sorted with the girls. Mum has offered to help out, and Susie could do more hours, but I was hoping you could work from home a bit more while I'm away and look after them over night. I don't want to disrupt their bedtime routines too much.' She knew this was a big ask given

Damian's apparent current workload, and the fact that he was spending more evenings staying over at his flat in the city, but for her plan to work she was relying on him being supportive.

'How long are you planning on being away for…. just a few days, or a week?'

'I'm not sure yet. I suppose it depends on what type of welcome I receive, and how he takes the news that he has a grown-up daughter and grand-daughters he knew nothing about. There's the distinct possibility that me suddenly descending on his life from nowhere might not go down too well,' she laughed to herself imagining the reception she might receive. 'I wouldn't think it would be more than a few days though.'

Whilst Damian had been as shocked as Amanda with the contents of Ken's letter, and was generally supportive of her researching who her biological father was, he had never expected everything to move as quickly as this, or for Amanda to be as decisive as she was in her response. They had discussed the letter in passing, but Damian was now being forced to recognise perhaps he had not given it as much weight as he should. He had naively or selfishly presumed it would be one of those things that could fizzle away over time, never fully realising how determined Amanda would be, or how single-minded she would become.

He supposed he could, if pushed, manage work and family life from home for a short period of time, but with all the pressures with the business at the moment he felt a little resentful that now was not the best time for him.

'I suppose I could manage from home, but how about you go in a month or so when everything has settled down a bit. You are still grieving. It's only been a few weeks since your dad died and it's probably a bit too early for flying over to America and opening up something that you have no idea about. Emotionally what you're suggesting is going to be quite tough on a lot of people. Why don't you do a bit more research first and perhaps meet on line or chat over the phone before racing over there?' Damian suggested, trying to buy himself some time, but also trying to put the brakes on Amanda's half-concocted plan.

Amanda had given some thought to what this could mean to Rob and his family, presuming there was an extended family; but in reality, she could not allow herself to believe he would not want to meet her. She accepted that he may not want a relationship with her, and she clearly wanted nothing from him, but out of curiosity if nothing else she hoped he would agree to them meeting. Above all she was intrigued to see what he looked like, and whether she could see herself in him. Her mum had mentioned how tall and good looking he had been back in the day, and how blonde he was, which is probably where she got her height and colouring from.

Amanda had on reflection never really seen a physical resemblance of herself in her dad, even though it was often remarked on how similar they were, but she supposed that was where the whole concept of nurture versus nature played in; because even though biologically she was not her dad's daughter, her value set, her sense of humour and above all her general approach to life were strongly influenced by the way her parents had raised her.

Amanda had no idea from speaking with her Aunt Jane what Rob's personal situation was either, but regardless she knew she did not want to go crashing in headfirst and upsetting his life; she just wanted to meet him and at least give him the opportunity to understand he had a daughter that he knew nothing of. Shocked as she imagined he would be, she still believed he had a right to know that.

That was the sum total of how far Amanda's thinking and planning had gone so far; other than an acknowledgement that there may be consequences, she had not really given any serious thought to what these could be. She simply imagined she would be home within the week, with everybody's lives then reverting back to normal, just with the added knowledge that she now had some new and distant relatives on the other side of the Atlantic, relatives that she would probably never meet again.

'No, I want to go and now is as good a time as ever. Also, if Aunt Jane is right and he is ill, I don't want to delay it too much. Something feels right about doing this; almost as if my dad is driving me towards it. Losing one dad is enough – I don't want to lose another one before I even find him!'

Damian realising he was not going to change her mind, resigned himself to supporting her through the next stage of the process – wherever that might take them. He knew a couple of weeks working from home would require a bit of jiggling of the diary, but nothing he could not manage with the help of his secretary, provided Monica and Susie were serious about looking after the girls during the daytime. Juggling meetings online with them playing and shouting in the background would not be fun for any of them.

Chapter 28

Three hectic days later, Amanda was touching down at Boston's Logan International Airport after enjoying a very comfortable flight, made even better by the free upgrade she had been offered at check-in, some excellent food and even a glass or two of champagne. It was early evening as they came into land. The sky had been almost cloudless for the last couple of hours of the flight, the sun was still bright with the views of the eastern coastline as spectacular as Amanda remembered them. It had been a couple of years since she had last visited, in fact not since the girls had been born, but Boston and the surrounding states of New England was a part of America Amanda did not think she would ever tire of. When she thought of the drizzly, damp late spring day she had left behind in Heathrow as she had boarded the flight a few hours earlier, she marvelled at how the weather, the temperature and even the time of day were all so different from home.

Damian and the girls had driven Amanda to the train station to catch her connection into Heathrow, and whilst she could tell he was not too pleased to be left literally holding the baby, he had wished her well and said he hoped to see her soon as he gave her a brief kiss goodbye. Amanda had booked an open-return ticket, so whilst she sensed his emphasis on 'see you soon', in reality she had no idea when that would be, knowing only that it would depend on what awaited her when she arrived.

Their relationship had become increasingly tetchy recently, for no apparent reason that Amanda could isolate. There was probably a combination of factors, but nothing that was giving her too much cause for concern. They were both busy people, who for whatever reason were focused on their own agendas, so finding common ground was proving a bit of a challenge. Amanda assumed most relationships went through patches like this, but secretly admitted to herself how much she was looking forward to a bit of a break from her usual routine, with the added benefit of some quality time to herself. Juggling her career, motherhood and supporting her family through what was proving to be a difficult time for all of them, let alone dealing with her own grief and this latest bombshell, had not allowed much time for them as a couple. Damian was the crutch she would normally turn to for emotional support, but with their relationship under a bit of a strain that outlet was not there either.

Other than the occasional chat with her best friend Lisa, Amanda could not think of the last time she had had any girly fun or even let her hair down, so whilst the next few days were a step into the unknown, and potentially could prove to be a bit of an emotional roller-coaster, she was nevertheless looking forward to the diversion it was providing.

Aunt Jane and Brad had offered to meet her at the airport, but she had politely declined, opting instead for hiring a car and driving the short distance to Salem. It was less than an hour's drive and having her own transport over the next few days would give her more flexibility to get around without being dependent on other people to taxi her about. With arranging everything at such short notice, Amanda was conscious that she did not want to disrupt anyone's plans more than necessary. It was kind enough that they had offered to let her stay with them, and were helping her with contacting Rob, without expecting them to put themselves out any more than necessary.

'Hello there. How wonderful to see you!' exclaimed Jane excitedly when Amanda eventually pulled into the drive and got out of the car, immediately hugging her aunt and her cousin Clara, who had both been waiting patiently for her arrival for the last hour or so and had started to wonder if she had got lost. Clara had driven over earlier that afternoon from downtown Boston where she rented a luxury waterfront apartment, to help form the welcome party and knew that the traffic was bad, but it should not have taken that long.

'How glad am I to finally get here. It's been a long day and getting through immigration and then the car hire was a nightmare!' exclaimed Amanda, relieved that she had then managed to get to Jane's in one piece without getting too lost. *Thank God for satnav* she thought to herself.

'Clara, I wasn't expecting you, what a lovely surprise. Have you just arrived? More importantly, is there a bottle of wine chilling – I could really do with a glass or two?', knowing that if her cousin was around, then that was bit of a rhetorical question.

The two cousins were great friends who had enjoyed a close relationship throughout their lives. They spoke regularly on the phone and always enjoyed being in each other's company whenever they got the opportunity to meet up. Being roughly the same age, they had quite a few shared interests, liking the same type of music, food and wine; but their lives had followed different paths, both emotionally and physically.

Clara reminded Amanda very much of Lisa, and presumed this was why they got on so famously. Clara too was unmarried, with no children, thrived on city life, driven in her career as an editor at one of the Boston daily newspapers, and currently without a significant other in her life. Her most recent relationship had been with a jewellery designer called Lucy who lived in Boston, but that had fizzled out about a year ago when Lucy started to get serious. Clara liked Lucy, but was not ready for settling down, she enjoying her freedom and independence too much and was not ready for commitment.

Amanda and Clara had spoken on the phone the previous evening, and whilst Clara still did not know the exact reason for Amanda's visit, assuming she just needed a break and a bit of family time, she was excited to catch-up and had several outings planned for the two of them if time allowed. She was hoping to take Amanda to a new bar she had just discovered on the waterfront if she got the chance, where the lobster was excellent and the margaritas to die for. She sensed her cousin was in need of a bit of cheering up.

Amanda had chosen to keep the reason for her trip just between herself and Aunt Jane so far; not because she did not trust Clara, but because she wanted to understand the lay of the land before she said too much to anyone else. Salem was a small town, and like most small towns gossip spread very quickly. Amanda was concerned about how people would react, and wanted to ensure that nothing got onto the grapevine before she had had the chance to speak to Rob herself. Her mum's story was quite incredulous, so telling it in a way that had meaning was important to her, and important for any future relationship she may have with her biological father. Amanda believed it needed to be handled with a high degree of sensitivity.

'Come on in, there's a bottle open, and another one chilling, so we're prepared. Dinner will be in around an hour's time when Dad gets back from golf, so plenty of time to freshen up before then if you want – or we could just get a glass now and head to the garden so you could tell me why you're here,' said Clara smiling, grabbing Amanda's bag and leading the way into the house.

'The garden it is then,' replied Amanda, translating the look her aunt gave her, and realising Clara would not settle until she knew what was going on and the real reason for the visit. Amanda also knew that Clara would have a perspective on what had happened that she would be interested to hear, recognising this may help in deciding how she approached the meeting with Rob. For all her fun and frivolity, Clara had a sensitive side and as a professional editor was use to making words work for her. Perhaps she could help Amanda find the right words for this occasion.

Chapter 29

Amanda woke surprisingly early the following morning; her body-clock deceiving her into believing it was much later and therefore time to get up, but her watch clearly telling her to stay in bed for another couple of hours. She was unsure what was most to blame for how awake she felt, or how muggy her head was. It could easily have been the long flight or five-hour time difference, or even the two bottles of wine drunk during dinner, or perhaps going over the story with Brad and Clara into the early hours, trying to formulate a plan over a glass or two of brandy once Jane had gone to bed, but whatever it was, Amanda knew she was not going to get back to sleep. *Best get up and see if I can find some coffee and perhaps a couple of paracetamols,* she thought to herself as she pulled on the fluffy dressing-gown her aunt had left out for her, and slotted her feet into her slippers that she had remembered to pack. The temperature promised to be a lot warmer than back at home as the day developed, but at this time in the morning there was still a chill in the air and too early for any heating to kick in.

The smell of the coffee must have woken Clara up, as no sooner had Amanda poured her first cup her cousin was standing in the doorway, still in her pyjamas, stretching and yawning away. She was not a heavy sleeper, which she put down to too many years in the newspaper industry and needing to be on call, regardless of the time or day, but normally when she came home and was back in her old room she slept like a baby. Sleep was a premium few editors could afford to waste whenever they got the chance, but last night Clara's mind had not switched off once she had gone to bed. She had spent the night tossing and turning mulling everything over, wondering if there was anything else she could do to help her cousin.

'Good morning. Is there enough coffee for two? I'm parched,' asked Clara reaching for a mug, bleary eyed and looking a little worse for wear. 'I think I'm going to need a few strong coffees to kick my system into gear today. I didn't sleep too well after last night's discussion. My mind seems to have been going over and over what we discussed. I still can't get over the shock or what we should do.'

Over dinner the previous evening the four of them had all discussed the best approach, from every conceivable angle, concluding that the simplest solution of ringing Rob to arrange a visit was deemed the easiest and preferable way forward. They all recognised though that a direct telephone call from Amanda, or even Jane, out of the blue would appear strange, so the plan involved bringing Brad's brother Will into the mix as their go-between. Will still lived relatively locally, just half an hour's drive away, and whilst his and Rob's lives had drifted apart over recent years, they had remained friends and still had occasional contact through the sailing club where they were both members.

Brad had offered to ring his brother later that day, invite him round for lunch, and then they would take it from there. The hope was that if Will was supportive, he could arrange for him and Amanda to meet Rob whenever he was free.

Amanda also hoped that Will would be able to provide a greater insight into Rob's life and his family circumstances before their visit, mainly so that she could lessen any risk of shock or insensitivity in the way she broached what she had to tell him, but also because she currently knew little more about her biological father than the brief outline her mum had provided of the young, good looking boy she had kissed under the moonlight all those years ago, and had probably promptly forgotten all about her, moving swiftly onto the next young girl he fancied. Amanda knew boys would be boys, sowing their wild oats whenever and wherever they got the opportunity, after all she had been a teenage girl herself. She also knew she would not be the first child that had sought out biological parents, but nevertheless Amanda was inquisitive to find out more, and had no intention of letting the circumstance around what had happened colour her view towards Rob, or equally towards her mum. As her dad had rightly said, without him she would not have been born, so no regrets or recriminations!

Rob's illness however added a further dimension that Amanda had to be mindful of, conscious that she currently had no knowledge what condition he had, or more importantly how serious it was. Having just lost her dad to cancer, at the back of her mind she feared a similar situation here, but did not want to jump to any conclusions until she had heard more.

'I hope Uncle Will is around this week and can help,' said Clara, stirring two spoonsful of sugars into her black coffee to give her that extra kick. 'I haven't seen him for a few months, so I'm planning on staying around if you don't mind and catching up with him too. If fact, I think I might phone the office and take a few days off and camp out while you're here. I had planned on inviting you back to Boston and taking you out to one of my favourite restaurants followed by a club, but the more I think about it, there's going to be enough excitement around here for the time being, don't you!'

'I'd love you to stick around for a bit if you're happy to do that,' replied Amanda, pleased that her cousin was being so supportive, adding 'You never know, I might need your shoulder to cry on if all doesn't go well.'

Amanda had played various scenarios out in her head, but until she met Rob and got a sense of him, she had no idea at all whether she would be heading home in a couple of days with a whole new family or simply a door shut in her face, hopefully only metaphorically speaking.

Chapter 30

'Well, I'm not sure what to make of all that' exclaimed Will the following day after listening carefully to them all recounting Amanda's story over lunch, outlining the plan they had concocted for meeting Rob and specifically where he fitted into it.

'Come to think of it, I do remember that day on the water and taking Monica with me in my old Jeep. If I'm right it was over Labor Day weekend. We had a great time I seem to recall, there were probably about a dozen or so of us. I was with a girl called Sonia, beautiful long legs, I wonder what happened to her?' he considered, laughing to himself, hoping he was not due a visit from an unknown son or daughter too!

Brad had phoned and invited Will over without telling him the reason, just saying it would be good to catch up. Will had welcomed the opportunity of a home cooked meal, particularly if Jane was the cook; as anything was preferable than the take-aways he was surviving on at the moment. He had not hesitated or asked any questions when accepting the invitation, just looked forward to catching up with his brother and family and having some well-deserved downtime.

But now listening to him recall the events in a similar way as her mum had done a few days earlier was reassuring to Amanda, but it also boded well for Rob recalling them too. If it had been such a memorable day, then perhaps her mum might not have been as easily forgotten as she had imagined.

As Will spoke, Amanda imagined him as a young lad, and having seen photos of him around Jane and Kitty's houses, with his youthful good looks and his happy go lucky approach to life, she could easily believe he and his friends would be great fun to spend time with. She sensed her mum had been almost captivated by the lifestyle she found here, particularly compared to what she had experienced back home in Manchester and Nana Moira's somewhat drab lifestyle and strict upbringing. The contrast was incomparable.

'I'm more than happy to help you, and I agree that meeting up with Rob in person would be the best approach. I've not seen him at the sailing club for a while, but I've still got his mobile number and can easily give him a call and see if he's around,' offered Will, happy to help. 'I had heard that he wasn't too well, but I'm not sure what the problem is. I know he lost his wife probably around ten years ago now. She died following a car crash when a lorry careered into her if I recall correctly, but thankfully their twin sons weren't in the car with her that day. I think she had left them with their grandparents. It was all very traumatic and Rob was badly affected and threw himself into bringing up the boys, probably by way of therapy. I think they will be around eighteen or nineteen now;

off at university I imagine,' reflected Will, recalling how badly Rob had taken it and how he had withdrawn from everyone for such a long period of time, consumed by grief as he was, but also scared of losing the boys too, throwing a protective net around them. Events like this remind you of how tenuous your hold on life is.

Will, being recently divorced after a short childless, and some would say loveless, marriage was now living on his own in a spacious new build apartment a short drive away from his old home. He had bought the apartment on impulse when him and his wife amicably split, but had not yet got around to fully furnishing the place, or even to installing a functioning kitchen. It just did not seem like a priority with all the other things he was juggling in his work life. Listening to Amanda's story though, and knowing that he could help, and in the process reconnect with Rob was probably the distraction he needed to get him out of his current doldrum.

Will had established a growing and lucrative fashion business, marketing and distributing designer leisurewear and clothing worldwide. After graduating and taking his gap year exploring Europe, he had joined the family business, but soon realised it was not for him. He loved the cut and thrust of business and particularly the import/export dynamic, but not the commodities his family dealt in, mainly foodstuffs.

Will had always had an eye for fashion, particularly sportswear and had spotted early on a niche in the market for high-end leisurewear. In the late 1980s he started a business sourcing quality merchandise and suppliers, both in America and overseas, initially for local customers, principally associated with and linked to the sailing club. His business had grown steadily as the leisure industry grew, but with the explosion of the internet in the early-mid 1990s and subsequent on-line marketing, it took off in a way he had never imagined.

His business was now worth a considerable amount of money, employed over three-hundred people in various countries around the globe, both directly and in the supply and distribution chains, and provided him with a handsome lifestyle. By anyone's standards he was very rich and successful. If only he had the chance to enjoy it, or even someone in his life to share it with, or just as important someone to pass it onto when he decided enough was enough.

Over the years his business had become all consuming. Will acknowledged he had poured his heart and soul into it at the expense of his marriage and his social life, but knew he would not have wanted it any other way. He had married for the wrong reasons, picking up a trophy wife who looked good on his arm, but in the end had paid the price for a loveless marriage with an expensive divorce settlement.

Now in his mid-fifties, he was seriously considering what direction his life was moving in. He knew he needed to get his act together, to start to focus on his work-life balance more, before it was too late, whatever that meant; but work was so demanding that it sapped all his energies. He really should learn to delegate more, but as it was his own business that he had built up from nothing, he struggled to trust anyone enough to fully hand over the reins.

On an evening when he eventually got back to his apartment, usually too late to do much more than eat his take-away before going to bed, he had no desire or inclination to start looking for furnishings, let alone enjoy any real social life. He tried to recall the last time he had gone out for a meal that was not a work event, meeting new clients or suppliers, and could not. Since his divorce he certainly had not dated or even seen another woman socially. He knew he needed to make some changes, and probably getting a designer in to furnish the apartment might be a small start. In terms of him managing the rest of his life, perhaps reconnecting with Rob might kickstart the social side too. At his age he was too young to give up.

Suddenly Will felt enthused by the way the discussion was going. 'So, when are you free?' he enquired of Amanda. 'And more importantly when I do call Rob, how shall I position that I am bringing a lovely young English girl to meet him?'

'The sooner the better,' replied Amanda, grateful that Will was on-board to help and excited, if a little apprehensive, to get started. 'I'll leave the positioning to you!'

Chapter 31

Around lunchtime the following day, whilst Aunt Jane and Clara were at the market getting some fresh fish and running errands around town, and Brad was playing another round of golf with some friends, Amanda had been left home alone. It was peaceful in the house and gave her a chance to reflect on the previous evening's discussion as she pottered in the kitchen preparing the vegetables for dinner.   As her mobile rang, Amanda smiled, recognising the ringtone and knowing straightaway who was calling.

'Well how are you and how's it all going? What progress have you made so far?' asked Lisa excitedly when Amanda picked up the phone. They had messaged regularly over the last week, but just a few short words to check in on each other. With the time difference and everything else that seemed to be going on in both their lives, finding time to connect properly had not been easy.

In fact, Amanda was finding it difficult to connect with Damian too, but probably that was for a different reason. Something was niggling away in her head, but she would need to deal with that another day when she had the energy. She had a growing sense from the way he responded, or more importantly did not respond, that something was happening at home that she was not aware of. Her mum had reassured her the girls were well, but there was still something at the back of her mind that suggested all was not as it should be.

Amanda knew that Lisa was in the middle of a big domestic abuse case and was having quite a tough and emotional time dealing with all the evidence that was emerging. Her client was a young woman in her mid-twenties, but due to client confidentiality Lisa had not told her too much, but it sounded like quite a complex set of problems she was having to untangle to get to the nub of the legal issues. Whilst Lisa presented to the outside world a calm persona, someone who was quite tough and carefree, Amanda knew the real person behind the mask; recognising that you did not have to scratch too deeply to find Lisa's vulnerable and sensitive side, and cases particularly where children were involved could hit her quite hard.

Amanda was mindful of not appearing too needy at times like these, understanding how stressful Lisa's job could be. When there was a big case on, she had learnt to read the signs to assess whether her friend wanted to confide, or just needed to be left alone. This time she had needed space, so Amanda had waited until Lisa was ready to talk, prepared as always to offer as much support as she was able. It was around 6pm at home, so Amanda presumed Lisa had just about finished up for the day.

'I'm fine thanks, lovely to hear from you. How are you doing with the case, is everything okay?'

Lisa updated her quickly on developments and what was happening as they prepared to go to trial, but soon moved the conversation on to what was happening with her. Amanda had previously told Lisa about their plan for lunch with Will, so she was eager to hear how that had gone.

'Well, we had a good lunch yesterday with Clara's Uncle Will. He was a bit surprised, but seemed to take it all in his stride. It doesn't look like much fazes him. He's great fun and I can imagine in his day he was a real stunner. He's roughly the same age as mum, but still very handsome and distinguished looking. He remembers the sailing trip vividly, and his recollections are pretty much the same as Mum's, which is reassuring.' replied Amanda laughing. 'By his own account, they all had a great time – and Mum and Rob weren't the only two to see some action it would seem'.

'That sound promising. So, what's happening next? Is he going to act as your go-between as you'd hoped?'

'Yes, he's offered to ring Rob and set up a lunch as soon as he's available. In fact, I think he's quite happy about getting involved. I get the sense he's quite excited to see how Rob will react.'

Amanda then went on to tell Lisa about Will's recent divorce, how he now found himself in a bit of a rut, unsure where his life was heading; the demands of his business allowing him little time to rebuild his life, particularly the social side. Amanda sensed he probably saw helping her as a catalyst to helping himself focus on turning his own life around. She also told Lisa about Rob being widowed, with twin boys who were probably in their late teens or early twenties by now, both presumably away at university.

'So, you have two half-brothers; wow, that's a surprise you weren't expecting. How do you feel about that, and have you decided what you're going to say to Rob when you eventually meet him? I presume you're not just going to blurt out, 'Hello, I'm your long-lost daughter!''

'No, I wasn't planning on being that insensitive, we do have his health to consider after all!' laughed Amanda, whilst recognising she still was not sure exactly how the subject would be broached. She just hoped that their conversation would present a suitable opening, which would then allow her to say what she needed to say, preferably avoiding killing him in the process with the shock.

'Will is going to take the lead, but as he's not sure either exactly what Rob's state of health is, until that's clear we agreed we both need to tread carefully. Will is going to do some discreet enquiries down at the sailing club tonight. Apparently, they are still both members so he'll see if anyone knows how he's doing.'

'That all sounds very positive. I'm looking forward to hearing the next instalment already. What does Damian think to the fact he has a couple of brothers-in-law?' enquired Lisa, keen to understand what support she was getting from her husband.

'Not much to be honest. I haven't managed to speak to him over the last couple of days, other than a few words when he video calls me for the girls to say goodnight before they go to bed. He's really busy with work, and with me being here he's having to pick up looking after Maisie and Alice too. Mum says he's dropping them off at her house quite early and it's after dinnertime before he's picking them up, so she feels like she's running a café as well as a creche, but I don't think she's complaining – not yet at least.'

Although Lisa knew Damian well, she had to admit to herself that over the years she had never grown particularly close to him, finding him a little standoffish around her. She sensed that there was an element of resentment, perhaps teetering on jealousy, on his side about how close she and Amanda were, how he occasionally felt excluded when Amanda automatically turned to her for support; but they were both civil and polite enough not to mention it whenever they met.

Lisa also sensed, reading between the lines, that her friend's relationship with her husband was going through a bit of a rocky patch. It was not what Amanda had said, more what she had not said that gave her some cause for concern. Amanda was very loyal to Damian, and although she confided in Lisa about almost everything, she rarely spoke of their relationship, preferring to keep her own counsel about the state of their marriage. Lisa never pried or challenged, but in her line of business was naturally attuned to the signals. It went without saying that if the need arose, she would act or respond without hesitation.

'Well just remember I'm here whenever you need to speak to someone, and if you need me to do anything back home for you, I can easily pop over at the weekend and check everything is okay. I'm long overdue a visit to see my parents, so it would be no trouble.'

'Thanks, I'll bear that in mind. I've got a feeling I may be here a little longer than the week I'd imagined, so I may need to call in the reinforcements,' admitted Amanda, adding 'the time seems to be going so fast. I'm already onto day four and we've still not set up a meeting, so it could be a few more days. If mum gets to the stage where the girls are driving her mad, I'll let you know. You can then waft in on your broomstick, do your fairy godmother routine and put the world to rights. They would love that,' laughed Amanda, knowing how much the girls loved their Auntie Lisa, and how the feeling was mutual.

'You're on,' replied Lisa, sensing that Damian would not be pleased to learn that the week had just turned into more of an indefinite period whenever Amanda got around to telling him.

Chapter 32

It was early the following evening before Amanda heard anything from Will. She had been anxious to phone him all the previous day to see if he had managed to contact Rob or whether he had learnt anything from the sailing club, but had not wanted to chase him or put pressure on him. Knowing how busy he was, it was kind of him to offer to help in the first place, without her haranguing him into the bargain.

Amanda was struggling to control her feelings. Everything was moving so fast, but so slow at the same time. It was difficult to comprehend that it was only a couple of weeks since she had been sitting with her grandad reading her dad's letter to her, and now here she was over three thousand miles away planning to set up a meeting with a man she had never even known existed; her biological father. Amanda was not usually one for nerves, but recognised a nervous excitement at the thought of what she might find out. Knowing she had two half-brothers had also sparked a feeling she had never expected. Being an only child was all she had ever known, so having siblings was a real bonus, but something she was not sure how to react to. She wondered what they would be like, and more importantly what their reaction would be to a half-sister landing on their doorstep and upsetting the status quo.

Amanda excitedly answered the phone on the second ring, immediately recognising the number. 'Hi Will, have you found anything out yet? I've been on tenterhooks all day hoping you would get in touch. I've been a nervous wreck thinking that he wouldn't want to see me and thinking that you hadn't rung because you didn't know how to break the news to me.'

'And good evening to you too,' laughed Will when Amanda eventually stopped babbling. When they had met over lunch a couple of days previously, he had sensed her excitement, but could see that it was controlled, whereas today the excitement was evident, but mixed with a nervous anxiety, anticipating that what he may say might not be what she wanted to hear.

Will had met Amanda a couple of times over the years during her occasional family visits to see her aunt, so whilst he had been impressed to see the confident women she had grown into when they had met a couple of days ago, today she reminded him more of the young excitable and spirited teenager she had once been. He realised he liked both sides equally, refreshing as it was to see a woman comfortable to express both her strong and vulnerable sides.

'You'll be pleased to know that I've spoken to Rob and I suggested lunch tomorrow. He was a little surprised by the call, but has agreed to meet us. He asked if we could meet at his house as he needs to be home in the afternoon, which I didn't have a problem with. I told him I was bringing a young lady with me to meet him, which he didn't question too much; I presume he assumed it was a new girlfriend of mine, so I'll deal with that when we get there.' Will waited a few moments allowing Amanda to absorb what he had said before asking 'If that's all okay with you, I'll pick you up at noon.'

'Yes, that's perfect. Thank you. I don't know what else to say, replied Amanda nervously, suddenly realising this was all becoming real and by this time tomorrow she will have met her biological father.

'By the way, did you find out anything about his illness or the state of his health?' enquired Amanda, still unsure what the problem was that Aunt Jane and Will had alluded to, but neither had been able to shed any light on.

'No, the guys at the sailing club said he's not been around for some months now. A few of them have called to his house and tried to get him out, but he's not wanted to go. Always some excuse or other, they said. After a while, they stopped calling and he hasn't been in touch. Whatever it is, it seems like it's keeping him at home by the sounds of it,' said Will, recognising that if he was honest with himself, he would prefer to go around by himself first to assess the situation, but he did not want to betray Amanda. She was after all a grown woman who would have to deal with whatever they found, and him being overly protective or attempting to sugar coat it would not help the situation.

'And did anyone know where his sons were?' asked Amanda, still anxious to understand a little more about Rob's personal circumstances before they landed at his door. 'Are they at home, or still away at university?'

'I believe they're both away, but I don't know for certain, or where they study. The guys at the club said they were both keen sailors like their father, but neither had been around for a couple of months either. It is term time though, so they are probably still away studying. And the sailing season isn't really at its height at this time of the year anyway.'

'Well, let's go tomorrow and see what we find. If it gets difficult or something happens that means I can't tell him, then we may need to find a plan B,' admitted Amanda, putting the phone down to Will, conscious all of a sudden that simply marching in there and saying '*Hi, look at me, I'm your long-lost daughter*' might not be as straightforward as she had perhaps naively imagined.

Chapter 33

The following morning Amanda woke up early to the promise of a bright sunny day, with a gentle sea breeze wafting in through her bedroom window. She had taken to sleeping without the curtains drawn and the sash windows open, something she would never consider at home at this time of year, where the weather was still unpredictable and the mornings still on the cool side. Here the weather was so much more pleasant, although she could imagine it getting insufferably hot as the summer approached. Spring and autumn were here favourite seasons, with temperatures more manageable, neither too hot nor too cold.

After her discussion with Will yesterday evening, Amanda had tried once again to phone Damian to catch-up, but had not been able to get hold of him, which given it was nearly midnight was disappointing, but perhaps not surprising if he was exhausted. His mobile was probably on silent. She had not really had a proper talk to him since she had arrived, and was getting increasingly concerned that there was something he was not telling her. It would just have to wait until tomorrow she realised, the time difference making communication that bit more of a challenge.

So, when she tried again the following lunchtime, knowing he should be home, or at least answering his phone, but still could not get hold of him, she phoned her mum to check everything was okay.

Monica assured her Maisie and Alice were both fine, 'Yes, they're fine, in fact they stayed over with me last night as Damian apparently had a late meeting in town that he couldn't do from home, so suggested he stay over at his flat, provided I was alright to have them for a sleepover. Do you want to speak to them? We were just about to have lunch, but I'm sure they would love to talk to you.'

'That would be lovely, but did everything seem alright when he left them? It's just he never mentioned anything to me about needing to go into the office, or staying overnight at the flat. I understood he was managing everything from home. I hope there's nothing wrong,' asked Amanda, with a growing sense of unease that she could not quite express, plus a feeling that her being away was only exasperating the situation, whatever '*the situation*' was. She knew Damian had not been fully supportive of her coming over to the States, and if he suspected she was going to be away longer he would not be at all happy.

'I'm sure there's nothing to worry about, but when he picks them up this evening, I'll let him know you were trying to get hold of him just in case you still haven't managed to speak to him,' Monica said in an attempt to reassure her daughter. 'By the way, how is everything going over there. Have you spoken to Rob yet?'

'No, I'm going later today with Will. He's arranged for us to go to Rob's house for lunch. I have to admit Mum, I'm starting to get a little nervous. This adventure is suddenly becoming real, and I'm not sure what to think at the moment. Part of me is excited about what I might find, but part of me is thinking about packing my suitcase and coming home. I'm getting nervous about what I could unearth when I open up Pandora's box. I know Dad said there would be '*consequences*' but I think it's finally hitting me that I haven't really thought these through, and I don't know if it's too late to stop.'

Monica had mixed feelings about Amanda's trip to America, but had kept these to herself, knowing that her daughter could be head strung, and once she had read Ken's letter, which had set her on this particular course of action, there would have been little, if any, point trying to deter her. She too was concerned about the consequences, but knew that whatever these were she would have to deal with them, and more importantly be there to support Amanda as she dealt with them too.

Monica recognised that one of her worst fears was that Rob would reject Amanda or want nothing to do with her, and she could not bear that thought for her daughter. Rob had no responsibility for her, and at his age would presumably not be looking for any upheaval in his life. His priority would be to protect his family, and Amanda might prove to be an unwelcome curve ball that he just could not deal with. Monica knew how hard Amanda had taken her dad's death; losing one dad had been difficult, but losing both would be unbearable, particularly if the second brought a sense of rejection with it.

'Darling, you can always come home if you feel that way, no-one other than the family would be any the wiser, and although I have some concerns about what you're doing, I sense that it's something you have to do anyway. Your dad told you for a reason, so perhaps you need to go with it, but if you feel at all uncomfortable, then just leave, pack your bags and come home. I'll be here waiting for you.'

As Amanda dressed and got herself ready, carefully choosing what she should wear, without any concept of what would be appropriate attire for meeting your biological father for the first time, she reflected on her mum's wise words; but her resolve was to go ahead with the meeting as planned. She acknowledged that any doubts and concerns she felt had not gone away, but at the same time she believed she owed it to her dad to carry out his final wishes, wherever they might take her. Throughout her life, his guidance and support had never let her down, so why was she be doubting it now? She needed to trust and go with her instincts, but as her mum had said, if all goes badly, head for the airport pronto whilst her dignity was still intact.

Chapter 34

For the last three hours, Amanda had tried on every conceivable combination of clothing she had with her, before settling on a pair of three-quarter length, smart cream linen trousers, a blue and white striped lightweight-knit jumper and her flat navy pumps. She had tamed her long curly hair into a sleek ponytail and applied a little mascara and lip-gloss. Amanda did not wear make-up often, but as she had looked at herself in the mirror, she noticed how her complexion had really benefitted from the last few days in the fresh air. Her eyes had regained most of the sparkle they had lost recently, her cheeks now had a healthy glow from being out in the sunshine and the smattering of freckles across her nose made a very attractive addition to her overall appearance. *Not too bad for someone in her thirties* she thought to herself.

She had aimed for the smart casual look, neither wanting to appear too formal nor give the impression she could not be bothered, but now as she stood in the hall waiting for Will she wondered whether she had achieved the desired effect, or whether it all looked a bit too nautical. *Oh well, too late to change now* thought Amanda as she heard

Will's car pull up outside the house as the clock struck noon. Will was nothing if not punctual!

'Good afternoon young lady, don't you look a picture,' said Will as he held the door open for Amanda, immediately sensing some nerves as she approached the car. 'Are you still good to go? Any second thoughts about today, because if you have, I can easily cancel?'

Amanda wondered whether it was written in big bold letters all over her face. Will had managed to sum up her feelings by simply looking at her, without her even saying a word. It did not bode too well for when she met Rob if her face and demeanour was so readable, how was she going to play it cool?

'I have to admit I am a little nervous, and there is a small element of me that's starting to panic and have second thoughts, but I can't back out now, can I?' asked Amanda, perhaps subconsciously looking for reassurance from Will, before adding with a bit more confidence, 'No, I've come this far and I need to know who my biological father is, even if it is the first and last time we ever meet.'

'Don't pressure yourself. You can still pull out, or if you're not ready we could rearrange for another day. I could easily make an excuse for turning up by myself, it's your choice,' replied Will, adding, 'In my view though, I think you would regret that. Rob is a lovely man, and even if you guys don't develop a long-term relationship, at least you will have met him. Don't worry, he won't bite, but even if he does, I'm there to protect you.'

'I know you're right, I would regret it, and I do believe you that he's a nice man. Let's go then, it's now or never,' resolved Amanda, finally settling herself into the car for the short drive over to Rob's house. She acknowledged though that however nice a man he was, the shock was still going to hit him hard, and the reception she would receive was not something she was prepared to bet on.

Will had said it should only take about fifteen minutes to drive there at this time of the day, as the roads would be relatively quiet, so Amanda belted herself in and tried to relax, at the same time praying that the churning in her stomach, due to nerves rather than hunger, was nowhere near as loud as she imagined it to be.

Chapter 35

When Will pulled his car into Rob's drive a short time later, Amanda had to hold her breath as she glimpsed the house in front of her for the first time. It looked unreal, almost as if it had been lifted directly out of a Hollywood film set. It was in fact picture perfect. The white double fronted property which seemed to sprawl over two floors was set back about three hundred meters from the road, thereby ensuring it was private and not overlooked. It had a sweeping driveway leading to a separate detached building that was either a garage or boat house, or potentially both it was so big, with what looked like a separate annex or granny flat above it. Amanda realised that building alone was probably bigger than her house at home.

The backdrop to the property though was what really caught Amanda's attention. It was one of the most amazing sea views she had ever seen, with a selection of pretty sail boats gently bobbing around on the clear blue water, almost within touching distance of the house. It was a perfect day for sailing, with a cloudless sky and the midday sun reflecting on the water, making everything shine as if it had been polished to within an inch of its life.

From what she could see from the driveway, the house was surrounded by well-established and beautifully maintained gardens, with species of plants and trees that Amanda would struggle to recognise even though she had been brought up gardening with her dad and took a great interest in understanding the various varieties. There was also to the side of the property, behind some ornate gates a furnished patio area overlooking the water, with a private jetty running alongside the house, where a small yacht was moored, presumably belonging to Rob.

'It's stunning!' was the only word she could summon up when Will opened the car door for her to get out. 'Are you sure we're at the right house?'

No one had ever mentioned what Rob did for a living, or whether or not he was well off, and it was not the type of question Amanda had even thought to ask. Money had never been her motivation for being here, and she definitely did not want to appear a gold-digger by asking too many questions. She remembered her mum telling her that it had been Rob's parents' boat that they had originally sailed on, but she had not given any further thought to that, and had probably naively never considered looking Rob up online to see what she could find out about him. As her Aunt Jane and Will knew him as an old family friend it had not seemed necessary. Now she was thinking that perhaps she should have done some research to prepare herself. Yet another part of her plan not really thought through she realised to herself.

'Yes, this is the right house. It's amazing, isn't it?' said Will noticing the stunned look on Amanda's face. 'Rob moved back home when his parents were ill some years ago and no longer able to run the house by themselves. I'm not sure if they have both died since or whether they're in a nursing home, but as far as I know they don't live here anymore. If I remember rightly though, his parents bought it when Rob was just a baby, so the property must have been in his family for over fifty years. His parents spent a lot of time and money renovating it over the years, and Rob has done more since he moved back, but I agree it really is stunning. The view from the back of the house is equally amazing, and the insides won't disappoint you either! Come on, let's go and see if Rob's around,' encouraged Will, putting his arm out to support Amanda, noticing how she seemed a little reluctant to move forward all of a sudden.

As they approached the house, the front door opened and Amanda caught a glimpse of Rob for the first time as he beckoned them forward; he had obviously been waiting for their arrival with some anticipation.

'Welcome, welcome, come on in. You're right on time,' said Rob in a voice that seemed welcoming, if a little strained. 'It's great to see you Will, and who is this beautiful young lady? I was intrigued when you said you were bringing a guest. It's great to have company. I seem to be rattling around in here at the moment with both the boys away.'

Rob Mason appeared tall, over six foot, cleanshaven with fair hair, a little overgrown, but not scruffy. Amanda could see the ends of his hair curling around his neckline, immediately conjuring in her head an image of Maisie's hair when she first woke up in the morning before it had been tamed with the hairbrush.

Whilst Rob's face looked quite drawn, his features were strong and the good looks her mum had warned her about were still very apparent. Amanda smiled at the fact he was dressed in a similar nautical theme to herself; pale blue trousers, a white striped polo shirt and cream deck shoes, but noticed his clothes seemed to hang off him a little, as if he had recently lost weight, evidence of his illness she presumed.

'Thank you, great to see you too. This is Amanda from the UK; she's over here visiting family. I'll introduce you properly when we're inside if that's okay,' said Will, obviously not wanting the have the discussion on the doorstep.

'No problem. Come on through then, I was thinking of sitting in the garden at the back. It's quite sheltered there and a good place to eat lunch. My housekeeper, Mrs. Reilly was here earlier and has prepared us something light to eat if that's alright with you,' enquired Rob, as he led the way indoors, proceeding through the house directly to the garden that ran the length of the property, manicured lawns gently sloping down to the waterfront.

So far Amanda had been too stunned to say anything or even offer her hand to Rob, she just smiled as she followed him indoors, through the house and outside to the patio area she had glimpsed from the front, which she noticed had already been set for lunch, presumably by the housekeeper. She did not take in any of the interior of the building, so completely dazed and taken aback was she by the similarities she saw in Rob to herself; his colouring, his build, his height. Suddenly feeling quite conscious, she wondered was it only obvious to her or had Will or Rob noticed it too?

She had never really considered the fact that she had little physical resemblance to her dad as a concern; their similarities were most obvious in their values and general approach to life, values he had instilled into her throughout her upbringing. She had few memories of her maternal grandparents, but always presumed she took after her mum's side; that her fair hair and height had come from there, although she knew both her mum and Aunt Jane were dark too. Ken had been a much slighter build, with ramrod straight dark hair, and although she had loved him to bits, he did not have the film star good looks that Rob had.

As Amanda waited quietly in the garden whilst Rob and Will had a bit of a catch-up in the kitchen preparing their drinks, her thoughts began to wander, trying to assimilate all that had happening over the last few days, leading up to this point now where she had finally come face-to-face with her biological father.

Having now seen him, she was left in no doubt whatsoever about her parentage. For some inexplicable reason though her feelings towards him were not as she had imagined they would be. She had expected to feel nothing more than a general curiosity, but now meeting him, albeit briefly and seeing the brave face he was so obviously trying to present to them despite his illness, she could not detach herself as she had imagined she would. If she did not know any better, she would probably say it was a strange feeling a protectiveness she felt towards him, but where that feeling came from God only knew.

Bringing her out of her reverie she heard Rob say, 'Is this okay?' as he placed a glass of ice tea in front of her, with a curious smile on his face. 'I could get you something else if you would prefer, there's wine in the fridge if it's not too carly?'

Will had been a little cagey on the phone when they had spoken about arranging lunch and bringing someone round to meet him, but having now seen Amanda, Rob did not think she was Will's usual type, and also much younger than his normal girlfriends, so presumed she was not his latest fling. But that still did not answer the question of who she was, or more importantly why Will had brought her along. He had a strange feeling about her, almost like he knew her from somewhere, but he could not put his finger on it.

'Thank you, that's perfect. It's not a drink I've ever drunk at home, but since coming here I am enjoying it. It's very refreshing, which you need on a day like today,' babbled Amanda a little embarrassed, adding, 'the view here is stunning,' in an attempt to further disguise the fact that she had been miles away day-dreaming, and had undoubtedly missed some of the conversation that had taken place between Rob and Will.

'So how are you feeling Rob? I've heard you've not been too well recently. Nothing serious I hope,' enquired Will in an attempt to move the conversation along.

'To be honest, I have good days and bad days. I won't bore you with the details, but I've been having problems with my kidneys for a while now. Recently it's got worse and I'm now on dialysis most afternoons at the moment. Thankfully I can do that from home, which explains why I'm not venturing too far. The doctor says I'm on the list for transplant if a donor can be found, but until then it's a case of keep taking the tablets!' he laughed, trying to inject a little humour into the mood. He did not want to get into health issues when there were guests in the house, and was much more interested in finding out who Amanda was than talking through his woes. That niggling feeling was still there; there was definitely something familiar about her.

'So, tell me Amanda, what brings you over here? Will said you were here to see family,' enquired Rob, turning to face Amanda so that he could give her his full attention. Will had been waiting to change the subject to something less direct, but Rob seemed to have another agenda. His and Amanda's plan had been to skirt around the issue until they had established the lay of the land, but it looked like that plan was about to backfire.

Rob noticing a look of almost panic on Amanda's face, and sensing she was looking towards Will for support realised he had probably been a little insensitive by being so direct. 'I'm sorry, that was rude of me to ask. I apologise if I have offended you, please ignore me.'

Amanda smiled, but kept quiet, afraid to blurt something out too soon.

'So where are your sons at the moment; remind me how old are they now? Time seems to fly by. I don't think I've seen them around for a few years,' asked Will trying to navigate onto a safer subject.

'They're twenty-two next birthday, in fact next week. Ben is at Harvard studying Medicine. He's not made any firm choice yet about what area of medicine to specialise in, but potentially paediatrics. Lucas is also at Harvard but studying Business and Economics. He plans on being an entrepreneur, but again not quite sure exactly what he's going to make his millions on,' laughed Rob. His mood then softened as he added, 'After their mum, Carrie died, nearly eight years ago now, they were both really shook up; everything was so sudden for all of us, so they decided to study locally to keep their eye on me. I don't think they liked the idea of me being in the house by myself, but now with my health the way it is, it's good to have them around.'

'Secretly though,' he continued, 'I think having the sailing club on the doorstep is the biggest pull. They're both as addicted to the water as we were. They're really good kids and very close, even though they're so different. They get home whenever they can, in fact they will be home for their birthday, so I'm looking forward to that.'

It was obvious from the look on his face that he adored his sons and took great pleasure in talking about them, and from what he said his feelings appeared to be reciprocated. Having such close ties must have been so important to Rob when they lost Carrie.

'Have you got anything planned to celebrate?' asked Will, anxious to continue the discussion on safe ground.

'No, it will be pretty low key, just a family dinner, Ben, Lucas, Myself and Greg – Lily's husband,' said Rob by way of explanation, but as soon as he mentioned Lily's name, he felt a strange sensation in his stomach. That was it, Amanda reminded him of his sister, Lily. Why had he not seen the resemblance sooner? Looking at her closely there was something about her eyes, and as he watched her, he could feel tears coming to his eyes too as he faced the memory it had brought.

Lily had been in the car with Carrie. They had been returning from a shopping trip to Boston to top up their summer wardrobes when they had their fatal accident. A sports car had been speeding on a winding coastal road, it lost control in the bright glare of the sun and careered into Carrie's car, forcing it to spin off the road and into a ravine, killing both women instantly, as well as the young driver of the sports car. Rob remembered being at home preparing dinner for them all when he received a call from the police. In one afternoon, he not only lost his wife, but his only sister too. His life, the lives of his two young sons and that of his brother-in-law Greg were changed overnight.

Lily had been four years younger than Rob, the baby of the family and spoilt rotten by her parents and everyone who met her. She was so bubbly, but also so easy going and fun to be around. She had also been one of Carrie's closest friends, in fact that was how Rob and Carrie had met, at one of Lily's student costume parties twenty-five years ago when they were at university studying fashion design. Rob, had been invited to bring along a group of friends to boost the number of boys. 'Invite the better-looking ones,' he remembered Lily instructing him at the time.

Greg had come along a couple of years later, meeting Lily in New York where she had moved for work after graduating with a first in Fashion Design from Boston University. She had secured an eighteen-month internship with a design house specialising in Children's fashion, living in a small converted loft apartment in the Garment district of Manhattan. She had only been in New York for six months, but already loved the buzz and the lifestyle her job provided, supporting VIP events, fashion shows and charity functions throughout the city being some of the regular highlights.

Greg and Lily literally bumped into each other in a bar after work one evening; Lily was out with a group of colleagues, having a few drinks to wind down after finalising their winter collection, and Greg was celebrating his birthday with friends when they collided as Greg was returning from the bar with a couple of beers in his hands, promptly slopping most of it over Lily. Their eyes met, and rather than being cross at having beer spilled down her dress, Lily smiled and offered to buy Greg another drink. Before long, their friends had been forgotten, they were exchanging numbers and had planned to meet up the following evening for a quiet drink.

From there, their relationship developed at an alarming speed, both realising they had found their soul mates, becoming inseparable almost overnight. They moved in together within a month, were engaged within six months and by the time Lily's internship was in its final month Greg had popped the question and they decided to marry as soon as possible, both excited about their future together.

Greg was working as a journalist with the New York Post and had been in the city just under a year when they met. He was originally from a small town in Canada where, by his own admission, nothing happened, so as a journalist he had no great desire to move back there. Being an only child with elderly parents who had resettled in Florida when they retired, mainly for the weather and the relaxed lifestyle, other than a few college friends there were no strings pulling him back or anchoring him to his home town.

They initially discussed staying in New York after they had married, but decided to move back to New England to settle nearer Lily's family, eventually buying a property just outside Boston that was in need of love, attention and a whole lot of renovation. Lily wanted to be closer to her parents and brother, and although she had loved the highlife of New York, after eighteen months she now felt a more settled environment would be preferable to raise their family.

Their greatest sadness was that the family Lily and Greg dreamed of never materialised; even a couple of rounds of IVF did not produce their much long for child, but rather than being downhearted, they threw themselves into their careers and their families, doting on Carrie and Rob's twins as if they were their own. Greg had transferred to the Boston Herald and was progressing up his journalistic career ladder, and Lily had founded a small niche business designing children's clothing. Both were doing well and knew they had to count their blessings.

After Lily's death, Greg closely considered his options. New England had become his home, and even though Lily had gone, his life was here. Rob and the boys were his family. He would still visit his parents occasionally in Florida, happy in their purpose-built retirement village, but he knew that to get through this, he would need Rob and the boys more than ever. In fact, they would all need each other.

Rob wiping the tear from his eye, sensed he needed to bring the conversation back to the present, but also try to find out a bit more about his guest. 'So, Amanda, is this your first time in New England, and are you planning on staying long?'

'No, I've been here a couple of times before with my parents, staying with my aunt in Salem. I've been here just under a week now, but it's all a bit open ended in terms of when I go back home …' Rob noticed a cryptic glance exchanged between Amanda and Will as she spoke; almost implying she was seeking his agreement to whatever she was saying.

Again, sensing a bit of an uncomfortable atmosphere, Rob decided it was an opportunity to bring lunch out. He placed a selection of meats, cheeses and salads on the table in front of his guests; a simple light lunch he had said, but his housekeeper had gone to town by the look of the plates Rob produced.

'I hope you're hungry. Mrs. Reilly got excited when I said I was having friends over for lunch and seems to have made enough to feed an army. Please help yourself. I think she's also left a cheesecake for later,' Rob added, placing fresh drinks down too.

'Thanks, this looks amazing,' said Will, 'You shouldn't have gone to so much trouble, but now that you have, I'm going to tuck in as I'm starving. I only managed a coffee before I left home, so my stomach is screaming out for food.'

Amanda watched Rob as the conversation continued between the two men whilst they ate, mainly about the sailing club and what the latest developments were around town. Rob admitted he had become quite a medical recluse recently, opting to keep himself to himself for fear of infection, but being out of touch made him anxious for whatever updates he could get. Will also regaled him about his own situation; his divorce, the new apartment and how the business was all getting a bit much. The conversation flowed easily and Amanda was able to blend into the background, comfortable to listen and watch.

It was obvious to Amanda that the two had been close friends, but over recent years had lost touch, so were now enjoying rekindling their friendship. But as the meal came to an end, she knew that the time had come to broach the subject she had come to discuss. She could not put it off any longer. She had noticed Rob looking at her curiously on a few occasions, and although she did not know what to think, she knew he suspected something.

'That was lovely, thank you,' said Amanda politely as she placed her knife and fork down, giving Will a look to indicate it was time. They had decided he would introduce the subject, by recalling their sailing trip once she had given him the indication she was ready.

'I'm glad you enjoyed it; now can I tempt you into cheesecake?' asked Rob keen to bring Amanda back into the discussion.

'Rob, before we go onto that, there's something we would like to discuss with you,' began Will, watching Rob closely as he continued. 'Do you remember that summer back in 1984 when a group of us went sailing over Labor Day weekend? We took your parents' boat out and had a picnic afterwards over on the bank, with a campfire.'

'I do. That was a great weekend. One of our last hurrahs after university if I remember correctly, before we all went our separate ways and had to start working for a living. Great memories. There were about twenty of us by the end of the day I seem to recall. But why bring that up Will, that's a bit of a random memory isn't it?'

'Well, do you remember, I brought along a friend from England, a girl who was staying with my brother Brad, his sister-in-law Monica?'

'Yes I do, in fact she was lovely. A proper English rose if I recall rightly. I seem to remember we had some great fun together.'

'Well, Amanda is Monica's daughter. And it would appear yours too.'

Amanda watched Rob's face throughout, noticing his expression changing to one of surprise and realisation, rather than shock as Will provided the final piece of the jigsaw.

'Oh boy, that explains it.' Rob, now looking directly at Amanda added, 'I felt there was a sense of familiarity when I first saw you, but I couldn't quite place it. Then when we were talking about Lily earlier, that feeling became even stronger, something about you was confusing me. I thought I recognised you, but couldn't place where I might have met you before. But now I can see it clearly, the resemblance is uncanny. You are so like my sister…' he said, with tears in his eyes 'I don't know what to say … I'm lost for words. You're my daughter. I had no idea.'

Amanda waited a few moments for the news to sink in, not knowing what to do next, but experiencing a great desire to get up and go over to comfort Rob. The feeling of protectiveness she had felt earlier was now stronger than ever, and seeing him with tears in his eyes was difficult to take.

Rob slowly rose from his chair and walked into the house, returning a short while later with a gilt framed photograph of his sister, taken when she was in her mid-thirties, presumably around the same age as Amanda was now. Rob handed it to Amanda and she saw instantly why he had been so spooked by her appearance; her likeness to his sister, her aunt was uncanny. For Amanda it was almost like looking into a mirror, she noticed how their eyes were the same shape and colour, they both had the same high defined cheekbones and even the sprinkling of freckles across their noses was almost identical.

Returning the photo to Rob, Amanda commented on how beautiful Lily had been, and how distraught he must have been following not only her death, but Carrie's too.

'Yes, she was beautiful, in fact they both were, and with both of them it wasn't just skin deep either, they had beautiful souls. Kind and considerate natures and the greatest of friends, always ganging up against me if either of them wanted anything. Not a day passes that I don't miss them or wish they were still here. I miss them both deeply,' said Rob in a melancholy way.

After a few moments of reflection, his mood lifted and a smile returned to his face. 'But I have a daughter! That was the last thing I was expecting to be told today. I'm not sure quite what to think, but looking at the evidence before me I don't think a paternity test is in order do you?' he laughed, but then more thoughtfully added, 'Why are you telling me now, why've I never known I had a daughter? Where've you been for the last thirty odd years?'

'I've been living in England with my parents and until very recently I was unaware that my dad wasn't my biological father,' Amanda began, soon realising though that although Rob was listening, he was starting to look tired. She remembered that he had mentioned earlier that he needed dialysis in the afternoon, so decided that probably it would be better to leave it there for now and allow him some time to absorb what he had heard before she went further. 'It's a long story, but if you'd like I can come around tomorrow, or later in the week and we can talk some more.'

Rob, acknowledging that he wanted to hear more, but at the same time recognising he was tired agreed that tomorrow would be good. He had been completely surprised, but at the same time delighted with the idea that he had a grown-up daughter, and the more he looked at Amanda and listened to her speak, the more he wanted to know about her and her life.

Driving home with Will later, Amanda commented on how pleasantly surprised, in fact delighted she was by how easily the discussion had gone, thanking Will for the invaluable support he had provided as go-between. But now she recognised she needed some time alone to reflect on the last couple of hours, to consider her own feelings on finally coming face-to-face with her biological father. The early nerves she had experienced had long gone, replaced by an excitement she had not expected. Rob had been polite, welcoming and charismatic, but more importantly he had been excited at the prospect of her being part of his life.

Amanda in reality had never expected much from the meeting, other than possibly a challenge to her assertions, or at best a nonchalance to her existence, but his reaction was off-the-scale in a positive way. Where did this leave her now, and critically what did she want from Rob going forward? A question she recognised would need some serious thought over the coming days as they got to know each other more.

Chapter 36

It was mid-afternoon by the time Will pulled into the driveway back at Jane's house. The sun was no longer directly overhead, and some of the heat had gone from it, but it was still a warm afternoon and promised to be a lovely evening. They had taken the roof off the car to appreciate the sea breeze as they had meandered back along the coastal roads, with the sounds of Fleetwood Mac, Will's favourite band, wafting through the music system. *The joys of having a convertible* thought Will to himself as he relaxed into the journey. Both he and Amanda had been quite reflective on the way back, both lost in their own thoughts.

Will had enjoyed catching up with Rob and sharing their news, but had been left feeling guilty that so much time had gone by without them being in touch. Both he and Rob had gone through their own personal challenges over recent years, and Will was saddened that they had not both been there for each other through these difficult times. He vowed to himself that as part of the rebuilding of his social life, he would invest more time in rekindling those friendships that he had allowed to slip.

No sooner had the car stopped, Jane and Clara both ran towards them anxious to hear how their lunch had gone. They had both been on tenterhooks all morning waiting for Will and Amanda to return, neither willing to believe anything bad would have happened, but at the same time unsure how he would have reacted to the news.

Sensing Jane and Clara were ready to pounce, Will remained in the car. 'I'm going to get straight off if that's okay with you, there're a couple of things I need to get sorted at the office this afternoon, but by the looks of it you have your audience waiting,' he laughed. He knew Jane and Clara would demand chapter and verse and he did not feel the need to relive it again. He could wait for a follow-up instalment at a later date.

'That's no problem, I agree, escape whilst the going's good, but thank you so much Will for all you've done. I really couldn't have gone through that without you. I really appreciate it,' said Amanda, leaning across to give Will a kiss on the cheek before getting out of the car. He really was a nice man, *and a great catch for someone* she thought to herself, hoping that their adventure would provide the catalyst for him to get his own life back on track. 'I'll let you know how I get on with Rob over the next few days if you like'.

'That would be great. Good luck' he shouted as he started the car waving to Jane and Clara as he headed out of the driveway towards his office. Today had given him a lot to think about and a few hours alone would be good for him.

Chapter 37

An hour later, Rob was sitting quietly upstairs in one of the spare bedrooms, in his comfy armchair positioned in the bay window to capture the best views of the ocean. He was watching the sail boats bobbing on the sea, their highly polished chrome reflecting the bright spring sunshine and the colours replicating the cheerful mood he found himself in. He knew it was the type of view he would never get tired of, feeling forever thankful that he lived in such a beautiful part of the world.

He recognised his share of heartache and loss over the years, but notwithstanding all the cards life had dealt him, he was an eternal optimist and regularly counted his blessings. His sons were foremost on that list, but as of this morning he now had to contemplate the addition of a daughter; *how had that happened* he asked himself, with a grin on his face. As he pondered Amanda's news, he realised rather than the shock he should have felt, it had actually come as a pleasant surprise.

Rob was honest enough not to pretend Monica, Amanda's mum had been the love of his life, or frankly that he had even given her a second thought once that summer was over and she had returned to England, but he did recall their time together and the memories were very pleasant indeed; just two youngsters messing around, enjoying a bit of harmless and inconsequential fun, or so he had thought. *It's amazing how life plays tricks on you when you least expect it,* he thought to himself.

Scattered around him was the dialysis equipment he had asked the hospital to install, a constant reminder of his health and the fragility of his situation. The hospital and his consultant had been very supportive, providing everything he needed to undertake the process in the comfort of his home, without the hassle of getting to and from the clinic each time he needed treatment. It was a bind having to wire himself up to the machine, but contemplating the alternative was not a pleasant thought.

He had developed a mild kidney infection a couple of years previously, after contracting a rare virus, but rather than clear up as the doctors had hoped with a normal course of antibiotics, the infection had worsened to the point that he now knew that without a transplant his chances of survival were significantly reduced. The only way to help prevent the condition worsening was to undergo regular dialysis, which for him meant hooking up to the machine for several hours, three times a week.

Rob was grateful that neither his condition nor the treatment itself was painful, but it was quite debilitating and was controlling the quality of his life in more ways than he liked to admit. Without it he knew that his condition would gradually worsen, but because of the risks of a relapse he never felt confident enough to stray too far from home. Arranging any social life, or simply meeting up with friends outside of his home was challenging, which was why the opportunity of catching up with Will today had been something he had really looked forward to.

Rob recalled how he had sensed something familiar about Amanda from the moment she had got out of Will's car; her walk, her look, her posture, that smile. There were so many different things that he could not quite fathom, but he knew at the back of his mind that there was something strangely familiar. Throughout the time they were there, that sense deepened, such that when Will finally introduced Amanda as his daughter, it was as if he already knew and the jigsaw just fell into place. Any shock was replaced by an amazing feeling of relief that the connection had been made.

There were so many questions going through his mind, not least of all why now, and why for over thirty years had there never been any hint that he had a daughter. Surely Will would have known and could not have kept that a secret? Also, what did it mean to Amanda? Had she been searching long for him, and now that she had found him what did that mean. Did she want a relationship, a future? Also, what would it mean to Ben and Lucas to know they had a half-sister; would they be upset, or would she even want to know anything about them? They had to remain his priorities.

So many questions and currently so few answers. Although as these spun around in his head, Rob accepted that he would have to be patient until tomorrow when Amanda had offered to return and fill in some of the gaps for him. Tomorrow suddenly felt so far away, and as he closed his eyes to rest whilst the machine did its job, it left him wondering how he was going to get through the next twenty-four hours until her return.

Chapter 38

The following morning brought another beautiful day, again with the promise of sunshine and cool gentle breezes to keep the temperatures at a manageable level. As Amanda awoke to the usual sound of the birds singing, she felt almost as excited as a child on Christmas morning. Her mind had been working overtime trying to process everything that had happened to her over the last few days, culminating in yesterday and finally coming face-to-face with her biological father. The detached, almost perfunctory feelings she had expected to have had not materialised, but in their place, she had experienced feelings of emotion with an overriding feeling of concern for the man who had sat opposite her, a man for whom only a few weeks ago she did not know even existed.

After replaying the events of the day with Jane and Clara, she had phoned home and spoken to Damian, followed by a call to her mum, and then finally to Lisa, who she spoke at length to late into the night. Whilst the reactions she got from all were positive, Damian seemed the most detached, concerned mainly with when she was planning on coming home, with an unspoken subtext of *how soon could we just get back to normal.* His empathy, or more importantly his lack of empathy, added to Amanda's growing concern that something was still not right at home, but when asked he insisted everything was okay, adding he was just tired and overworked.

Monica was relieved that the conversation with Rob had gone well and equally pleased that he had remembered their time together after all these years. Her concern had been that Rob may have simply dismissed Amanda's claim, taking little or no interest in what she had to say. No one was asking him to accept any responsibility, financial or otherwise, for what had happened, but her fear had been that their meeting could have backfired, which would have left Amanda feeling abandoned and potentially embarrassed, not to say rejected and disappointed.

Lisa with her considerable experience in family law, plus a legal brain trained to assess risks, had feared scenarios at both ends of the spectrum. Throughout her career, she had encountered many cases involving long-lost families, where family members were unearthed as wills were being read; noxious sibling rivalries resulting from second families; cases when adoptions or childcare orders were needed; examples where there was a history of physical abuse that had meant the family member had gone to ground, but rarely had she come across cases that resulted in a happy ever after. Hearing Amanda's story though had encouraged her to believe this could prove to be the exception to the rule.

Driving to Rob's mid-morning, Amanda had to keep checking her emotions, unsure how she would feel as she retold her story, or more importantly her dad's story once he had uncovered the truth about him not being her real father. She loved her dad unconditionally, so regardless of all that had been unearthed since his death, those feelings would not change and no matter what happened now, she would not be disloyal to him concerning the actions he took or his motivation at the time. He had enabled the life she had lived, and she would not have changed that for anything.

She also recognised that Rob would have had time to think through what he had learned yesterday, so today his feelings may be less conciliatory, more on guard and potentially a little suspicious of her intentions. His initial surprise will now be more considered and balanced. Having had time to think through the impact on his sons, on his wider family, he may have reached the conclusion that introducing Amanda into the mix at this time, particularly with the added concerns for his health, might not be the best idea. An arm's length relationship might be his preferred way forward.

Any concerns Amanda may have had were soon laid to rest later that day. On arrival at Rob's house, they had headed directly to the garden to sit and talk, Amanda once again marvelling at the small boats and private yachts bobbing about on the water.

Over lunch, prepared and left out by the housekeeper as previously, Amanda recounted stories of her life in England, describing her parents, her children, her husband. She painted a vivid picture of the upbringing she had enjoyed, being raised in the beautiful Cotswolds, learning to appreciate nature and value the simpler way of life.

It was clear to Rob as he listened that it had been a happy childhood, one filled with love, family and support.

When Amanda explained she was a lecturer at the local college, they found that they had a shared love of Art, but where Amanda's heart lay in art history, especially some of the great renaissance painters, Michelangelo and Leonardo da Vinci being particular favourites, Rob admitted his leaning was more towards some of the emerging contemporary artists, and whilst he was not a serious collector, he had managed to pick up one or two good pieces during his travels.

As each new page unfolded, Amanda could sense Rob's joy at her apparent happiness, but also his loss at all that he had missed in her life, so when she eventually shared the final part of the story, including the letters her dad had written to both her and Monica, there were tears in both their eyes.

Rob had at no stage passed judgement or even commented on the decision Ken had taken to keep his secret, he just listened attentively and with an appreciation of the dilemma Ken had obviously found himself in. He wondered to himself what he would have done in a similar situation, questioning whether he would have been brave enough to bring up another man's child without ever mentioning it, and with such obvious love and devotion.

He also sensed the underlying guilt Ken must have felt in keeping the secret to himself, including the fear he harboured should the truth ever be revealed, especially the risk of losing the love and respect from both his daughter and the wife he obviously adored. That final drive to reveal this secret, effectively on his death bed, Rob did not see as a weakness, more as further proof of the love he had for his daughter and his desire that she should not only learn the truth, but also learn it for her own benefit, and that of her daughters. Even after his death, this risk was immense given the way it could have tarnished their memories.

'That's quite a story, and quite a journey you've been on,' Rob said when it was clear Amanda had finished recounting what she knew, including the part Will had played in acting as a go-between. 'I really don't know what to say, other than how happy I am that you came to find me, but also how sorry I am about the circumstances that preceded it. Your dad was obviously a loving, caring man and it's a shame you've lost him in such a devastating way. To have the strength to come and find me, when you're still grieving, must have taken great resolve and determination, even though by the sound of it I wasn't too difficult to track down, thanks to Will,' he added smiling.

'Yes, it has been difficult emotionally, and it was a real shock at the time', replied Amanda. 'I suppose I can understand though what my dad's motivation was for keeping his secret, but I am very grateful that he had the courage to tell me before he died, without taking that secret to his grave. I just wished we could have discussed it rather than finding out the way I did in a letter after it was too late. To have lived for all those years with a fear of being found out must have haunted him, but I know from what his letter said, he couldn't feel anything bad against you or mum, because without what happened he would never have had me. I think he transferred any guilt to himself, rather than direct this at Mum.'

'Yes, I can see that he loved you both very much, and did all that was in his power to protect you. What a very special relationship you must have both had. But also, from what you say, it was as much a shock to your mum. To believe he was the father of her child and then to be told otherwise must have been incredible, particularly when she was in mourning herself; so to add a sense of guilt on top, without the opportunity to discuss it with him must have been very difficult for her also. I know when I lost Carrie I felt as if my world had fallen apart for so long, and the one person I needed to speak to wasn't there.'

They sat for a few minutes, both lost in their thoughts before Rob asked, 'So what happens next? When do you plan to go back to England? From what you say your husband and daughters are missing you.'

'I don't know to be honest. I haven't really thought that bit through,' replied Amanda honestly. She recognised now how much she had been knifing and forking her plan from the outset, never wanting to think too far ahead for fear of the unknown. Coming looking for her biological father had always been a gamble because no one could have predicted what she would have found.

Now, having met Rob, and sensing a desire on his side to get to know her more too, she realised she was in no real hurry to rush home. She knew Damian expected her back within a day or so, and accepted the girls would be missing her, but in her heart, she knew she needed to stay a while longer.

'It would be lovely if you could hang around for a few days and meet Ben and Lucas, but I would understand if that was too much, too soon.

They're home the day after tomorrow for their birthday weekend. I haven't mentioned anything to them yet, but I'm sure they would want to meet you. You could join us for dinner, and meet Lily's husband Greg too.'

'I don't know,' replied Amanda cautiously, 'I'm not sure how that would work. It's their birthday weekend after all, and I don't want to spoil everything for them by just turning up. They might not be too comfortable finding a long-lost sister at their table. You might want to discuss it with them first.'

Whilst Amanda accepted if she wanted any relationship with Rob, then that would undoubtedly include his sons, but she did not want to impose or just expect they would greet her with the same open arms. She had to consider their feelings. It may take time and a bit more than a piece of birthday cake to win them over.

'Before we decide anything, why don't you have a chat with them and let me know. I'll leave you my mobile number so you can ring me after you've spoken to them. I'll look at flights for Monday anyway, but even if we don't catch up again before I fly, we can talk more once I'm home.'

'That sounds like a plan,' accepted Rob, conscious that he didn't want to make Amanda feel uncomfortable by pushing too hard, but at the same time trying to balance his desire to catch up over thirty years of lost time. 'Right, shall we eat that lunch, all this talking has made me hungry.'

Chapter 39

A couple of days later it was Saturday evening and Amanda found herself nervously getting ready for dinner over at Rob's house. She and Clara had taken a trip into town earlier in the day to find something suitable to wear, settling on a pretty summer dress in pastel shades that provided the perfect complement to her blonde colouring, with a lightweight pale pink jacket that made the outfit a little more formal, but also gave Amanda more confidence.

'That really suits you,' exclaimed Clara as Amanda tried on the outfit in the shop, wriggling around in front of the mirror. Whilst it was not something she would normally wear, it somehow felt right in this setting. Casual wear was more her style, but she wanted to feel like she had made an effort.

'Great, that's the outfit sorted then,' said Amanda, relieved that Clara agreed it looked good. 'Now for the presents.' As it was Ben and Lucas' birthday she did not want to turn up without a small gift, but what to buy was a bit of a dilemma.

'Any ideas Clara?' She asked her cousin hopefully.

'How about a nice pen each, if they're studying pens are always useful. And if you wanted to make it special you could always engrave it with their initials,' offered Clara.

'What a great idea, personal without being too personal. I like it,' agreed Amanda.

They stopped off at the little gift cum jewellers shop on the high-street and found two matching pens that were perfect. Leaving them with the engraver they popped for a coffee in the delicatessen across the road.

Amanda hoped the gifts would strike the right note. She acknowledged to Clara she was worried what to say, and more importantly what not to say when she met her half-brothers and their uncle Greg. She had developed a mental image of them from what Rob had told her, and seen photos around the house, but nothing could really prepare her for the actual meeting. She knew twins had a telepathic way of communicating, so whilst she was normally relatively good at reading people, dealing with this may prove challenging.

'Just be yourself and they will love you. You've nothing to worry about,' reassured Clara, 'what's the worst that can happen? If you don't feel comfortable then make your excuses and come home. I'm going to stay up and wait for you anyway, so we can either celebrate or drown our sorrows whichever proves most appropriate.'

Amanda had spoken to Rob a couple of times over the phone since their lunch and they had developed an easy manner in their conversations, both happy to share and explore each other's lives, trying to cram in whatever they could before she went home. This openness had come about in an amazingly short period of time, both appreciating the value of speaking from their hearts and avoiding the strain any more secrets would create.

Rob had told her more about his illness and the impact it had on his life, not just on a day-to-day basis, but also the longer-term prognosis should the transplant not materialise. His condition was not improving, but with dialysis the doctors were managing to stabilise it, however they had warned that the older he got, the more difficult and riskier it would be for him to undergo surgery should a kidney become available. He spoke with such openness and honesty, treated Amanda as if he had known her forever, sharing his fears and concerns for his sons should anything happen to him.

Whilst speaking with Rob felt easy, Amanda had no idea what it would feel like to be with Ben and Lucas, especially as Rob had assured her, they were *intrigued* to meet her, or what Greg would be like, sensing it may be upsetting for him to meet her if she resembled Lily as much as Rob implied. They would all feel very protective of Rob and potentially suspicious of her and her motives, so she needed to do nothing to provoke their concerns.

When Amanda had spoken to Lisa the previous evening, she like Clara had advised her to relax and just be herself, but tonight she sensed she would need more than her glittering personality to get through. She would need to tread very carefully, be sensitive to the atmosphere but more importantly as Clara wisely advised, be ready to head for the hills if it all got too uncomfortable.

Chapter 40

Rob was waiting on the doorstep when Amanda's car pulled up at seven that evening, a broad smile on his face, dressed in an open neck shirt and smart suit, that she noticed hung on him, perhaps more than it should have done. Having not known Rob before his illness, Amanda had no real sense of how big a man he had been, or how much weight he had lost, but his clothes could not hide the fact that there had definitely been an impact.

'You look lovely,' he remarked as Amanda got out of the car and straightened her dress, grabbing the present bags and a couple of bottles of wine as she went.

'Thank you.' Amanda accepted the compliment with a smile, knowing that she looked good after all the effort she had gone to. Her make-up had been done by Clara and her hair trimmed and styled by Jane, who although she had sold the salon several years ago, retained her skills by regularly cutting the hair of any family or friends that dropped in. She had left it long and curly, but layered it in a way that flattered and emphasised Amanda's pretty face, to which Clara then applied a very light foundation, a touch of mascara and a pale eyeshadow to bring out the blue in her eyes.

Handing over the wine, Amanda was ushered into the house by Rob, her nerves abating a little, but still leaving her stomach fluttering. As she walked through the door, she instantly saw Ben and Lucas standing in the hallway ready to greet her, along with Greg, Lily's husband. They all waited until Rob spoke, no-one wanting to make the first move.

'Amanda, let me introduce everyone first,' he started as soon as he had closed the door behind her, 'and then we can go and get some drinks and talk. Dinner isn't for another hour. Mrs. Reilly has given me strict instructions about that.' He laughed, explaining his housekeeper had prepared the meal, was staying around to serve it, but then leaving them free to relax and enjoy themselves.

As introductions were made, Amanda noticed that Ben and Lucas, although twins were far from alike. Although they were similar builds, Ben was fair like herself and looked similar to Rob in his features, whereas Lucas was darker and presumably took more after Carrie's side. They both politely came forward and shook her hand.

'I hope you don't mind, but I've got you both a gift for your birthday,' said Amanda handing each a gift bag containing their pen. 'It's nothing special, but I've had your initials put on it, so I'm sorry you can't return it. I hope you like it.'

'Thank you, that's very kind,' said Lucas as he opened the gift, 'that's really thoughtful, and yes I love it.'

'Yes, me too,' added Ben, obviously taking his lead from his brother. He appeared shyer and more reserved than Lucas, and from what Rob had said was the more sensitive of the two.

All the while, Amanda sensed Greg's eyes on her. Having seen photos of Lily at her age, she knew how similar they looked so appreciated how unnerving it might be for him.

'Hello Greg, lovely to meet you,' she smiled as she stretched out her hand, trying to put him at his ease.

Introductions over, they moved into the lounge and as Rob poured drinks, they all stood around nervously wondering who was going to break the ice.

'Well, this has all been a bit of a surprise.' It was Lucas who eventually spoke, looking directly at Amanda, but including the rest of them with his remark. 'When Dad told us we were having company for dinner, we didn't know what to think, but then to find it was a long-lost sister, well I have to admit, that wasn't what I was expecting for my birthday. It's all come as a bit of a shock to be honest.'

'Yes, it was to me too,' replied Amanda nervously. 'As I've told Rob, I knew nothing about this either until a few weeks ago when my dad died. I was shocked, as was my mum, but as it was my dad's last wish that I try to find my biological father, I thought I had to give it a go. Thankfully it wasn't as difficult as I imagined it would be.'

'And I for one am pleased you have found me,' said Rob, obviously trying to fend off any uncertainty any of the others might have felt. 'I don't know about you Greg, but Amanda is so much like Lily, it makes me happy and sad all at the same time.'

'Yes, it's remarkable. There's definitely no need for a paternity test, I'll agree with you on that,' he laughed in an attempt to disguise the emotion he felt. From the moment he had seen Amanda, memories of Lily at that age came flooding back. Happy memories that he had packed deep into his heart were suddenly exploding within him, making him feel quite disorientated. Rob had prepared him by pointing out there was a resemblance when they had spoken earlier in the week, but he had never expected it to be so obvious. As he watched Amanda, almost mesmerized, he noticed even her mannerisms were similar to Lily's, the way she shook her head and wrinkled her nose when she smiled.

When Mrs. Reilly announced that dinner was ready sometime later, they made their way into the dining room at the rear of the house overlooking the patio area and the incredible view Amanda had previously only seen at lunchtime. With the evening light as the sun set, the view was equally stunning, but without the sailboats out it was much more peaceful and relaxing.

Over dinner the conversation flowed easily, with relaxed banter between the boys and their father, allowing Amanda an opportunity to observe the family dynamics, without the pressure of having to join in. It was obvious there was a lot of love in the family even recognising the sorrow they had all suffered. The occasional question was directed towards Amanda, but largely the talk was about the boys' studying, their plans for the coming summer and updates on Rob's health. Ben was anxious to understand whether there was any change in the donor situation, as a medical student he was particularly close to the science and liked to keep himself informed. Both boys had been tested to see if they could donate, but neither was a suitable match he advised.

As they were finishing coffee, the atmosphere had become very relaxed and talk returned to Amanda and her plans for returning back home.

'I'm booked to fly back on Monday. Now I've met you all, it would have been great to stay longer, but with Damian and the girls I really need to get home. Apart from which I think Aunt Jane wants some peace and quiet after all the drama of the last few days.'

'When will you return?' asked Lucas, in an encouraging tone that suggested he would like to spend more time together.

'I don't know, I haven't made any plans. As you pointed out earlier this has been a shock to everyone, so we probably all need to take stock. I would love to keep in touch though, if that's something you'd be interested in?' she asked to no one in particular.

At no stage over the last week had Amanda hinted at a longer-term relationship with Rob, put any demands on him, or made promises to keep in touch. Her motivation when she set out on this discovery had only been to make contact, not upset their status quo or force herself into their lives, but the more she had got to know Rob, and now her half-brothers, the more she hoped there could be a chance of that. There was a family here that she was part of, which despite all her reservations had inviting her in, and not only made her feel welcome, but gave the promise of making her feel loved.

'You're family now, so you're not shaking us off that easily,' laughed Rob, 'and apart from that, I've got two granddaughters to meet, so if you're not planning on coming back here soon, then I might have to fly over there to meet them. Once I've had my transplant that is,' he added ruefully.

As Amanda drove home later that night, she reflected on how well the evening had gone, meeting Greg and her half-brothers for the first time. She had expected her motivations to be questioned and pressure to be applied as to why she had sought to find Rob, but had received nothing but positivity and acceptance. She remembered her dad's warning that there would be consequences should she meet up with her biological father, but at no stage had she predicted these would be good ones, always at the back of her mind fearing the worst and coming home feeling dejected, with her tail between her legs.

But now as she anticipated her return home, it was with thoughts of what it might mean to her family; her mum, Damian and the girls, and whether they would accept her American relatives. Was there hope that they could make this work, and what would that life look like in years to come? A lot of food for thought for the flight home.

Chapter 41

By late spring, Amanda had spent four weeks at home trying to resume the life she had left, finding it increasingly difficult to balance the old with the new. She could sense deep down that something about her had changed but could not quite pinpoint what, and that feeling was making everything very unsettled.

The girls had obviously missed her and were excited to have her home, especially as she was the bearer of presents. At four, Maisie was still very sad to have lost her grandad. Death for her was one of those subjects that made her worry and provoked those innocent 'what if' type questions, the repetitive nature of which only a child can dream up, and result in parents running out of answers, and patience, very quickly. Alice at two was still a toddler, so did not really have a concept of death; to her she just knew that grandad was not around for bath-time any more, but as long as someone was there to play with her, she was happy. Any attempt to explain finding another grandad to either of them would be difficult. A subject to be put off for another day.

Her mum had missed her. Monica had sat and listened intently as her daughter recounted her stories about Rob, meeting his family and being made to feel welcome and accepted. Monica was pleased it had gone well, but part of her was left to wonder what it would mean now Amanda was home. Monica had sensed a new level of excitement in her daughter, an excitement that was being fuelled the more she and Rob spoke over the phone or Skyped each other as the weeks passed. She had even started to chat online to Ben and Lucas, tentatively building a relationship with the siblings she had never known existed. Monica knew how much Amanda had always longed for siblings, so could understand the lure not only one, but two ready-made brothers would bring.

Damian said he was pleased to have her home, but Amanda suspected more from a domestic perspective than anything else, recognising she could now take back some of the heavy lifting with the girls and running the house while he got back to the office. He had coped admirably, with both Maisie and Alice being well looked after, but at no time soon would he be applying to be a full-time stay-at-home dad. He had had a taste of that and as much as he loved his daughters, that concept would never wash with him.

Amanda also feared his interest in what she told him about Rob was superficial, with him appearing preoccupied whenever she tried to initiate a conversation, the reason behind which she could not quite fathom. Communication between them was not as easy as it had been, but after nearly seven years of marriage she was not sure if that was to be expected. Did couples simply run out of things to say, or did they learn to communicate more telepathically she wondered. Their relationship had begun to get tetchy before she left, but sadly the old adage that absence makes the heart grow fonder had apparently not proved to be the case from either of their perspectives.

'All couples go through patches like this, and at the moment you have a lot on your plate to deal with,' Lisa had said to her the previous evening when Amanda mentioned how she was feeling. 'The question is do you both still want the same things? You really need to talk to Damian and tell him how you feel and see what he says. You may be reading too much into all this, or more probably you've got yourselves a bit muddled with everything else that's been going on. Why don't you arrange a date night with some time to yourselves to work out between you what's important?'

Amanda found they were spending less and less time together, with Damian opting to spend an increasing number of nights at his flat, arguing pressure of work and a need to catch up with so much in the office now she was home. Amanda had not tried to dig too deeply, but the more she thought about it she could not remember the last time they had cuddled up on the sofa together with a bottle of wine, or spent time together, just the two of them. Was the adage about the seven-year itch the more appropriate one here she wondered to herself, and was Lisa right? Did they need to try harder with their relationship and to focus on what was important to them as a couple? Perhaps she had a point, and rather than trying to unravel what had been niggling away, Amanda had found it easier to avoid or dodge the discussion, fearing an argument.

She recognised her priorities were changing, but it was clear that Damian was not on the same page. She had been sure time would sort it out one way or another, but the longer it seemed to go on she felt she could not side-step the issue any more. She had never dealt with conflict well, relying on time to heal most things rather than facing them head on, but she sensed that her tried and tested approach might need a bit of rethinking.

An idea started to develop in Amanda's mind, that with careful planning and a bit of help might work. She got out her phone and messaged Lisa:

> '*How do you fancy babysitting the girls tomorrow evening and staying over? I'm planning a date night and could do with your help*!'

Chapter 42

Using the spare key Amanda had eventually found tucked away in Damian's underwear drawer, she let herself into the building and headed towards the lift up to the second floor. Her heals echoed as she crossed the tiled landing; the atrium of the building feeling very cold, hollow and antiseptic. The flat had never been somewhere she enjoyed being; it represented their old city life and all that had involved. Her life had moved on, and in her view for the better since they had moved back to the countryside. The flat to her now was just a convenient bolt hole for Damian when work became pressurised, and an investment should they ever need to release some capital.

It was however a nice flat; quite small, just one bedroom, but in a new purpose-built block centrally located in Cheltenham, great for city life. It had all the modern appeal any young executive would want, and very tastefully decorated for a bachelor pad at least. Damian had lived in it for a couple of years before Amanda moved in with him, but when she had attempted to prettify it with a few cushions and flowery prints, she had sensed more than a little resistance to her ideas for feminine touches, so had left well alone. It remained very much Damian's space.

Today the flat appeared more dishevelled than usual, with cushions and papers littered all over the floor, and by the look of the kitchen, her husband had left in a hurry that morning without having time to tidy away the breakfast things or wash last night's dishes. In fact, the number of wine glasses and dirty dinner plates sitting on the draining board suggested the washing-up had not been done for at least a couple of days. The bed was unmade too, with the look of the crumpled bed sheets indicating a change of bedding was definitely in order before any planned seduction took place, and perhaps some clean towels, spying the damp ones on the bathroom floor, presumably abandoned after this morning's shower.

Damian had stayed over the previous evening and had already let Amanda know he was staying that evening too. Since she had returned home from America, he had developed a habit of staying at the flat a couple of nights a week, arguing that working late and then travelling home was draining, claiming it would be more efficient for him to stay over. Knowing how hard working he was and how committed to building up his business into the successful IT and Communications company he dreamed of, Amanda had supported his decision, never questioning his judgement.

It was already around four in the afternoon, so without any idea how late he would return, she quickly set about getting the flat clean and tidy, excited that he would be pleased to see her, especially as she had come prepared with all the ingredients to make his favourite dinner. Amanda had called at the supermarket en-route, buying prime fillet steak with all the trimmings, plus a couple of bottles of Damian's favourite red wine, and had even splashed out on chocolate souffles that just needed popping into the oven. She had not been prepared to take the risk that his cupboards or fridge would have anything worth eating in them, so had bought everything she could think of to ensure their date night was a success.

The plan was relatively straightforward; prep the food, make herself look irresistible and wait for him to come home. She could not decide whether food or bed should come first, but resolved to be spontaneous and take her cues from how he reacted to her surprise visit. If all went to plan, by tomorrow morning their relationship would be back on track, and although the difficult discussions may have remained parked, they would at least have rekindled their relationship and be in a better position to talk about their future and importantly to what extent that involved her new found father.

When Amanda heard the key in the door a couple of hours later, she was just putting the finishing touches to her hair in front of the bathroom mirror. The food was all prepared, but she had decided not to start cooking until he arrived home and had time to relax with a glass or two of wine. They had the evening ahead of them, without the girls to distract them. There was no need to rush, just settle back and enjoy some quality time together.

Amanda resisted the urge to shout out to him, preferring instead to see the surprise on his face when he saw her, and had deliberately left the hall lights off so that he would not suspect her of being there. She could not see the front door open, but was conscious straightaway of two voices in the small hall way; Damian's she recognised instantly, but also a woman's voice that was lighter, and by the sound of the tone laughing at something Damian had just said or done.

'Stop it, can you not wait until we get into the flat at least,' she heard the giggling voice say, 'or at least let me take my coat off before you pounce…'

'I know, but I've not been able to get my hands on you all day,' came the reply Amanda was least expecting to hear from her husband, as she stood silently watching him backing into the lounge, his arms clearly groping the woman, his lips nibbled away at her ear, oblivious to the fact that his wife was surveying the scene as it played out in front of her; an unsuspecting gooseberry.

Amanda waited, almost transfixed in the bathroom doorway, unsure what the correct etiquette was for a situation like this. To say she was shocked was the understatement of the year. Had she walked in on them, already suspecting her husband was being unfaithful would have been one thing, but to have them walk in on her, when she had been completely unsuspecting and totally unprepared was another thing entirely. It was a situation she had never found herself in before, or to be honest never thought she would, but now she was here she felt surprisingly emotionally detached.

Some of the niggles she had felt over the previous few months about their relationship and Damian's behaviour now started to resonate in her head; worries she had laughed off initially were now like individual jigsaw pieces suddenly forming a picture in her mind.

Was a polite cough to let them know she was there appropriate when meeting her husband's lover, or should she just throw a heavy object at them hoping that would do the trick, perhaps causing a bit of damage in the process if she aimed it correctly? No, if she was going to win the war, today was probably not the right time to fight a battle; perhaps better to retain the moral high-ground. It was undoubtedly going to be an interesting couple of minutes, and ones she was intent on determining the outcome of. So, rather than be furious and launch herself at the other woman ready to fight for her man in an archetypal cat fight, she remained calm and perversely just thought how pleased she was that she was looking her best, almost dressed for the occasion.

'Damian, sorry darling to interrupt you,' she started, opting to play it cool and go for the polite, confident approach, even if deep down this was the furthest from how she really felt, 'but I don't think we've been introduced. Hi, I'm Amanda, Damian's wife,' smiling at the leggy brunette who was probably around ten years her junior and dressed in a short skirt with knee high boots, wearing a cropped T-Shirt and leather jacket, neither of which were quite covering her bare mid-drift.

On hearing Amanda speak, Damian turned, completely dumbfounded and momentarily caught off-guard. He saw his wife standing a few feet away, smiling at him almost serenely and looking beautiful in a dress he did not recognise, with her hair curled up framing her face just the way he liked her to wear it. She was smiling at him mischievously, without any hint of suspicion, which he found unnerving.

'Amanda, this is a surprise. What are you doing here - Is everything okay at home?' he asked in a faltering voice, immediately disentangling himself from the young woman and straightening his jacket, unsure what Amanda had seen or heard, or how long she had been standing there.

Seeing the bemused look on his wife's face as she continued to smile at him, he added 'This isn't what it looks like, I've just come back to the flat to pick up some papers and then we're going back to the office. We're in for a late night's slog.' Then remembering his companion, he added, 'Chloe has just come in to use the bathroom before we set off back.'

Amanda continued to stare at him, desperately trying to read the confused expression on his face. There was definitely a look of surprise at being caught out, but at the same time a clear look in his eyes of love for her, a look she recognised but had not seen for a while. She had made a real effort this evening with her hair and choice of clothes, and by the reaction on his face it had created the desired effect. Had Chloe not been in tow tonight, he would have easily got away with his cheating, which made Amanda wonder how long he had managed to keep this affair from her; obviously he was more versed in the act of deception than she gave him credit for, she thought to herself.

She decided not to comment on the takeaway in Chloe's hands, or the obvious surprise on his colleague's face when Damian had tried to cover his tracks, or the fact that none of the evidence supported the lie Damian had so easily concocted about them going back to the office and Chloe needing the bathroom. No, she was not prepared to react to his response and was determined any argument or fallout from this was not going to be carried out in front of this woman. She would let Damian stew and have any discussion at home on her own terms, once she had thought through what these terms might be.

Clearly the romantic surprise she had planned had backfired, but Amanda was not going to allow the situation to unnerve her. With more confidence and assertion than she felt, she casually walked towards the armchair, picked up the bag and coat she had left there only a matter of hours ago, and turned to Damian.

'I had come to make you a surprise dinner, but I see you have other plans, so I'll leave you to them and speak to you tomorrow.' Then aiming her look more towards the young lady, who had remained uncomfortably rooted to the spot throughout, obviously wondering what she had walked into, she added, 'I've changed the sheets for you; they seemed to be a little grubby. No need to thank me.'

And with that she waltzed out of the door, head held high, unprepared to show any emotion until she was in the privacy of her car, where no-one could hear no matter how loud she screamed or how choice her vocabulary was.

Chapter 43

Lisa was surprised to hear the key in the lock as she was finishing tucking Maisie and Alice into bed later that evening. Other than Amanda and Damian, only Monica had a key and it was unlikely to be her at this time of night. It was nearly eight o'clock and the girls should have been in bed an hour ago, but she had been enjoying spoiling them and spending time with them, so had not wanted to rush them off too early. She knew she would probably pay for it in the morning when she was getting them up before dropping them off at their childminder's, but hey-ho those were the joys of being a godmother. It was not that she got to be in charge too often.

She had been asked to drop them off at Susie's around 8.30am, which traffic permitting should get her into the office before her 10am meeting. Recognising it had already been a long day, Lisa had opted for an early night herself as soon as the girls were settled, so when the door had opened, she was not only surprised but a little disappointed.

'Hello, it's only me. Sorry if I've surprised you, but there's been a slight change of plan,' said

Amanda as she saw her friend's shocked face at the top of the stairs.

'Hi, I wasn't expecting you. I thought you were staying over with Damian at the flat. Is everything okay?' asked Lisa, sensing immediately from the look in Amanda's eyes that something was wrong. She watched as her friend dropped her bag in the hall and made her way straight to the fridge. *So much for an early night* thought Lisa as she saw her friend reach for the bottle, suddenly wondering what was going on.

'In fact, quite a big change to the plan,' laughed Amanda as she poured herself a large glass of wine and took a glug, almost emptying the glass in one mouthful. 'How stupid of me, but I hadn't considered Damian might have made arrangements for the night, or the fact that he might want to spend the evening with some floozy from the office instead of his wife, but it would appear I was mistaken.'

'Hold on a minute, rewind. What are you talking about?' asked Lisa, shocked at the way this conversation was going. 'You must be mistaken. I'm sure there's an explanation why he wasn't home. Presumably he was caught at the office and had to work late.'

'No, you misunderstand me. He was home alright, but complete with a take-away and a bit of sauce on the side too. I wouldn't mind but she was old enough to be his daughter. What was he thinking of? Crazy fucking idiot?'

The calm and serenity Amanda had displayed as she left the flat had quickly dissipated when she got into the car, and throughout the drive home she had got increasingly mad at the situation.

What had he been thinking of, how long had this been going on, why had she missed the signs? A complete jumble of questions kept going around her head, so that by the time she got home she was ready to explode. She was so angry, having been taken for a complete fool, duped by her own husband.

Lisa decided to pour herself a glass of wine too as she listened to her friend recount the events of the evening, opting not to cast judgement or offer comment too soon, although if she was honest, she had noticed a lot of tell-tale signs over recent weeks that had indicated things were not quite right. She realised their relationship had been going through a difficult patch, but at no stage had she suspected Damian of having an affair. She did not think that was his style; too much to lose, but evidently not.

Lisa had just put it down to the pressures of everything that had been going on in Amanda's life, her dad's death, discovering the truth about her biological father and then finding him, and not only him but two brothers plus a whole new family. It had been a lot for her to take in, and also a lot for Damian too, particularly as he was in a supporting role and not the leading one he usually preferred. She had always sensed he liked the attention, so probably had found it difficult to find he was not the centre of proceedings this time around.

'So, what are you going to do?' asked Lisa sometime later, once she sensed Amanda had either calmed down a bit, or more probably just run out of steam. 'Are you going to give him a chance to explain, or has the jury already delivered its verdict?'

'I don't know, I was just so taken aback. I accept I've been preoccupied over the last few weeks, and perhaps I've relied on Damian too much, but this is something else,' she sighed, 'I've no idea how long this has been going on, but it was obvious from the way they acted that this wasn't a one-off. She was too relaxed with him for that. If he's found someone else though, it might not even be my decision. It would appear I've been too trusting and foolish; I've probably only got myself to blame.'

'Wait a minute, you're not to blame here,' said Lisa, ready to defend her friend at all costs. 'The fact he has allowed his head to be turned is down to his ego and his mid-life crisis – not you or anything you've done. And if his head has been turned by a 'floozy' as you termed her, then that's his problem. Men, they always think the grass is greener! You just need to decide whether you're prepared to forgive and forget, or not, but don't be too hasty or jump to conclusions until you've calmed down and spoken to him. I know in reality it's not that simple, but in truth that's what it boils down to in the end. Assuming he is prepared to fight for your relationship and that it's not something more serious with Miss Floozy?' questioned Lisa, unsure what in reality had taken place or whether her friend's marriage lay in tatters or not.

As Amanda lay in bed later that evening replaying the day's events over and over in her head, she was at a loss to know how she truly felt. Did she want to fight for Damian and the life they had, or had he inadvertently just handed her a get out of jail free card and an opportunity to live a different life. Had they run out of steam, or just hit a bit of a bump in the road?

Her life, but more importantly the emotional roller coaster over the last few months, felt like everything was in a tumble dryer, being repeatedly tossed and turned, never settling long enough to allow Amanda to get a real grip or sense of perspective. The highs and lows, the dramas and disappointments, the opportunities and consequence all mingled to blur the picture, distorting any roadmap there might be out of this.

She recognised she was still grieving for her dad, and that her mum and daughters needed her support as much as she needed theirs. They would always remain her priority. Before today she had never questioned that Damian would be at her side to be her rock, to provide her with the sustenance she needed to get through this, the love and dependability she relied upon. Had she taken their relationship for granted?

But when she was in America with Rob and her new family, she became a different person; almost reborn, feeling an excitement she had never known before. Gone were the everyday responsibilities and pressures that form part of the job description for a working mum and wife. This new found part of her desperately wanted to discover more about herself; and she was almost frightened by the strength of the pull towards a family she never knew existed, but now did not want to be apart from.

The two lives were so distinct, different cultures as well as different continents, but at the same time intrinsically linked. These two halves might currently be separated by an ocean, but neither one would survive without the other, and whether she or anyone else liked it or not, the conundrum was now how to move forward and combine them in a way that worked for everyone.

Amanda by no means underestimated the enormity of the challenge, or to quote her dad did not recognise there would be consequences along the way, but as she drifted off to sleep, she pondered for the first time what trade-offs she would be prepared to make to get a workable combination, and whether her marriage would be first on that list.

Chapter 44

As Amanda was preparing an early lunch the following morning in lieu of skipping breakfast, her phone buzzed indicating another incoming message. She had not spoken to Damian since the botched date night the previous evening, although he had tried to phone and text several times, even leaving a couple of rambling apologetic messages begging to speak to her when she did not answer. She was not ready to speak to him yet; she would let him stew a little longer until she felt clearer in her mind about what she wanted to say, and equally what she needed to know from him.

By the time she and Lisa had eventually gone to bed around one in the morning, they had both drunk themselves sober, but nevertheless she still felt rotten this morning. Her head was aching and she had no real appetite or enthusiasm for anything. Making herself a sandwich was taking more effort than usual, and in truth she was not sure she really wanted to eat it anyway. She felt for Lisa who had not had much sleep either, but had still left early to get to her meeting, even dropping the girls off as planned at the childminder's house to give Amanda some time to herself. Thankfully the girls had not asked any difficult questions this morning, just accepting as normal that their mum was there as well as Auntie Lisa.

Girding herself as she reached for her phone to see what Damian's latest message contained, she thought *what a mess everything is this morning, how has my life come to this?*

> *'Hi, hope you're well. Can you please phone when you get a chance? Dad's not too well and Lucas and I thought you might want to know. Thanks Ben'*

Reading the message was neither what she was expecting, nor what she wanted to read. Since returning home both Ben and Lucas had messaged occasionally, but conversation had always been relatively light. They were all very much in the exploratory stages of building a relationship, so everything was casual and chatty.

This time it was short, sweet and very much to the point, and obviously for them to message her they must be worried, particularly as it was so early in the morning for them. She dialled the number, unsurprised to hear it was answered on the second ring.

'Hi Ben, I've just got your message. What's the problem?' she said, unsure exactly what she could say or do three thousand miles away.

'Hi, thanks for getting back. I just wanted to let you know that Dad was taken into hospital yesterday. He's been fighting an infection for the last few days, but the doctor got concerned so he's admitted him for tests. We're worried whether he can fight this, but also it kiboshes his chances of a transplant. He needs to be well to undergo any surgery, so if a kidney became available now, he wouldn't be able to take it. It's all a bit of a mess!'

Amanda could hear the emotion in Ben's voice, sensing he was holding back the tears and putting a brave face on. For someone in his early twenties it was a lot to ask. 'I just wish Lucas or I had been a match and we could have given him one of ours.'

'What do you mean. I don't understand?'

Until this point, although she vaguely recalled Rob mentioning that both sons had been tested, Amanda had never considered or even understood the concept of being a living donor, so over the next few minutes she listened as Ben explained the process involving donating a kidney and how it was a relatively standard procedure in the US, with minimal risks to the donor. He and Lucas had done quite a bit of research when it was originally mentioned to them, and as Ben was medically trained it was all quite 'matter-of-fact' in the way he explained the procedure.

'So does that mean I could donate?' asked Amanda, unsure why she was even offering this without really considering the consequences.

'I suppose in theory you could,' replied Ben, surprised what direction this conversation had suddenly taken. He had only phoned to let Amanda know where Rob was in case she rang and became worried when he did not answer. 'Anyone can be a living donor provided they meet certain criteria, and I suppose being a daughter would mean you have as much chance as we had. But it's a big thing and you hardly know Dad, so it would be too much to ask.'

'You're not asking though are you, it's me who brought this up; anyway, there's no guarantee that I would be any better a match than you or Lucas, but I could at least be screened couldn't I?' Something within Amanda spurred her on, 'I known I haven't known Rob too long, but he is my biological father, and I had hoped to build a relationship with him, and get to know you all better.' *Having just lost one dad, I'm not sure I'm ready to lose another one so soon* she thought to herself without worrying Ben.

'That's great, but please have a think about it and don't be too hasty with your decision. Talk it over with Damian too and see what he thinks before you go any further, because if you were to have it done you would need to be in the States, and you would need to spend quite a bit of time over here both pre and post the operation. It's a big ask for anyone.'

'Okay leave it with me. By the way, please give Rob my love when you next speak to him and let me know if there's any change' said Amanda as she hung up the phone, Ben's final words suddenly reminding her that she had unfinished business with her husband, but if she did decide to go to the States again so soon, she would certainly need him on side to support her.

Today was not turning out at all as she imagined. That recurring mantra kept ringing in her head: there would be consequences, but she had never quite expected them to mount up so quickly or be so far reaching. The last few weeks had been a real roller coaster. This morning her biggest challenge had been dealing with her husband's infidelity with a girl who looked old enough to be his daughter, but now she was considering being a living donor for a man she hardly knew, and it still was not even lunchtime. God only knew what this afternoon would bring; life was definitely far from boring at the moment.

Chapter 45

As Amanda sat in the waiting room flicking through old editions of Country Life and Hello! magazines, she pondered the last couple of days, replaying some of the difficult discussions she had gone through with not only Damian, but her mum and Lisa, who most surprised her with her reluctance to wholeheartedly support what she was considering.

Her discussion with Damian had been the first hurdle. Whilst she had been avoiding him over the 'date night' fiasco, she realised her latest idea was not something she could just park or avoid, so called him straight after lunch. He was at the office and unsurprisingly his secretary put the call through straightaway, without the usual polite excuse that he was in a meeting and would call her back.

Although Amanda made it perfectly clear it was her decision to put herself forward as a potential donor, she accepted that they had a joint responsibility for their children, so anything that affected the girls needed to be discussed and agreed. He was not at all supportive, but at a time when he was in no position to take the moral high ground, he agreed to Amanda at least exploring the options so they could make a more informed decision.

Damian was relieved that the question of Chloe, and what she was to him was not raised, but he was astute enough to realise that was a discussion reserved for a later date, rather than one that had been brushed over entirely.

Monica was equally concerned, but more from the perspective of the health risk to her daughter. The idea of her having surgery to remove her kidney to give it to a man she hardly knew, and incidentally had no responsibility for, was difficult for her to grasp. Why should she put herself and her family at risk? In her eyes, Ken would always be Amanda's father, and nothing Rob said or did would ever replace him as far as she was concerned. She was worried that Amanda might airbrush her dad out of her life now that Rob had come along with his shiny new lifestyle, uneasy about how much prominence he and his sons already seemed to have in her daughter's life.

Lisa with her risk adverse approach to life as well as her understanding of some of the legal hurdles, was also fearful of what her friend was considering. This was a big step and she felt Amanda had not fully thought through the pros and cons, failing to weigh up the implications and effect it would have not just on herself but others around her. She sensed Amanda was allowing her heart to rule her head, and in Lisa's experience that was a dangerous stance to take. She knew Amanda was sore at Damian, and rightly so, but did not want this decision to be a reflex action to the anger she felt. Punishing him by rushing off to America again was not the best way of addressing their problems; she needed to face up to them, not run off and add another layer of complexity to the already confused mix.

The only real supporter had been Grandad Tom who understood what she was contemplating, and although he was not overjoyed at the prospect of his grand-daughter going under the surgeon's knife, he recognised her motivations were driven predominantly from the realisation that she had been powerless to save her dad, so was viewing this as her second chance. He knew how proud Ken would be of her and the way she had reacted to the events of the last few months. She had chosen not to be angry with the world and all around her after not only losing her dad in such distressing circumstances, but then having to deal with the fact that he was not really her biological father. Some people would have gone to pieces, but she had acted both positively and maturely by facing up to the situation, and was now even considering taking on a responsibility that was not hers to assume. He too was proud of her, and for that he was prepared to support her all the way, even if he would secretly be counting the days down until she was safely home.

'Mrs. Reynolds, Doctor Greaves is ready to see you,' said the receptionist, bringing Amanda out of her reverie and back to the real world. She put down the magazines and walked into the surgery.

Doctor Joe Greaves had been one of her dad's oldest friends as well as their GP, so in addition to seeking medical advice Amanda wanted to use him as a sounding block to what her dad might have thought about what she was considering. She knew from her dad's letter that both Dr Greaves' had known for many years about Ken not being her biological father, and that they had faithfully kept his secret, accepting they would have taken it to their graves had her dad not chosen to allow the truth to come out following his own death.

When Amanda had asked for an urgent appointment to see him, Joe had at first wondered why, but as he waited for her to take a seat, he realised he had not had the chance to properly speak to her since Ken's death, so presumed it was related to that. He naturally offered his condolences, adding that like everyone in the village, he had been stunned by the suddenness of Ken's death. As a doctor he had assumed with the right treatment his friend would have had a few more years in him, but the complications brought on by pneumonia had been difficult to predict.

'Thank you, it has been a very difficult time for the family, the shock was awful...' started Amanda, grateful for his condolences, but anxious to move on. 'I need to talk to you today though about something I'm considering and I would really value your opinion; not only as my GP but as a family friend. I'm also hoping for an insight into what you think my dad might have thought about what I'm considering doing.'

Once she had Dr Joe's attention, she calmly told him of the process she had gone through to follow her dad's wishes to find her biological father; how she had found Rob and particularly his state of health, especially the challenges of finding a donor, and the fact that neither of his sons was a match. She managed to condense all her feelings into a couple of succinct statements, trying to contain the emotion as much as she could.

'So, I'm considering whether to be tested to see if I could become a living donor. I've read-up on the Internet all what the process involves, the risks and the pros and cons, but before I take it further, I want to understand whether you think my dad would approve. He told me to find my biological father, follow my heart and deal with the consequences – which in my mind is kind of his endorsement of what I am thinking...'

'All I know is that your dad loved you very much. He would have done anything to protect you and his granddaughters,' reflected Dr Joe. 'I remember he agonised for a long time whether he should tell your mum when he initially found out, but at that time his overriding worry was losing you both. I don't think he felt guilt about your biological father to begin with, but over the years he probably felt he had inadvertently stolen something precious from him. As your GP I can't advise you to have this procedure, but as a friend I think your dad would be very proud of you, and perhaps would feel in some small way it rebalanced what has obviously been a very sensitive situation.'

Amanda felt quite emotional as she listened to Dr Joe recalling those events from nearly thirty years ago, events that had until recently been unknown to her. The empathy she felt as Dr Joe articulated the feelings and emotions her dad had experienced, and the dilemma he had been in was palpable. She tried not to judge either the ethics or the morals of what had been done, accepting that there was no malice in the decision that had been taken. They were simply the actions of a man desperate to do the best to protect his family.

As Amanda left the surgery, she realised she too had been facing her own dilemma, a difficult decision to protect her newly found family. With this now resolved, she felt a weight had been lifted from her. Dr Joe had explained the process was complex, with no guarantee of her being a match, but the blood tests he had carried out were the first step. Now it was just a case of going home, discussing with the family what might happen and then waiting.

Although she knew the risks of being a match were low, embarking on the process provided a sense of empowerment she had severely lacked when trying to protect her dad. That total loss of helplessness was something she never wanted to experience again.

Chapter 46

Amanda was in a confused daze for most of the following week, her emotions in a maelstrom as she waited patiently to learn her fate should the tests show a potential match, whilst brooding over what she felt for Damian. Her quiet, predictable suburban life had definitely taken a surprising turn over the last six months.

Lucas and Ben had been pleased to hear she had started the process, both remaining equally hopeful but realistic about the chances of success. Having been tested themselves they knew better than anyone the probability of a match was low, but they were thankful Amanda had offered to at least be tested, and was prepared to go through with the surgery if a match was made.

They had informed Rob and his consultant straightaway. The consultant was optimistic and kept close to the hospital, ready to take the next steps should transplantation become an option. Mercifully Rob's health had not deteriorated significantly over recent weeks, so his ability to undergo surgery was still viable. Rob had mixed emotions about Amanda's offer; relieved that a potential donor had come forward, but at the same time unsure whether it was an abuse of their fledgling relationship. He had tried to reason with his daughter directly to outline the risks, but intuitively recognised her stubborn streak, sensing that once she made her mind up nothing would swing her.

Time was of the essence in situations such as this, and one of the benefits of private healthcare meant that everything could move at speed should the need arise. Amanda was amazed at how efficient the process appeared, even comforted when understanding organ donations to a nominated recipient was not an uncommon process in the States. Thankfully Rob had offered to cover all the costs and insurances, so at least that was something Amanda had no need to worry about.

Damian was less pleased, but given their relationship was finely balanced or more correctly on a knife edge at the moment, he felt it prudent to keep his feelings under control and not declare what he really thought. Amanda had listened patiently when he had pleaded that the episode with Chloe was a one-off moment of madness, a mid-life crisis, a play for attention. He assured his wife that nothing serious had happened, apart from flirtatious behaviour on her part that he had admitted to being flattered by, but read the signs all wrong. He professed to being a complete fool and begged for her understanding and forgiveness.

Amanda was unsure what to believe if she was honest; neither the evidence at the apartment nor his behaviour over recent weeks supported the theory that nothing had happened, but rather than react by throwing him out, she decided to give him the benefit of the doubt, or at least appear to do so, for the time being.

When she forced herself to reflect over recent months, she realised there had been many small tell-tale signs that all was not rosy in their relationship, but with everything going on with her dad she had chosen to overlook them. Perhaps it was a play for attention, but one with high stakes. She realised forgiveness and understanding were a long way off, and frankly the jury was still out, but selfishly she knew that if she did go ahead with the procedure, she would need Damian on side to help with the girls.

As she was just finishing tidying away the breakfast pots, her mobile started to ring.

'Mrs. Reynolds, It's Dr Joe's secretary here. Are you available for a quick chat with the Doctor?'

'Thank you, yes. Do you need me to come into the surgery?'

'No, I'll put the Doctor through now.'

As Amanda waited, her heart was in her mouth, unsure whether she was prepared for what she was about to hear. The concept she had been toying with was either about to become a reality, or another failed attempt to help save the life of someone she was close to. Either way it was a momentous moment that would have serious consequences. She decided to sit down, just in case.

'Amanda, lovely to speak to you again,' started Dr Joe, hesitating a little before continuing. 'I just wanted to let you know that your results have come back and these show that you are a very close donor match to the potential recipient. So much so that your biological father's consultants have suggested that it would be worth you having further tests in the States to determine whether the donation could go ahead.

I must inform you that you are not obliged to go ahead, and that if you've had any second thoughts, or need further information then that's okay. You still have the opportunity to change your mind. There's no commitment at this stage,' he said, obviously not wanting to either push Amanda into a decision or imply he was fully supportive of what she was considering. He admired her motivations and knew the medical risks were manageable, but nevertheless he could not disguise his reservations.

'Thank you for phoning. I'm glad the results are here as I've been on tenterhooks for the last few days waiting,' she began, taking a deep breath and buying herself time whilst she considered her response. 'I've given this a lot of thought and tried to prepare myself emotionally and mentally for whichever way the results went, but now they're here it's suddenly become real. No, I want to go ahead. I'm determined to do this if at all possible. What do I need to do next?'

Over the next few minutes, they discussed next steps, with Dr Joe agreeing to inform the consultants, who would likely be in touch with Amanda directly. He anticipated the tests would be conducted as soon as she could fly over, recognising time was not on their side, but as he spoke his words became drowned out by the practicalities of travel and childcare that started to whirl around her head, now fully focused on making this happen.

As Amanda put the phone down, she was left in no doubt that this was real. The tentative plans she had discussed with her mum, Damian and even calling in all her favours with Lisa, now needed to be enacted at speed. The ball was rolling; it would gather momentum and a life of its own that would not stop unless she had second thoughts or withdrew her consent, which was highly unlikely now her mind was made up.

Time to get her bags packed and dust off the passport again she thought before quickly ringing Ben to give him the news and let him know she was on her way. Rather than apprehension, she suddenly realised that excitement was her principal feeling. Life was full of surprises and this one was certainly up there as one of the biggest of her life, so far!

Chapter 47

Ben had met Amanda at the airport a couple of days later, driving her straight to the hospital to meet with the medical team that was responsible for Rob's treatment. Assessments both of her physical and psychological capacity to be a donor were required, with the necessary legal and disclaimer tick boxes needing to be signed. Normally a donor would undergo a series of counselling sessions to confirm the risks and procedural elements were understood, but Amanda made it clear that she was in no way prepared to delay the treatment or go through any unnecessary hoops. She gave her consent to the removal of her kidney, and in doing so, made it abundantly clear they needed to do it as soon as possible.

Delaying was not in anyone's interest, least of all Rob's. Whilst his condition thankfully had stabilised, no-one wanted to contemplate what would happen if the transplant did not go ahead, or the risks should his body reject it. Finding a donor had been a long process, so to now get an almost perfect match from a direct blood relative was the answer to a prayer, a situation that had never been considered a possibility once Ben and Lucas had failed to provide a match.

Surgery was booked for the following day.

After Ben and Lucas left, Rob and Amanda had spent the evening talking in the hospital, both anxious about the procedure, but hopeful about the outcome. Rob had again tried to talk Amanda out of taking the risk, but soon gave up once he recognised the seriousness of her determination and understood the strength of her feelings. Until that time, whilst he had realised from the first moment he had met her, how much her coming into his life had meant to him, he had not felt like those feelings had been reciprocated. She had been abundantly clear early on that she had a dad, and was not looking for a replacement.

He assumed, quite correctly as it transpired, that she was just looking to scratch the itch of finding him and putting a name to a face, never expecting an emotional attachment to develop, or to finding a family that would welcome her with open arms. How wrong had they been, and how much in just a few short months had things changed for both of them. Once Amanda realised fighting against nature was impossible for her, but more importantly how going with her heart made her feel, she accepted the inevitable. It was as if she had found the missing piece in her life, a piece that until now she had not even known was missing.

'I'm going to go now so sleep tight, you need to get your rest,' she said as she got up from her chair and prepared to leave his room to return to hers a couple of doors down the corridor. The hospital staff had been extremely considerate in allowing them so much time together, but she did not want to abuse it. Also, if she was honest, she was tired as well, and whilst it was too late to phone home, she needed some time to herself to reflect on all the things they had spoken about over the last hour or so, the plans they had discussed, the dreams they had shared.

'Good night, Dear. Tomorrow is a big day for both of us, so see you at the other end,' smiled Rob as she left, adding 'thank you Amanda, I love you...'

And before she knew what she was saying she replied, 'I love you too Dad'.

Chapter 48

A couple of weeks later, Rob was at home recuperating after his surgery, relaxing in the sunshine and taking it easy, gradually building up his strength and doing some gentle exercise in the pool. For both of them their operations had gone remarkably well and from the early signs had been a success. So far, his body had shown no signs of rejecting the kidney and although he knew he would need immunosuppressant drugs for the rest of his life to maintain this, it was a small price to pay for having a functioning body again. The promise of life returning to normal, or as near normal as possible was exciting and a prospect he had long given up on.

Amanda too was making a good recovery, still tired but generally well. She had undergone a small laparoscopic surgical procedure, which had been less invasive, with the advantage of a shorter recovery time. She knew she needed to relax and let her body heal, and most importantly follow the doctor's advice, which included no flying for a minimum of six to eight weeks. The medical care in the states was proving to be top-notch, and as Rob was picking up all the bills, she just had to sit back and go with it.

Amanda had moved in with Rob after being discharged as it was not only convenient but seemed the right thing to do. Rob had engaged a nurse to be on hand for the duration, so with that and Mrs. Reilly doing all the cooking and cleaning, her biggest fear was putting on too much weight from all the lounging around and eating her delicious homemade treats.

Thankfully the prognosis was good for both of them and they settled into a comfortable routine around the house that involved them spending quality time together, but also allowing each other space. Amanda missed Maisie and Alice but spoke to them daily, either with Damian or her mum dependent on where they were or what time of day it was. Lisa was on hand to help out whenever called upon, but so far Monica and Damian seemed to have it all under control.

'Hi Darling, how are you doing today?' asked Monica when she video called to let the girls tell their mum all the exciting things they had been doing at their childminder's that day. 'The girls are here to talk to you,' she said passing her iPad to Maisie. Although it was early evening at home, it was only mid-day in the States. Amanda had been having a lazy morning pottering around the house, but was just starting to feel her stomach rumble as aromas from the kitchen of Mrs. Reilly's lunch wafted up the stairs.

Maisie was due to start school in a few weeks' time, so was getting really excited about that. Her uniform had been bought just before Amanda left, but the chance of her getting home before her first day was now questionable. It was already mid-July and her flying ban would probably not be lifted until the end of August, which was really pushing everything to the wire. She had not mentioned that to Maisie yet, planning to cross that bridge when she came to it. Alice was her usual happy self, content to be playing out with her friends in the sunshine, taking in her stride the fact that mummy was not around to tuck her in as daddy was getting quite good at reading bedtime stories and making their teas.

After a few minutes of listening to the girls, Amanda asked 'Mum, what do you think about bringing the girls over for a couple of weeks or so for a bit of a holiday, my treat. I know they'd love the adventure and it'd give you a break too. You could also see Aunt Jane; you've not had a proper catch up for a couple of years. I haven't mentioned it to Damian yet, but what do you think?'

'I don't know Dear, it sounds a lovely idea, but it's a long way to go with two little ones all by myself,' replied Monica wistfully. The idea of seeing her sister again appealed, but she was not too sure about meeting Rob. She fully understood the connection between him and her daughter, but did not know where she fitted into this new family. She knew she would need to address it some time, but now felt too soon. Perhaps she could put if off just a bit longer.

'Well, what about if I ask Lisa to join you and help with the girls? There's more than enough room here for all of you, and I'm sure Rob would be delighted to meet you again and meet Maisie and Alice. Shall I speak to Lisa and see if she's free to come?'

'Well, I don't suppose it would do any harm to ask,' replied Monica a little reluctantly, but at the same time mildly excited at the prospect of a visit. Since Ken had died, she had not left the house much, spending her time mainly helping with the children or keeping herself to herself. Even though she had not been short of callers or offers, most of her friends and hobbies had been put on the back burner whilst she allowed herself time to adjust to life without her husband. Perhaps something like this might be the impetus she needed to force her into getting her life back on track. What harm could a couple of weeks in the sun do she thought?

'If I do come, I'll stay with Jane if that's okay. I'm sure she'll have a bedroom spare and I wouldn't want to put Rob out. I'm ringing her later, so I'll ask.'

'And I'll phone Lisa and see if I can get her on-board too,' said Amanda, sensing her mum's anxiety about meeting Rob, but suddenly excited at the prospect of the visit. She closed the laptop and went downstairs to speak to Rob to double check he would be alright with a British invasion.

She smiled when she saw him gently doing a few strokes in the pool, pleased at the way he had recovered and the improvement he had made over the last couple of weeks. Every day he seemed to be getting stronger and stronger, challenging himself to do simple little things he had avoided for so long, pushing himself.

Neither Ben nor Lucas could believe the transformation of their father either, both pleased to see not only his energy and health returning after the operation, but to see him so happy at building his relationship with Amanda. They too were enjoying building their own relationships with her, each confident enough to feel neither jealousy nor unease about her coming into their family. She was welcomed with open arms; and having now given this renewed life to their father, it made her even more special in their eyes. Having a big sister was providing a whole new dimension to all of their lives.

Once Rob had got out and towelled down, Amanda asked 'What do you feel about me inviting some little house guests to stay for a couple of weeks?', sensing from the look on his face that she did not even need to name his grandchildren to get his attention and approval. 'If it's too much trouble, let me know, but if you fancy seeing your granddaughters then let me see what I can arrange.'

She did not need to wait for an answer. The tears in his eyes and the smile on his face spoke volumes all by themselves.

All she now needed was to get Lisa onboard, oh and get Damian's agreement of course. Where to start first, and which one was going to take most persuading mused Amanda, trying to work out which strategy should most effectively be deployed with each of her hurdles.

Chapter 49

Damian had not been too happy with the proposal for Lisa and Monica to take the girls to America for a short holiday to meet their new grandfather and see their mum, but he sensed arguing or putting up barriers would not help any chances of winning back his wife's affection. Whilst they were both cordial with each other, he suspected Amanda was biding her time over the incident with Chloe, fearing the debate was parked rather than forgotten. The story he had concocted in the heat of the moment to deflect the fact that whilst he had not actually been caught in-flagrante was tenuous, but he was far from innocent of what he was being accused of.

He and Chloe had been having an affair for nearly a year. It had started as an innocent office flirtation, but when she responded and even encouraged him Damian had been flattered by the younger woman's attention. She was fun and fresh; she pandered to his ego and all the sneaking around spiced up his life, which he felt had become mundane, the clichéd 'married with two kids and a mortgage' type existence. The typical male mid-life crisis.

Sneaking around and lying to his wife all this time had become challenging, fun at first, but over time more difficult. Whilst he had tried to end it after Ken died, feeling guilty and a bit of a shit, for one reason or another he could not quite get around to it. Amanda was absorbed in her own struggles and grief, and selfishly he felt abandoned, or at least neglected. The attention Chloe paid him was good for his soul and he felt he needed that more than ever. Having a young, attractive girl who looked up to him made him feel attractive again, giving him a boost in confidence and overall level of satisfaction that he was struggling to get within his marriage.

Now that he had been caught out though, any excitement he had felt suddenly paled, leaving it all feeling a little sordid. He realised how much he wanted his wife and his old life back, but knowing Amanda, that would not be an easy fight to win. They had not really talked it out; Amanda trying every tactic possible to avoid having the debate or even show her true feelings, being so accommodating it was frightening. She was never one for arguing or conflict, but even faced with this, Damian had been left in a vacuum unsure where his fate lay from his wife's perspective. He knew he had to play the long game and agreeing to let the girls go was in his mind part of that.

Lisa had proved surprisingly easy to talk into taking the trip. She had just finished a difficult case that thankfully she had won, but had left her quite drained emotionally. Another broken family, another abused wife, children caught in the cross-fire of psychological abuse to their mum by a dad they loved but feared in equal measure. Her job was never going to be easy, but this time it had been tougher than usual, requiring all her legal wiles to get the woman to open up and help her build the case she needed.

As she was owed some holiday, the promise of a couple of weeks of sunshine relaxing in luxury, with a private yacht on hand and all expenses paid seemed too good an offer to turn down. Apart from which she was desperate to meet Rob, who had obviously made such an impression on her friend that she had literally risked her life to save his. Lisa had massive admiration for what Amanda had done, but was unsure if faced with the same dilemma she would have made the same decision. Lisa was risk adverse by nature, so coupling that with someone cutting you open to remove your organs was not something she would be at the front of the queue for.

Lisa had travelled quite considerably both with work and socially, so navigating airports and taking charge was all in a day's work for her; but travelling with two infants in tow was a completely new challenge, saying nothing about Monica, who although she loved to bits, was proving to be a bit of a struggle. She was forever fussing over the children and panicking at the slightest of things, acting more like a nervous teenager than a mature grandmother. Thankfully Lisa had had the foresight to buy a couple of paperbacks in the airport, so provided the kids obliged and went to sleep, her plan was to get stuck into one of those or perhaps catch a movie to pass the time.

As they boarded the aircraft, she longingly wished she could turn left into Business Class as was her norm, instead of right into economy with the rest of the passengers. Without trying to be stereotypical, Lisa judged they were mainly holidaymakers from the look of their clothes, bags and the sound of their excited chatter; children probably hyped up on the promise of Walt Disney World if they were en route to Florida via Boston. Others perhaps touring New England or even heading further east. Boston was one of the major hubs for flights across the States so people could literally be going on anywhere: the options were endless.

As they took their seats, Lisa saw the airhostesses buzzing around preparing the cabin, offering around activity packs for the children and soft drinks and face towels to anyone who wanted one. So much for her usual tipple of champagne or a G&T before take-off. Today a soft drink would have to suffice; being tipsy in charge of children was not an option. No, today's flight would be a sober experience, but God help Amanda if there was no stiff drink, or preferably two waiting for her on arrival. If the journey so far was anything to go by, she would most definitely have earned it.

After what seemed and eternity, they had finally arrived in Boston, cleared Immigration, collected their bags and were approaching Arrivals. Although Ben had offered to collect them, Amanda had asked Brad and Jane to, believing her mum would feel more comfortable and less flustered being met by a friendly face. She planned on introducing her mum to Ben and Lucas in a day or so, but for now Brad and Jane would collect them, drop Lisa off with her, before taking Monica, Maisie and Alice back to stay at their house.

'Monica, over here!' Jane called, waving her arms trying to attract her sister's attention. She could see the two women in the distance looking a bit frazzled, struggling with cases, a buggy and the two children, unsure exactly what direction to head in.

'Here, let me help,' said Brad as they finally caught up with them, as Jane pulled her sister into her arms before bending down to kiss the girls. Alice was asleep in the buggy and Maisie was trying desperately to stay awake, but she too looked fit to drop. Hopefully they would sleep in the car on the way home thought Jane.

'Have you got everything?' enquired Brad as he took charge of the cases. 'How was the flight? It seemed to arrive ahead of schedule, which is always a bonus.'

'Everything was fine, and thanks, I think we've got everything,' replied Lisa as she relinquished her luggage to Brad, 'I'm Lisa by the way, I don't think we've met before,' she smiled at Brad. He took in the petite brunette, dressed casually in jeans and sneakers, but wearing a smart jacket that suited her perfectly. He guessed she was a similar age to his daughter and there was something about her that reminded him very much of Clara. He was not sure what it was, but the confidence she exuded and her smile were infectious.

'Pleased to meet you, and welcome to Boston. I imagine you're in need of a drink,' he smiled back, correctly reading Lisa's expression and knowing straight away they were going to get on.

'That's the best thing I've heard all day,' laughed Lisa, 'I hope Amanda is well stocked up. I think I deserve it. My Goddaughters are a delight, but I'm not sure I'm cut out for motherhood full time.'

Brad led the way to the car, talking comfortably to Lisa, assuring her that they would be home in less than an hour and he was sure drinks would be waiting. Jane and Monica followed in their wake, Jane, taking charge of the buggy and Monica tightly holding Maisie's hand for fear of losing her.

True to form, no sooner had the engine started Maisie and Alice were fast asleep, remaining that way until the car eventually pulled into Brad's driveway. They had stopped off briefly at Rob's to drop Lisa off, but even then, the girls did not stir. Tomorrow would be a big day for them not only catching up with their mum, but meeting their new grandad for the first time, so tonight they were staying with Grandma.

Chapter 50

'This house is amazing!' announced Lisa when Amanda had finished the grand tour early the following morning. They were sitting on the veranda eating a healthy breakfast prepared by Mrs. Reilly and the sun was already reflecting off the water, promising another beautiful day. 'I think I've stayed in less glamourous five-star hotels than this.'

'Yes, it's great, and I shouldn't say it, but it's already starting to feel like home. And now that you, Mum and the girls are here, I'm not sure what I'm missing about the UK. It's definitely not the weather or Damian come to think of it,' laughed Amanda, realising how little she was thinking about him or even considering the state of their marriage and what she had to face when she got home. 'Perhaps we should just consider squatting and see how long it takes Rob to throw us out.'

'Count me in on that, after the last few months I'm in no hurry for rushing back either. It's ages since I took some time off, so your suggestion couldn't have come at a better time. This last case took more out of me emotionally than I would have thought possible, and it's left me feeling exhausted and in need of a battery recharge. Some cases are more draining than others, and this last one definitely fell into that category. What some people have to contend with is really upsetting and it just makes me feel so thankful for the upbringing you and I have had. We don't appreciate how lucky we are sometimes.'

'Yes, you're right. We are very fortunate. I don't think I'd have the strength to deal with half of what you deal with in your job. Teaching a few grumpy teenagers is as bad as it gets for me,' reflected Amanda, knowing that whilst Lisa played down a lot of what she did, it was a harrowing task having to deal with a whole myriad of family situations and their inevitable legal ramifications when things went wrong, as they sadly so often did in today's dysfunctional society.

'Well, you've come to the right place. I'm sure we're going to have a great time, and I know the family will love you. It sounds like you've already won Brad over. Wait until you meet the rest of the crew later today.'

It was true though, being here was so relaxing and stress free. There was still convalescing to be done, which accounted for the fact Amanda was not doing much other than resting, eating and sleeping, but the whole atmosphere was welcoming and she felt so comfortable around Rob and her wider family. Ben and Lucas were in regular touch, coming over at the weekends to spend time with them. It was the summer holidays, so no studying, but both were busy in their own way; Ben with work-experience at the hospital, helping out on the children's wards and Lucas mooching around the sailing club, picking up whatever seasonal work he could find. His healthy allowance meant he did not need the money, but he loved being around the yachts, so any skippering he could land or coaching he could give was a bonus. He was still dreaming of becoming an entrepreneur, but whilst he waited for his 'big idea' to materialize, keeping busy doing what he loved was his priority, not to mention the fact the sailing club was a magnet for pretty, bikini-clad girls, which was a bonus.

Will had become a frequent visitor too, him and Rob picking up their friendship easily, with Rob eternally grateful for the role Will had played in bringing him and Amanda together. Their lives had diverged over recent years, with each having their personal struggles, so reconnecting was something they both found cathartic. Will had been more affected than he liked to admit by Rob's illness. Being roughly the same age, it brought it home to him how fragile life is, giving him the impetus he needed to get his own life back on track. Work and the successful company he had built was important, but not to the extent of everything else. His focus now was all about enjoying life and putting more spice and variety back into it. He hoped he had many years ahead of him and wanted to enjoy these, not be tied down behind a desk, or jetting off somewhere new every week dealing with buyers and suppliers. The fun had gone out of that; he had enjoyed the challenge in building up the business and seeing it grow, but unless he really wanted to keep on expanding or diversifying there was not much challenge left for him and, he admitted to himself, it had become a little tedious. No, he needed to think of his exit strategy, improve his delegation skills, even develop a succession plan so someone much younger with new ideas could run the business and allow him to step back. It had definitely given him a lot to think about.

He had chatted to both Rob and Amanda about this, both men being pleasantly surprised by Amanda's knowledge of the fashion world, specifically her ideas on design and the history of fashion. Rob recalled how Lily had studied fashion design, so whilst Amanda had majored in Art History their interests again showed a lot of parallels.

She had also got to know Greg, Rob's brother-in-law a lot more and found him great company. He had quite a dry sense of humour, which Amanda found endearing once she managed to zone into it. Knowing how much she reminded him of Lily at first had been awkward, but that soon melted away the more they spoke and got to know each other. Greg was interested to observe the same mannerisms and expressions in Amanda that he missed from his wife, but it amused him rather than saddened him. At times he wondered if he and Lily had had a daughter, how similar she and Amanda would have been, but it was no use grieving over what had not happened. He just made a conscious decision to enjoy Amanda's company, finding whatever comfort he could in the memories it evoked.

Aunt Jane and Brad were only a few miles down the road too, and they thought nothing of popping in unannounced to check up on her, or drop off homemade baking – as if what Mrs. Reilly made was not enough – or something that they had just happened to pick up in town that they thought she would like. Any excuse, not that they needed an excuse as far as Amanda or Rob were concerned.

One of the best things though was being almost within walking distance of Clara. They had always been close, but now they were virtually within the same postcode and time zone, they realised how much more in common they had than they had previously recognised. Clara was still living in Boston working as an editor on one of the daily newspapers, but coming home to spend time with Amanda whenever her schedule allowed. They had sneaked a couple of girly trips to Salem for a coffee and a mooch around the shops, but nothing too energetic so far given the need to take it easy and follow doctor's orders for convalescence, but as soon as she was fit, there were plans afoot for many more raucous adventures. Clara's luxury two-bed apartment on the waterfront was apparently going to be party central once the okay from the doctors had been given, with Amanda being introduced to all her friends and the Boston nightlife.

It was many years since Amanda had last visited a nightclub, or disco, or whatever they called them these days, so although there was no knocking her enthusiasm Clara's plans did leave her a little wary. Her life had been devoted to being a good daughter, mother and wife; neither partying nor socialising featuring high on her list of current pastimes. A new wardrobe would definitely be in order too if she needed to glam up!

'So, what's the plan for today?' asked Lisa as she finished her second cup of coffee. They had stayed up talking later into the evening than she had intended, so the caffeine was essential to get her body kickstarted. She had woken early, given the jetlag and time difference, but she was not going to let anything spoil the first day of her holiday.

'Mum is bringing Maisie and Alice over for lunch later. It will be their first chance to meet Rob, but it will also be the first time Mum's seen him since before I was born, so that will be interesting. I think they are both a bit nervous, if truth be told. I believe Clara is coming too. I hope you will get on with her as she's a real scream. I don't know if you remember her from the funeral.'

Lisa recalled seeing a young woman sitting close to Amanda, but as she had rushed straight off after the church service, there had not been any time for introductions and she had not thought to ask Amanda since who the woman had been. She recalled how smart the woman had looked, very attractive and fashionable in a tailored black suit emphasising her long legs. Her hat had masked her hair, but she presumed she was probably blonde by the colouring of her skin and her clear complexion, and would have guessed she was probably about 5'8" if asked. Lisa blushed as she recalled the effect the woman had had on her at the time; wondering now if she was Clara, and secretly hoping that was who was coming around later.

'I do recall a lady there. She looked similar to you if I remember correctly, but I didn't give it a second thought,' replied Lisa trying to play down her almost total recall.

'Yes, that will have been Clara, we're often mistaken for sisters.'

'I didn't see her husband with her,' fished Lisa, still a little unsure what she was asking.

Amanda was aware that Lisa had dated men early on, but over recent years she suspected she found women to be a bit more her style, although nothing had ever been confirmed. It was a part of herself that Lisa kept very private and even with her best friend it was not a discussion they ever got into. Amanda could not recall Lisa ever having had a formal or long-term relationship with anyone: lots of casual friends and dates, but nothing serious.

'No, she's not married, in fact she's not in a relationship at all at the moment. She's very independent and likes her social life too much,' laughed Amanda at the thought of Clara settling down and being married. 'She was living with a girl called Lucy, but I think that finished a while ago. I think Lucy was more serious about things than Clara was, so they parted company. Thinking about it, you two will probably hit it off nicely – both party animals, looking for fun over commitment. The ideal combination. I'll have to make sure I don't get left behind.'

'Well, I best get my party clothes out ready then' said Lisa, suddenly feeling quite excited about meeting cousin Clara. This holiday was improving by the minute she thought to herself smiling.

Chapter 51

'Mummy, Mummy!' squealed Maisie and Alice as they got out of Clara's car and charged straight towards Amanda that afternoon, throwing themselves against her. They had both rested that morning and were now full of beans, chattering excitedly to Amanda about everything and anything that had happened to them. Maisie as always was taking charge, but Alice was no shy violet and was holding her own in the competition for their mother's attention.

'Be careful you two,' cautioned Monica as she saw Amanda flinch a little as the two girls launched themselves at her ready for their long-awaited hugs and kisses. 'Don't you remember me telling you that Mummy's just had a little operation, so we need to be careful with her until she gets better.'

'Thanks Mum, but I'm okay. In fact, I'm feeling a lot stronger than the doctor predicted I would be by this stage. Apparently, I'm a model patient and I'm making good progress,' said Amanda as she went over to hug her mum too. 'It's great that you're all here now. Lisa was filling me in last night about the journey. She'll be down in a minute. She's just having a quick shower after her morning swim before we have lunch. I think she's made herself at home already. Anyway, come on in. We can't talk on the step all day. Rob's waiting to meet you all,' added Amanda ushering her mum, daughters and Clara towards the house, straight through to the veranda at the back where Rob was sitting patiently, if cautiously, waiting to meet them.

'Hello Monica and welcome to my home. It's lovely to see you again after all these years. You're looking well,' said Rob as he rose from the chair and reached out his arm to shake hands. He was genuinely pleased to see Monica and equally pleased to see that the pretty girl he had known over thirty years earlier had matured into such a beautiful woman. He had seen a few snapshots of her that Amanda had shown him taken the previous summer, but they had not done her justice.

'And who are these two young ladies?' he asked spying Maisie and Alice peeking out from behind Amanda's legs, the bravado of only a few minutes ago temporarily gone.

'Well, this is Maisie and she is nearly five, and Alice who is nearly three. Maisie starts big school in a few weeks so is very grown up, and Alice when she starts talking will never stop,' replied Amanda on behalf of the girls.

Rob crouched down to be at their level, realising how imposing he must look to the girls. 'Hello. I'm Rob, and it's lovely to meet you both. Your mum has told me all about you. Would either of you like a drink before your lunch? Mrs. Reilly has made you both a special treat in the kitchen if you want to come and look', and with that both girls moved forward, each taking one of Rob's hands and allowed themselves to be led towards the kitchen and the promise of a treat.

'Well, that was a lot easier than I'd imagined,' laughed Amanda, realising how calmly her daughters had gone to Rob. She had feared their shyness might prevent him getting to know them, or at least take some time before they opened up, but by the sounds of their chattering as they walked towards the kitchen the opposite appeared to be the case. She could hear him laughing as he answered their questions, the girls giggling too at something that was being said. He obviously had a way of charming the ladies.

Lisa appeared in the doorway just as Rob was leading the girls out, so stood for a moment taking in the scene; a family drawn together under unconventional circumstances, unsure what their future would hold, but intent on finding a path forward. She was pleased to see Amanda relaxed, knowing how anxious she had been about this moment when Rob would meet his granddaughters for the first time, as well as being reintroduced to Monica, no longer the girl he had had a brief summer fling with, but now a mature woman recently widowed, who was having to face the consequences of a relationship she had had over thirty years previously. It could have gone either way, so the fact it had gone so well was amazing. So far so good.

As Lisa watched from the shadows, she saw Clara in the background and suddenly felt nervous about entering the room. Clara looked so sophisticated and elegant, not a hair out of place. She was dressed in casual wear, simple cropped white linen trousers teamed with a navy blue lacy sleeveless top. Lisa noticed how tanned her skin was and how smooth it looked, making her feel awkward with her plain looks, pale English skin, freckles and short dumpy legs. She was only 5'2" and Clara was at least another few inches taller, even in her flat sandals, and she was beautiful.

In her professional life, Lisa was naturally bubbly with a level of self-confidence that made her a strong character, essential when dealing with some of the dubious individuals she got involved with, but where personal relationships were concerned those natural behaviours were less apparent. She found it easier to put herself down, refusing to see what anyone else saw in her. Most of her relationships had ended prematurely because she felt inadequate and found it easier to ditch than be ditched, never having the confidence to trust what others said about her. As she watched Clara now, she was already mentally preparing herself for rejection and disappointment. Why would Clara even look at her, she was well out of her league?

'Lisa, I didn't see you there. Come on in and meet Clara. Rob's just taken the girls for a treat to the kitchen, so we can have a few minutes peace before they return,' said Amanda beckoning her friend over.

'Lisa, welcome to America. It's so lovely to finally meet you in person,' said Clara as she approached Lisa and put her arms around her in a friendly hug. 'I feel I already know you given Amanda never stops talking about you. I believe you're a top-notch lawyer when you're not playing at being fairy Godmother to Maisie and Alice. I bet those two are easier work than most of your clients.' As Clara spoke, Lisa noticed how her face lit up and displayed the most beautiful smile she had ever seen.

'You're right, although some of my clients act more like children than the girls I have to admit, but mainly the cases I tend to get involved in are quite harrowing. Family law rarely has great outcomes for all concerned, we just have to do the best for the children caught up in the middle, whatever the case is,' replied Lisa, surprised how relaxed she was feeling speaking to Clara. 'When Amanda invited me over, I jumped at the chance. Coming away for a couple of weeks is light-relief and a well needed break I can assure you!'

'Glad to hear that as I've got some treats in store for both of you when Amanda is cleared to go out again, in fact whilst she's still recuperating there's nothing stopping me showing you around if you fancy that and Amanda doesn't mind me hijacking you?'

'What a great idea. I don't mind at all and it will give me chance to spend time with Mum and the girls,' replied Amanda, delighted to see that the two women seemed to have hit it off straightaway.

'Well, that's a plan then. I'll pick you up tomorrow morning and we can start exploring,' said Clara to a startled Lisa who could not quite believe her luck. Not only had Clara been warm towards her, but she had offered to spend time with her without any hesitation or prompting from Amanda. 'Right, what's for lunch then? I'm starving,' Clara added just as Rob and the girls came back all smiles and laughter from the kitchen.

Chapter 52

The next couple of days were like a whirlwind. Monica came over both mornings to spend time with Amanda and the girls, who had now moved into Rob's with their mother, but also to make sure they were not tiring her out too much. Amanda still needed her rest and whether the girls were there or not she still had to follow doctor's orders for another few weeks.

The girls enjoyed playing in the pool and generally running round the house exploring. They loved their bedroom, sharing a big king-sized bed covered with more cushions and pillows than they could imagine. Great for them to play hide and seek under. Rob had ordered toys and games for them too to keep them occupied and Mrs. Reilly was in her element looking after them, feeding the girls all sorts of fancy treats and generally regarding them as royal princesses. For her having a household to look after made her job worthwhile, bringing life and joy back into the family, both of which had been sorely lacking over recent years.

Rob was in his element too. Getting to know Amanda had been remarkable, but now to finally get the chance to know his granddaughters was beyond his wildest dreams. He could not believe his luck, not only in finding out he had a daughter, but Maisie and Alice too and even reconnecting with Monica, who after all these years he still found attractive in a mature sort of way. He loved reminiscing with her about their brief time together, but also about life in general, and being the same generation, they found they had a lot in common.

Most importantly though was how well he felt and how grateful for the selfless act Amanda had taken. The doctors said both their operations had been a success with all the signs continuing to be positive. When he considered his life less than twelve month previously, with endless dialysis and patient waiting for a donor, the prognosis he faced was less than positive. Now approaching sixty he could see a life ahead of him and a life that had not only changed for the better, but suddenly was full of promise.

Rob was sitting on the deck enjoying a morning coffee with Monica, both watching the girls splashing in the pool with Lisa. She was a real trooper with the girls, instinctively taking control when Amanda needed space to rest, but equally making herself scarce if Amanda or he wanted time with the girls. Lisa was bubbly and full of life, but sensitive to the needs of the family. A true friend and a lovely young woman in Rob's view; but he sensed there was something missing in her life, something that he could not quite put his finger on at the moment.

'Hello Dad...' brought Rob out of his thoughts, as he turned to see Lucas and Ben unexpectantly walking into the garden.

'What a great surprise, but what are you both doing here this early, I wasn't expecting you for another couple of hours at least?' asked Rob. 'Is anything wrong?'

'No, we're both fine. Ben thought we should make an early appearance and help Mrs. Reilly with some of the prep for the BBQ tonight,' said Lucas casting his eyes around, 'but now that we're here, I think I might join the girls in the pool as that looks like much more fun!' which was typical of Lucas.

A family BBQ was on the agenda for the evening, with Brad and Will in charge of the cooking, giving Mrs. Reilly a well-deserved evening off. In fact, she was taking the rest of the weekend off and going to spend a couple of nights with her sister in Rockport a short drive up the coast, leaving them to their own devices. Although with the way she had stocked the fridge before she left, it was fair to say no-one would go hungry for at least a month.

'Before you do that, let me introduce you properly to Monica and Lisa,' said Rob, prompting the introductions, as Lisa lifted the girls out of the pool and wrapped beach towels around them, before going up to say hello. Lisa had heard a lot about Rob's sons from both Rob and Amanda, but seeing them close up she was impressed, not only with their looks, but also their manners and obvious attention to their father.

'Hi, I'm Lisa and it's great to finally meet you. I've heard a lot about you both,' she said confidently as the girls shyly hid behind her legs. She was sure Rob would not have any problems marrying either of them off when the time came; the young ladies would no doubt be flocking! 'And these two little wet imps are Maisie and Alice. Come on girls say hi to your uncles and try not to soak them through…' she added gently easing the girls forward.

'And this is Monica, Amanda's mum. We've been enjoying a great catch up' added Rob, smiling as he said this, gently patting Monica's arm. He was really enjoying her company, and she seemed to be relaxed in his too, finding that although their lives had been very different, they had many shared values and common interests. Their conversation never dried up and they both felt comfortable in each other's company, even sharing the odd joke or two. They had both loved and lost, which meant there was a great deal of empathy and understanding between them, so to find an unexpected friendship at their stage in life was something they were valuing.

Today was all about relaxing around the pool and spending quality time together as a new and extended family. Rob was hopeful it would create the foundations from which they could all build on for the future, blending his new and existing families together. Before long they were joined by Greg, Will, Clara, Brad and Jane, extending those family branches even further and creating a grouping that less than twelve months ago could never have been imagined.

He reflected on how life occasionally throws curved balls from such unexpected places; knowing that sometimes these create sad situations, acknowledging not only his illness and the loss of his wife, but also the losses that Greg and Monica had experienced too, but from those dark places for him had sprung so much joy that it was fair to say no-one around the table today would have seen coming.

Chapter 53

One noticeable absence from the family gathering was Damian. Amanda had spoken to him a couple of days earlier assuring him the girls had arrived safely and were settled, but other than that, their conversation had been limited to practicalities, and if she was honest both of them remained a little tense, with neither making an attempt to delve into the state of their relationship. Some discussions were best held face-to-face, but the more thinking time she was allowing herself, Amanda realised this was not a discussion she was looking forward to, equally though not a discussion she could put off for too much longer.

Chloe had never been mentioned again, so Amanda had no idea whether she was still around or if whatever had been going on had finished, but in her mind, it was immaterial as it had merely provided the catalyst for her to review her own life and what she wanted going forward. Her dad had told her to follow her dreams, be happy and not put her life on hold, and the more she reflected on this for herself and the girls, she knew that she could not go backwards into her old routines.

With each passing day, America was feeling more like home and definitely more where her heart was, that heart slowly being opened more and more to her new family. As she weighed up the reasons for returning to the UK, she realised the balance was not in its favour. Apart from anything else, if she was to have a break from Damian, the prospect of being single in the village, coping with work and two small daughters was not something she would like to entertain. Money was thankfully not something she had to worry about as her dad had left her well provided for, so perhaps she could give up work for a while, but then what would she do with her time, and if anything, having no focus would make that position even more difficult.

'Hey, penny for your thoughts,' said Clara bringing Amanda out of her daydream. The BBQ was in full swing and the girls were enjoying the attention and playing happily with Lisa and their new uncles, who were both acting like big kids themselves.

'Oh, I'm not sure they're worth that much' replied Amanda. 'If I'm honest, I'm thinking about Damian.'

'Is everything okay, are you missing him?'

'No, and that's the problem…… I think we've come to the end of the line and I'm not sure what the next steps are. I'm dreading the thought of going home and having to face up to it all.' Clara was fully aware of what had been happening with Damian, so this came as no surprise to her, but until now had been careful about offering her counsel. The more she saw and heard though, the more she supported her cousin in the direction she was thinking. Staying in any relationship that did not feel right was not the answer, and if trust had gone then that was one of the most difficult components to repair or replace, especially if there was no desire or imperative to try.

'Why don't you think about a break and stay here for a while longer? I'm sure there would be no argument from Rob on that front, and I'm equally sure he'd have the right connections to work through the legalities of visas and everything for you and the girls if you needed him to.'

'You don't know how tempting that is, but I'm not sure it's that easy. I'm sure Damian would have something to say about me keeping the girls from him, regardless of what his thoughts were towards me.'

Lisa wandered over and joined the conversation, wrapping a towel around herself to get dry, 'Can I join in, or am I disturbing you? I need to catch a breather as the girls are exhausting me. I think I'm going to develop webbed feet I've been in that pool for so long.'

'With pleasure,' said Amanda, 'I'm just having a bit of a down moment, thinking about the future and mulling over my options.'

Like Clara, Lisa was fully aware of the situation and although her and Clara had not spoken about it their views were similar. Lisa had always been friendly with Damian, principally for Amanda's sake, but if truth be told he was not someone she had a great affinity with. She suspected for some time that things were not as rosy as her friend made out, but as she had always kept her emotions quite close, it was only supposition on Lisa's part, but a feeling based on years of experience untangling the legal threads of families going through similar situations.

'How about I go and get us some food and we can chew this one over?' offered Clara. 'I've no doubt the three of us can resolve anything!'

As she walked in the direction of the BBQ, Lisa watched her go, feeling a confused mix of admiration and desire, both of which she was feeling difficult to handle or to hide.

Amanda watched her friend curiously, 'Am I missing something here? Is there something going on between you two that you're not telling me about?'

Lisa turned to Amanda embarrassed to have been caught out, 'Oops, no sorry about that, but I think your cousin is hot. She's gorgeous. Was it that obvious?'

'Only to me,' laughed Amanda, pleased to have been lifted out of her gloom. 'You'll have to get to know her. I'm sure you two would get on like a house on fire. And more importantly there's no-one on the scene at the moment, so your timing is brilliant.'

'As if, she wouldn't give me a second glance. A dwarf brunette compared with a blonde Goddess,' chuckled Lisa, always conscious of the fact she was only shoulder height even with her heels on.

'You're gorgeous, stop putting yourself down. In fact, you're both similar in so many ways. I think I can feel a bit of matchmaking coming on here. That will definitely keep me distracted from thinking about Damian!' smirked Amanda just as Clara was returning with plates of food in her hand and Will in her wake carrying a tray of drinks.

'I think I'll join you if that's okay. Rob and Monica are in deep discussion about something or nothing, but it looks like they don't want disturbing, and as I've no intention of getting wet, I'll sit over here and find out what you ladies are up to. In my line of business, it pays to keep up with fashions and trends, and you three are clearly in my target market. In fact, I should employ you and steal your design ideas as you all look fabulous as usual,' he flirted shamelessly.

Will's business in designer leisurewear was still taking up most of his time, but recently he had started to step back and delegate more. Rob's health scare had really shaken him up, giving him the wake-up call he needed to get his own work-life balance sorted. He had even started to get out more, with a view to potentially dipping his toe in the dating market again when the time was right. No hurry though, he certainly did not want to make any hasty or costly mistakes again.

'Well, I'm already spoken for as my newspaper won't edit itself, but Amanda or Lisa might be game,' laughed Clara.

'Not me either, I'm afraid, my legal career doesn't allow much time to draw a bath let alone design an outfit,' chirped in Lisa, enjoying the banter. 'My fashion sense isn't that great either; no, your best bet is Amanda. In fact, she's even got the qualifications, so no need to waste time or money on training her.'

'Ha, ha. Yes, although I studied History of Art at university, to be fair most of my teaching since then has been around the fashion and design aspects. I found that a lot more stimulating to teach than art history, and much more up my street,' spoken with a lightness of tone that showed she loved her work.

'Well, that's sorted then. Amanda, when can you start?' laughed Will, joining in with the spirit of the conversation, but as he watched her reaction, he could almost see cogs whirling around in her head, sensing that there was more going on in there than met the eye. It was not what she said, more the way she looked when she spoke, almost dreamlike.

Will knew that now was not the right time as today was all about relaxing and having fun, but if he had read her body language correctly, and he prided himself on that particular skill, there was definitely a discussion waiting to be had at a later date. He was excited at the prospect.

Chapter 54

Over the following weeks as summer drew to a close, a comfortable routine developed around the household. Rob and Monica fell into the role of doting grandparents, noticeably becoming more inseparable every day, subconsciously searching the other out whenever they were not in each other's company. They found endless things to talk about, even falling into the trap of finishing off each other's sentences as if they were an old married couple, not two people who had not seen each other for over thirty years.

Maisie and Alice were settled and had adapted well to their new surroundings, accepting their extended family as if they had always been there. They wanted for nothing, enjoyed being totally spoiled by everyone they came into contact with, and managed to delight everyone with the joy they found in all their new experiences. They were flourishing in the sunshine and had even learnt to swim, albeit in Alice's case it was still very much doggy paddle.

The new term was only a couple of weeks away and Maisie was getting excited about starting school, and looking at how much she had grown over the summer in height and confidence, she was definitely ready for it.

Amanda's health continued to improve, restoring back both her strength and energy, resulting in her becoming fidgety, but more importantly in need of a purpose. She had been waited on hand and foot by Mrs. Reilly, and had appreciated being pampered by everyone else whilst she was recuperating, but now looked towards reinstating her independence and finding something fruitful to occupy her time, other than simply relaxing by the pool or getting lost in a good book. She knew she was not suited to being a lady of leisure, having worked every day since graduating, and although she was not missing teaching per se, she was starting to miss the challenge it gave her. Technically she was still on a career break, but she knew that could not continue much longer, and in her heart sensed it was time to throw herself back into work.

But the danger of having time on her hands was more time to think, and recently those thoughts had drifted to whether teaching was something she really wanted to continue or whether it was time for a change. Will had really spooked her with his flippant offer of a job, but the more she thought about it, the more a new challenge seemed to appeal. He had not brought the subject up again, so she was sure he had only been joking, but the comment had sparked her imagination about all the possibilities and permutations with the skill set she had. Art, Design and Fashion were her passions and a career to meld these was something that could present a real possibility. Just where to start?

She knew she had to focus on making some tough decisions about her future and above all face the possibility that it might not involve Damian, other than as the girls' father. He had spoken to the children frequently over the last few weeks, always relaxed and happy to hear their news, but on no occasion had he suggested he fly over and visit them, or make any move to meet their extended family. Amanda had hinted at it a couple of times, but as there was a distinct lack of interest, and always something more pressing at work, she had not pushed too hard. The girls did not seem to be concerned, and if she was honest, she was not sure she wanted or needed to see him either, or how his presence would change the dynamic; this feeling of ambivalence leaving her certain she needed to make a change in her life. They had certainly drifted apart, but neither seemed bothered to stop the drift or attempt to close the gap.

She continued to surprise herself how openminded she had become as each new aspect of her life unfolded or change presented itself. Never normally a risk taker, Amanda was amazed at how her attitudes had shifted and how willing she now was to seek out and embrace what life had to offer. Those solid foundations she had felt were unmovable were now gently rocking; leaving the concept of her marriage crumbling not only plausible, but highly likely, something she would never have previously thought possible.

She realised now how much she had just 'settled' for a comfortable marriage, head down and blinkers on. They had been together for around ten years, married for nearly eight of these, during which time she and Damian had established their routines and simply got on with life. They were good parents to their children, both working hard in their careers, sharing the domestic chores and responsibilities, but somewhere along the line they had become stale as a couple, too relaxed in the status quo, both seemingly unprepared to rock the boat or challenge what they had.

But Amanda now recognised the spark had long since gone for both of them, and if she was right about Chloe that spark had gone even earlier for Damian, seeking out his excitement elsewhere. No, for Amanda settling no longer seemed a good option. Still not thirty-five, there had to be more to life, and recent events had demonstrated that beyond anything else.

In terms of the rest of the picture, there was no clear path visible at the moment, just a jumble of moving pieces roaring around her head; each having its own weighting on the debate. The people that were important to her: principally her daughters, and with Maisie starting school shortly that was a key focus; her mum and her new found friendship with Rob; Rob and her half-brothers, who she had got attached to against all the odds; her grandad left back in England, pondering what has become of his family; the many friends who had been there to support her. These were her priorities. But also, the practical issues: where would she live and call home, clearly not with Damian; what would she do as a career? Thankfully she was financially independent and had property in her own name, but protecting that should she and Damian divorce would also present a challenge, let alone a debate over custody of their children, which was one certainty she would not compromise on.

The events of the last year had provided a real catalyst for change. Having set out on the journey with no real expectations, other than to find her biological father and let him know she existed, the 'so-what-happens-next' was something she had never really factored in. Her dad had written about inevitable consequences should she embark on her search, without himself having any concept of what these might be, but now Amanda accepted in the early days she had not only been naïve, but blind to this as a reality.

Recently though, she had mulled over what could have been going through her dad's mind when he wrote his letters. She recalled his interests in genetic diseases and the risks to both her and his granddaughters of not knowing their true gene pool, but that could not have been his only motivation. The deeper she thought about it, the more she sensed he recognised her unhappiness long before she did, hence imploring her to follow her dreams. But as each event unfolded, and her feelings towards Rob strengthened, it left Amanda questioning what price she was willing to pay to achieve those dreams, and find the life her dad clearly had wanted for her.

The picture had become even cloudier when she met Will for lunch around ten days after the BBQ. He had invited her out to a swish restaurant on the quayside on the pretext of exploring her thoughts and plans about her future, offering to act as a sounding block to help get these into focus. But after a long and searching discussion, he ended up confusing her further by seriously offering her a dream job that would not only allow her to tap into her creative side, but provide her with a career change that would establish her as a fashion designer, albeit initially a trainee, with his financial backing and support. He had even said he was prepared for her to work from the UK if that helped, with occasional travel to America whenever necessary. What more could she ask for?

The time had come for decisions and actions, and whilst she valued the inputs of Clara and Lisa, who incidentally she noticed were spending a lot more time together and seemingly enjoying each other's company, she had a good sense of what each would say - neither being shy in offering their inputs so far. She was sure they would encourage and support whatever made her happy, their responsibility and loyalty clearly with her and not Damian. Both would be there to help her manage the fallout whichever way this went and their unconditional support was something she had no doubts about whatsoever, in fact it was the clearest thing in her mind.

No, she needed to get some time alone with both her mum and Rob for their insights. They were critical to whatever decisions she made, and theirs was the support and approval she needed, whichever path she chose.

Chapter 55

The flight back to Heathrow was not something Amanda had looked forward to, but knew was inevitable. The summer had come to an end and it was time to go home and face her future. The last few months had literally been life changing, not only for her, but for Rob and the wider family who were all impacted by what they had gone through.

For Rob, there was now hope where previously there had been none, now a family that he would have the time and energy to get to know and enjoy, and rekindled friendships that he valued more than he realised. He had not recognised how much he had missed the friendship of Will and others down at the sailing club, but more so was his friendship with Monica that had developed in a way he never thought possible. If ever he had a reason to live it was now; the years of bad health, self-enforced isolation and mourning were behind him. Life was there to be lived and he had every intention of doing so.

For Amanda, now fully recovered and physically fit to fly, she knew that although she could have thought of numerous excuses to stay, the time had come to go back home and face the music and more importantly Damian. She had a life ahead of her that could not be put on-hold indefinitely. Staying coddled in the safety and security of Rob's home was no longer an option and whilst she had hoped to stretch out the stay to encompass the Labor Day weekend celebrations, Maisie was desperate to start school and she could not deprive her of that. Eventually in the last week of August the flights were booked, cases packed and the long journey home, and back to reality began.

Brad had insisted on driving everyone to the airport, but he was not alone. Jane accompanied him anxious to see that Monica was alright. Her and Rob had enjoyed a farewell meal the previous evening at a romantic quayside restaurant, and although nothing had been said directly, Jane suspected that there was more to their friendship than anyone was admitting. Jane had enjoyed having her sister close for the last few weeks, appreciating spending quality time together and allowing her sister the space to talk and grieve. She noticed though how youthful and relaxed Monica became whenever she was around Rob, and how attentive Rob was in return, but sensed Monica was treading cautiously, presumably unable to accept as a recent widow she was deserving of happiness again. No doubt balancing familiar feelings of love and grief for Ken, with feelings for Rob that made her act and feel like a teenager again was obviously something she was struggling with.

Clara had also offered to drive to the airport to see the group off. She was going to miss them all, but more than anything she was going to miss Lisa, who over recent weeks she had developed strong feelings for. Clara, normally one to hold back and be cautious is terms of relationships, ever fearful of commitment, was taken aback not only by the suddenness of her feelings for Lisa, but also how strongly these developed over a relatively short period of time. She had never understood love at first sight, believing it to be the product of fairy tales or romantic novels, but there was something indescribable about how she felt.

She had not really noticed Lisa until the night of the BBQ when they had been having a laugh at Amanda's expense over the designer's job Will was trying to tempt them all with, but the more she watched and listened to her, she was captured not only by her wit, her intelligence or her sense of fun, but the allure of her eyes. They were the smoothest brown she had ever seen, almost like melted chocolate, that just drew her in, making her feel that Lisa was reaching deep down into her soul, not only reading her mind but playing tricks with her senses. Lisa intuitively knew she was being watched, and as she smiled back, her eyes lit up in a way that had Clara instantly hooked.

Lisa later admitted to Clara that she had been smitten from the first time she saw her walk into Rob's hallway, but uncertain of the situation had stayed in the background, too embarrassed to make her feelings known. Normally not lacking in confident or afraid of getting a pushback, she had felt Clara was well outside her league, so had resigned herself to just admire from afar and safe from humiliation. For Clara to make the first move had consequently left her both speechless and delighted.

They had met casually a couple of times since the BBQ within a group, but each time the electricity between them became more charged. Within the week, Clara had invited Lisa back to Boston for a night out to meet her friends. She stayed over, invested in a toothbrush and neither of them had looked back since or spent a day apart. Lisa had even extended her holiday, initially only intending to stay a couple of weeks with Amanda and the girls, but with more of a reason to stay she had been in no hurry to return to the office.

Now that she was going back though, she too had to give some serious thought to her future. With Clara it did not feel like a holiday romance, but more substantial with a potential longevity that left her questioning her life choices. As with Amanda, she had some serious thinking to do over the coming weeks, but one thing was certain, she was optimistic about the future.

'Right then, hugs all around,' said Amanda to Maisie and Alice as Brad lifted the luggage onto a trolley for them. There were definitely more bags on the homeward leg than there had been coming out, he thought to himself, mainly filled with toys and presents he suspected. Everyone had spoiled the girls, and although a lot was being left at Rob's for their next trip, most of the presents were heading home, the girls unable to be parted from them.

'Have a safe journey and message when you get home,' said Jane as she hugged Monica, unsure when she would see her again, but hopeful it would not be too long. She suspected as with Lisa, Monica had a reason for returning, even if she was not prepared to admit it to herself yet.

Jane watched on as Clara and Lisa embraced as they all said their final goodbyes and walked towards check-in. She was happy to see her daughter so content with Lisa, who over a short time she had grown to like, but equally concerned how their relationship would develop with an ocean between them. When she had met Brad all those years ago in Manchester, she had similarly felt heartbroken when he had initially returned home, unsure if his feelings would last once normality returned, but when he returned and proposed to her a few weeks later, her decision to marry him and emigrate to a new land had been her easiest one ever.

As she waved the family away with tears in her eyes, she wondered whether her daughter would have a similar fate and what the future held for all of them.

Chapter 56

Damian had met them at Heathrow as planned. The atmosphere Monica noted, had been a little tense in the car as they drove her home, but she tried not to read too much into it. She and Rob had spoken with Amanda at length the previous week so knew where her daughter's mind lay, so rather than say something she later regretted, she remained quiet in the back seat with the girls until the car pulled alongside her house just under a couple of hours later. She was tired from the flight, so forcing conversation was not top on her agenda anyway, but also the journey gave her space for her own thoughts.

Leaving Rob had proved more of a wrench than Monica had imagined, never really appreciating how close they had become until it was time to say goodbye. She remembered the gentle kiss at the restaurant as their lips met, the way he tenderly held her in his arms and the searching look in his eyes as her taxi pulled away. They had talked non-stop it seemed for weeks, but still there was so much left unsaid, questions never asked or answered, feelings never truly explored.

They had talked about meeting up again soon, but was it a friendship they wanted or were they ready for something more? Both had loved and lost, but was either of them ready to risk trying again at this stage of their lives? That was the question neither had dared to voice.

Lisa had arranged to get a connecting train from the airport to Bristol, so equally had time on her hands to reflect on what had been a crazy few weeks; not quite the holiday she had anticipated when Amanda had originally invited her out to help look after the girls. She had never imagined how things would pan out, certainly never factored falling head-over-heels in love, or meeting someone she potentially wanted to spend the rest of her life with into the bargain. Lisa had never been serious about anyone, or even met someone she wanted to spend more than the odd night or weekend away with, but Clara had changed her perspective completely, so now she just needed to work out what her next move was and what she truly wanted.

Clara was equally astounded by how fast their relationship had developed, feeling as Lisa did that this was the start of something meaningful for both of them. They had talked about the trials of a long-distance relationship, and agreed that neither of them wanted that, but at the same time both recognised that it was not as simple as throwing caution to the wind and crossing the ocean lock, stock and barrel. They needed space and distance to test their relationship, to work out what a long-term solution could look like, and then plan around that. Both were independent professional career women, with responsibilities that could not just be disregarded, and both were sensible enough to know that their whirlwind romance needed to develop some depth before any lasting commitments could be made. Time would tell, but the signals they gave to each other before they parted, and the words they exchanged left neither of them feeling this was not real.

Damian had been delighted to see the girls and listened as they chattered in the car all the way home, each trying to outdo the other for their father's attention, easing the pressure on Amanda to make conversation. Seeing Damian again after so long apart had left her confused, the feelings of ambivalence she had expected were replaced with an emotion she could not quite identify. He had obviously made an effort when collecting them all, prepared with drinks and snacks for the journey, ensuring nothing was a problem; courteous and patient with Monica and the girls and relaxed with Amanda. He had obviously made an effort with his appearance too, wearing clean chinos and a blue shirt she did not recognise, and had even grown a close trim beard, which she had to admit quite suited him.

As they drove, Amanda watched the familiar scenery, the fields and farmlands showing familiar signs of the harvest going on all around them, cereal crops being cut for transportation to market or for processing, bales of hay stacked along the waysides waiting to be taken for storage, tractors dragging trailers carrying their spoils, spilling the odd potato and spewing clods of wet earth behind them as they meandered down the country roads at their own speed, regardless of the cars stacking behind them. Driving in the countryside was an artform, with patience a virtue.

Beeping the horn got you nowhere fast, so years of experience told you just to relax and enjoy the ride.

Although she had loved being by the sea, had enjoyed the gentle breezes and marvelled at the brightness of the light created by the sun as it gleamed off the water, now back among the rolling hills of the Cotswolds it was evoking deeper feelings for home than she realised she had. This was her home and against her better judgment, she felt like she had come home.

The house felt different too, much cosier than she had remembered after the enormity and openness of Rob's home. Rob's had been professionally decorated some years earlier in very traditional New England styles, very nautical in its appearance, blues and whites dominating the colour scheme, with clean lines and uncluttered surfaces. The windows had blinds shading the indoors from the strength of the sun, and although it did not lack warmth, it lacked any feminine or personal touches.

Here felt much more autumnal with its russet-coloured sofas, cream carpets, all complemented by the bright colours and patterns of the cushions and curtains. The shelves and cabinets proudly displaying the books, photos and trinkets that summed up their life and the happy memories they had shared as a family, with toys tidied neatly away in boxes around the room ready to be dragged out at any opportunity. It was very much a lived-in house, with a family at its heart, whereas Rob's felt more like checking into a five-star hotel, glamourous, comfortable but very stylish, with the décor giving little if any clues about its owner. Two completely different styles to complement two completely different lifestyles.

Damian carried their bags indoors leaving Amanda to settle herself. As she wandered from room to room, sub-consciously touching the occasional piece of furniture or ornament, her feelings once again becoming disorientated. The girls took no time in opening their bags and displaying their presents to their dad, who sat down on the floor with them anxious to hear all about their time away. Amanda watched his face as he listened intently, pleasantly surprised to see how he engaged with them. Gone was the indifference she had experienced on the video calls, replaced by a real interest in what they were saying and the people they were excitedly talking about.

'I have missed you all so much, but it sounds like you've had a great time,' said Damian, with a smile that showed he was really engaging with them as they spoke. He pulled the girls into his arms cuddling each with a genuine sensitivity and added, 'I think I'd like to come with you next time if that's okay. I've heard so much about everyone and I can't wait to meet them. Shall we ask mummy and see what she thinks?'

In saying that, he turned towards Amanda and as their eyes locked, his searched deep into her soul, with a look that summed up so many emotions and questions, feelings they had not been able to speak about over recent months. It was a look that spoke volumes. Not only did it say I'm sorry, or seek to be forgiven, but most importantly it was a look that declared above anything else, I love you and want you in my life. Please give me a second chance.

Amanda recognised the look, understanding its meaning as clearly as if he had screamed it from the rooftops. She knew it would take some time to fully process what she was feeling at the moment, or where her life was destined, but without saying a word, she smiled encouragingly and then said, 'That would be nice.'

Chapter 57
Nine months later

The sun was shining, the sky was clear blue now the ominous clouds that had hung over the village for the last couple of days had finally cleared, leaving a crisp late spring morning which augured well for a lovely day ahead. Although there was still a bit of a nip in the air, which was a little unusual for late May, the long winter was finally over and the bulbs had thankfully sprung back into life after their slumber. The promise of summer was just around the corner once again.

'Amanda are you nearly ready, the car will be here shortly and the girls are getting fidgety?' Damian shouted upstairs urging his wife to hurry up as he struggled to keep Maisie and Alice from making themselves dizzy, so excited were they about what lay ahead. They had been up at the crack of dawn, for once not needing any encouragement to eat their breakfast or get themselves ready.

As she sat in front of her mirror applying the finishing touches to her make-up, Amanda reflected on how she had been in exactly the same position just over fifteen months earlier, then preparing herself both physically and mentally for the journey to the church to say goodbye to the dad she adored. Today was a similarly thoughtful time, but for completely different reasons. Where had that time gone, it seemed just a heartbeat away; but at the same time, so much had happened, not only in her life, but to the lives of those around her that it seemed like another lifetime.

No one could have imagined how prophetic her dad's words had been when he had urged her to seek out her biological father; there will be consequences and you need to be prepared to embrace them and live your best life, was what he had said. How true had that turned out to be thought Amanda as she headed to the door, stealing a final glance in the mirror, satisfied she had not smeared lipstick on her teeth. She picked up her pashmina and bag as she went out, quietly closing the door behind her.

'I'm coming now; Maisie, Alice will you both please calm down or you're going to be exhausted before you get there, and those beautiful dresses will be ruined,' she pleaded from the top of the stairs as she admired the tableau of her two little princesses ahead of her with Damian at his wits end in the middle of them. He looked very dapper she thought, dressed in an impeccably tailored suit, a crisp white shirt with a navy cravat that set off the colour of his eyes perfectly. Her heart ached with love every time she saw her daughters, but with each passing day the love she had had for her husband was returning, gently building back the trust and respect they had so nearly thrown away.

If nothing else, the last twelve months or so had taught Amanda how precious family was, but more importantly how precarious and fragile relationships can be. She now appreciated how much relationships needed time and space to grow, how they should be nurtured and not taken for granted, a trap both she and Damian now recognised they had inadvertently fallen into.

As Damian watched his wife descending the stairs, looking stunning in her pale blue chiffon dress, he recalled how terrified he had been at the thought of losing her, never truly knowing how perilously close he had come in reality to splitting up his family, and in the process condemning himself to the life of a part-time dad. How much would he have missed out on, not just seeing his children growing day-by-day and being part of their lives, but missing out on the love of his wife, a love that only now could he fully appreciate the strength of.

What a fool he had been, allowing his pathetic male ego to be piqued by the attentions of a much younger woman, and how easily he had allowed himself to be charmed and misguided into believing it was a risk worth taking. He remembered with shame the day Amanda had come to his flat to surprise him, and how that surprise had backfired so dramatically, leaving him so close to throwing everything away. Had Amanda not been there, then no doubt he would have been stupid enough to continue his affair with Chloe, but seeing Amanda and the hurt on her face had jolted him back into his senses, leaving him not only embarrassed but fearful of his future. He knew at that point the risks of carrying on were too huge to contemplate and knew he would do whatever it took to rebuild his family.

When Amanda had first returned from America, the atmosphere had been tense; each wary of the other, both knowing the inevitable discussion could not be put off any longer. All the time she had been away, they had skilfully avoided the subject, sensing a video call was not the right medium for dealing with such a sensitive topic.

Damian feared the extent of the damage he had caused, but felt incapable of doing anything about it with his wife thousands of miles away. He had considered jumping on a flight and facing it head-on, but was reluctant to cause further distress whilst his wife was recuperating, but also, he was anxious it could cause a scene that he would not be able to control or recover from. So, he bade his time and concentrated on putting his house metaphorically back in order at home, throwing himself into his work and clearing the decks as much as possible by delegating and appointing a team around him that he could trust, so that when they eventually returned, he could spend more time with his family and devote himself to the real priorities in his life.

Chloe was a distant memory, a huge mistake and not his proudest moment. Thankfully she had handed in her notice shortly after the incident so at least she was no longer around as a constant reminder of his stupidity. He would not be tempted into anything so reckless again; the stakes were too high, and it had been an expensive lesson to learn.

Damian had been honest eventually about his affair, but convincing Amanda that it was not as serious as it appeared had been a rough ride, so intent was she on believing the worst and that there was no coming back. Damian had managed to win her around gradually, piece by piece, but the damage it had done to their relationship was not an easy fix or a crack that could just be papered over. Patience and time were needed to fully repair the hurt, rebuild the trust, and above all re-establish the natural and easy friendship that had once been there. Thankfully they were both willing to try.

Each day felt a little less like treading on egg shells, but at no point did Damian feel complacent or take anything for granted. Amanda had given him a second chance, and he was determined he was not going to let her, himself or his family down ever again.

Chapter 58

As Amanda, Damian and the girls were getting into their taxi, Lisa was meeting Clara from the airport. They had known from the outset that a long-distance relationship was not a solution for them, so had spent the last few months working out what the future could look like. It had involved some serious soul searching and deep discussions, which was not always easy over the internet, both balancing challenging careers and having to deal with unwelcome time difference between them.

Being really open about what was important in their lives, weighed against what they were prepared to compromise on was the balance they had to strike, but as both were fully committed to their budding relationship, they found the planning fun and exciting, if a little exasperating at times. If nothing else, the debates they had reinforced their love for each other, both respecting and appreciating the values of the other, both entering the relationship as equals with their eyes wide open.

Above all, they had agreed they needed a base in one continent, with a bolt-hole in the other, because wherever they settled there would still be a need to travel for work commitments, apart from families to consider. Lisa's career was the ultimate deciding factor; working in family law was her passion and being qualified in English Law was not something that would easily transfer to the US legal system.

Clara as an editor was by comparison much more flexible, and once she started asking around and using her extensive network, had no difficulty finding a position working for one of the major British magazines as their fashion editor. She had spent ten years slogging away on the daily newspapers, so was excited about the challenges of the magazine industry, but to be heading up the fashion desk was something she could not wait for. It was for her the dream ticket.

'Oh my goodness, how much luggage have you brought with you! I thought you'd emptied your wardrobes last time you came over. We might need to rethink that apartment we've just committed to and get something larger!' remarked Lisa as she saw Clara struggling to push her over-ladened trolley with cases and holdalls perched precariously on top of each other.

'I'm pleased to see you too!' replied Clara taking Lisa into her arms laughing. 'I'd forgotten I hadn't emptied my closets at Mum's house too. I think I've got everything now; I just need to sort out what I want to keep, and what else I'm going to need to buy for your British weather. I don't think I even own an umbrella!' Both women had a great love of fashion, each having more clothes than they could ever need, so buying somewhere with enough wardrobe or closet space, as Clara was insistent on calling it, was something they certainly had not compromised on.

'Well, we can sort that out later, for now we need to get a move on or else we'll be late. I've booked us into a local hotel, so I suggest you can get showered and changed there before we set off, and hopefully the bedroom is large enough to store your bags in or we might have a problem,' she laughed in a mildly concerned manner. Some of these local country hotels have rooms that are not large enough to swing a cat in, and knowing what she had paid for it, she kept her fingers crossed they had been upgraded to something bigger than a cupboard.

'Great. Are Ben and Lucas staying there too did you say?' Clara had not seen much of them recently as both were in their final year, so deep in revision and exam preparations they rarely came up for air. Taking time out to visit the UK was not something either could easily afford the time to do, but equally neither was prepared to miss out. It would just mean a few more late nights' cramming when they got back.

Ben had been offered a conditional junior doctor's position in paediatrics at one of the teaching hospitals in Chicago starting in August, so was determined to get his grades. Lucas on the other hand was still considering his options, but equally determined not to let his brother outshine him. The business world still beckoned for him, and although there were a couple of internships he could probably walk straight into with his family connections, he was still unsure exactly what he wanted. Nevertheless, the competitive spirit remained alive in both of them and he was not going to rest on his laurels as far as his grades were concerned.

'Yes, they flew in yesterday morning with Will. Apparently, Ben and Lucas spent the night at Monica's, but they're at our hotel this evening. We'll get a taxi back together unless they wimp out early. I'm not sure what your mum and dad are doing though – have you heard from them?' asked Lisa.

'Don't worry, they arrived a couple of days ago. They caught the train up from London but not before Mum had spent a few days rinsing Dad's credit card around Harrods and Selfridges. What is it about Americans and London? Their hotel is a bit more upmarket than the one we're slumming in I think,' laughed Clara in a playful mood, conscious not to hurt Lisa's feelings. Accustomed to staying in large American hotels whenever she travelled on business, the thought of a small country Inn was something she was not too sure about, but Lisa had made it sound quaint and romantic, so she had decided to go with it. Looking at Lisa's reaction to her luggage though she was no longer sure.

'Mum messaged me from their hotel's Spa yesterday morning whilst Dad was on the golf course with Will and Rob. Apparently, they were all meeting up last night for dinner, which gave everyone the chance to meet Maria properly before today. Will, I understand is quite smitten with her. I'm happy he's finally found someone and is getting on with his life. Mum was planning on going to Monica's this morning and Dad was in charge of collecting Tom. According to Mum he's having the time of his life with all this attention' said Clara speaking ten to the dozen in an attempt to get all her news across in one go.

Both Lisa and Clara had always had a soft spot for Amanda's Grandad Tom so were delighted he had adapted so well to the sudden influx of American relatives he had got to know over the last few months as they came and went across the ocean at increasing regularity. Although now eighty-four he still had a lot of fight in him, and a lot to say for himself, so today was going to be memorable no doubt, but hopefully for all the right reasons.

When he had lost Ken, Tom realised that other than Monica, Amanda and the girls he had no other family left, so was determined to fall in with whatever made them happy. He had managed to outlive everyone, which was a sobering thought, and not one he really wanted to dwell on.

When Amanda had initially set out on her mission to find her biological father, Tom had harboured mixed feelings. He knew it was what his son would have wanted, but selfishly he realised his bloodline had come to an end, with the risks high that Amanda would seek and find a new life for herself, one that did not involve him. Tom, like Ken adored her and his grand-daughters, so the possibility of this was something he privately feared, and the longer Amanda remained in America after her surgery, the more anxious he became. Having her home and settled had been a great relief for him.

So now for them all to return, with such a positive outcome was something Tom silently said a prayer of thanks for each evening. Old age was bad enough, but loneliness was not something he intended throwing into the mix; hence he resigned himself to wholeheartedly going along with whatever faced him and whatever made his family happy. Life was for the living and hankering after what had been was not Tom's way of thinking.

Now standing at the back of the church with Monica on his arm, he was overwhelmed with so much genuine happiness he could not put it into words. Having never had a daughter of his own, he had never had the opportunity to give anyone away before, so being asked by Monica to do this for her had been a huge honour and privilege for him. He was convinced that somewhere among the congregation his son would be watching on, willing his family to find their own way forward, their happy ever after. They had a second chance at life and Tom was sure Monica was making the right decision and that wherever he was, Ken would be happy for her.

Chapter 59

At the other end of the aisle, Rob waited patiently as Monica approached him on the arm of her father-in-law. She was wearing a fitted oyster-pink three-quarter length gown that reinforced her still youthful figure. She looked as beautiful to him now in her mid-fifties as he remembered her all those years ago as a young girl. He counted himself the luckiest man alive. Not only had he found a daughter, two grand-daughters and been given a life-saving transplant, but somewhere among all that he had reconnected with Monica.

They had instantly struck up a deep and meaningful friendship, surprisingly so given the vast differences in both their lives and upbringings, but the speed with which that friendship had developed into a mature and profound love was astounding. They both realised after just a month of being apart, forced to rely on video calls and emails to keep in touch, that remaining simply as friends was not what they truly wanted; companionship was lovely and something they both valued, but their strength of feelings for each other left them wanting more.

Marriage after such a short period of time together initially seemed too huge a step, each fearing the other would not want to make such a big commitment, or their families and friends would have reservations, especially given Monica was so recently widowed, but when Rob built up the courage to propose, Monica did not hesitate to accept, with everyone else almost taking it as a given, sensing its inevitability.

Whilst she would never forget Ken, Monica had been given a chance to love again, something she would never have thought possible only the year before when the bottom had fallen out of her world and challenged everything she had held dear. Now with hopefully years ahead of them, she could not think of a better way to spend her life than with Rob by her side. She was sure Ken would both understand and approve.

When they had decided to get married shortly after meeting up again over the Christmas period, having Tom give Monica away was the first of many things they had immediately agreed upon. Tom had been the constant in Monica's life, and although he could have chosen to be difficult about them deciding to get married so soon after Ken's death, in reality he had embraced it and continued to provide whatever support he could give. Seeing the smile on his face now as he approached the altar, careful not to trip on the petals Maisie and Alice had strewn before them, you could almost sense the pride he felt, and the gratitude at being included in their special day in such an important way. As Tom placed his daughter-in-law's hand into Rob's, there was not a single dry eye in the church.

Chapter 60

'What a lovely service, and what a handsome couple they make,' remarked Will later in the day as he and Maria relaxed after the reception in the grounds of the Spa hotel talking with Clara and Lisa. The weather had behaved itself all day, and although there was a little nip in the air now, it was just about comfortable to sit outside, thanks to the patio heaters. 'And this hotel and grounds are amazing. We all had dinner here last night after an excellent round of golf, and the food was fantastic then too. I hear it's haunted though. I'm not sure if that's true or just the marketing blurb that helps keep bookings up,' he laughed, gently patting Maria's hand.

He was feeling a bit more relaxed now that his best man speech was out of the way and had not been a complete catastrophe. He was not a particularly good public speaker, but had been delighted when Rob had asked him to perform the task.

He too could not believe his own good fortune over recent months, not only reconnecting with Rob, but finding his life had taken a surprising turn for the better. Everyone had said the secret lay in getting his work-life balance back, and although he had not initially fully subscribed to that concept, he now knew there was a lot of truth in it. Over the last nine months he had consciously stepped back from the business, and six months ago put a managing director in place to oversee the day-to-day operations of the business, leaving himself more time to do those aspects he enjoyed, but above all more time to relax and appreciate the simple pleasures in life. It was early days and he was still taking baby steps in terms of letting go, but with each day it was becoming easier.

He had met Maria in the local supermarket of all places, both looking for inspiration in the frozen food aisle about what to have for their respective dinners. Maria was the principal at one of the local high schools and had just finished a drawn-out parents' evening that had overrun, so had called in looking for something quick and easy to put in the microwave before collapsing into bed after a stressful day. She lived alone now that both her children had grown-up and flown the nest, so only had herself to worry about, apart from her cat Tinker, who was a relatively self-sufficient and independent tabby who was happy, provided fresh food and water were left out for him daily.

They had struck up an unlikely conversation, laughing after they had both reached for the identical item at the same time, knocking over a display in the process, sending boxes and tins flying down the aisle. It ended up in neither of them buying any groceries, just heading straight to a local Italian restaurant for a pizza and a half decent bottle of wine to drown their embarrassment. It was all very low key and relaxed; Will dressed simply in jeans and a polo shirt, with Maria still in her smart grey suit and polka-dot blouse wearing her sensible shoes and carrying her bulging briefcase, neither concerned or conscious about what they looked like.

Will had not wanted to come over as pretentious or showy, so had played down his business interests and lifestyle, preferring instead to spend time listening to the anecdotes Maria was telling him about life in the classroom and the challenges of dealing with so many adolescents on a day-to-day basis, or worse still their pushy parents. Having never had children himself, or ever acted in a parental role of any sort, Will could not offer too much in support, or contest her theories on why people acted like they did, but nevertheless found her entertaining and witty at the same time; easy company to be with.

Physically she was not his usual type, much more petite than the more statuesque women he had previously dated and even gone onto marry, with a clear complexion that suggested she was not fixated on her looks. She had dark wavy hair casually tied back in a clip, with the odd grey hair on show that suggested she did not angst about her appearance either. He would guess her age somewhere in the early to mid-fifties if asked based on the things she spoke about, but on looks alone no more than mid to late forties. So definitely not the young, trophy, high maintenance blonde model that was more his usual downfall.

After that initial pizza, they agreed to meet again as friends, and over a couple of months met several times each week for dinner, or to go to the cinema, or simply for a walk in the park to get some fresh air after a long day. Will opened up a little about his recent divorce and his business, whilst Maria spoke about how her husband had divorced her when the children were young, leaving her to raise them by herself. He had supported them financially for a few years, but that had dried up once his new wife and subsequently a baby had come onto the scene. Listening to her speak, it was obvious she had had a few tough years and life had not been a bed of roses by any stretch of the imagination.

Faced with being the main bread winner, Maria had been forced to go back to work full time. She had thrown herself into her career to make a good living for herself and to support her family, gradually rising through the teaching grades until she was eventually appointed as a principal three years previously. It was a role she loved and a profession she felt committed to.

Neither was looking for a relationship, but the chance of some companionship and a bit of a social life was a luxury they both recognised and welcomed with open arms.

When crossing a busy road one evening after walking through the park, Will instinctively reached for Maria's gloved hand to navigate the traffic. The sun was just setting and the late autumn air had a nip in it, showing signs that the winter was on its way. They continued to walk and thought nothing of it until arriving at Maria's house sometime later to realise they were still holding hands. It felt comfortable and as their hands let go neither felt embarrassed. Will went to give Maria a gentle kiss on the cheek as he said goodnight, but anticipating it, she turned towards him and instead their lips met. They stared into each other's eyes, trying to read what was happening, neither sure of the next move, but both sensing that somewhere along that short walk home the dynamic in their relationship had inexplicably changed for the better.

The business had also taken on a different perspective for Will too. Amanda had eventually decided to accept his offer and had started working with him shortly after she returned from America. She had handed her notice in at the college and taken the plunge into the unknown world of business. She was still learning the ropes, but some of the designs she had come up with so far were really promising, moving the children's range into a whole new and interesting direction. She was working alongside some of his more established designers, but the feedback he was receiving was really encouraging.

As he sat there surrounded by family and friends, Will could not fail to count his blessings.

Chapter 61

Rob and his bride, the new Mrs. Mason, smiled as they approached their guests arm in arm. They were delighted that all their family were together, celebrating with them and enjoying their happiness. The last year or so had certainly been a whirlwind of emotions for all concerned, so it was reassuring to see that everyone had come out of the maelstrom unscathed.

Love and friendships had been found in some of the least expected places; Lisa and Clara a perfect example of that, closely followed by Will and Maria, and rekindled love in the relationship Damian and Amanda had fought to preserve. Following the conversation she and Rob had had with Amanda just before leaving America, Monica had feared that her daughter's marriage would not survive the return home, so intent was she in believing Damian had been unfaithful and that their relationship had run its course. To see them now, you would struggle to believe there had been problems with their marriage, and if Monica was reading the tell tail signs correctly, she was sure it would not be too long before Maisie and Alice had a little brother or sister to contend with. There was definitely a glint in her daughter's eye that she had not noticed for a long time.

Brad and Jane were staying over for a few days after the wedding to help Rob and Monica move into their new home. It was a luxury modern three-bedroom apartment in a lovingly converted period property that originally had been an old private hospital about five miles outside of the village, on the main dual carriageway heading west towards Bristol. It was a great location, accessible but well set back from the noise of the traffic, and in its own extensive grounds that backed onto open countryside. Monica had shown Jane around the apartment the afternoon after she and Brad had arrived from London when Rob had taken Brad and Will for the final fittings of their suits for the wedding, and Jane could understand why they had fallen in love with it. The current owner had agreed to rent it to them for three months whilst the conveyancing went through, but with the hefty deposit Rob had made, for all intents and purposes it felt like theirs already.

They were also keen to spend some time with Clara to explore the area where she and Lisa would be living. Jane had seen some initial photos of the waterside complex taken when they had initially made an offer on the property just after Christmas, but had not seen any recent ones as Clara was being cagey about the renovations they were having done. She knew they were planning on moving in in a couple of months, all being well, but hoped to get a sneak preview before they went home.

The property was in the centre of Bristol, and from the photos it looked amazing. Jane thought it looked very similar in style to the place Clara had rented in Boston, but the one in Bristol appeared much bigger. It was part of a residential complex that also had a gym and an indoor swimming pool in the basement that residents had access to, plus a coffee shop and bakery on the corner, with a private seating area and maintained gardens.

The apartment itself had three bedrooms, the master suite overlooking the quayside with an en-suite and spectacular views, then two smaller bedrooms that could easily act as guest rooms, but instead unbeknown to Jane were being converted into walk-in closets, one for each of them. Both had so many clothes and accessories that Lisa and Clara had agreed they did not want to spend their time arguing over who had which drawers or hanging space, so they had designed and commissioned identical closets that would be the envy of anyone visiting, and force whoever was visiting to book into the nearby Premier Inn or find alternative accommodation. They had agreed though on buying a big corner settee that converted into a king-sized bed should they decide that, by exception, the odd visitor could stay.

Lisa and Clara had finally got the keys the previous month and immediately got the workmen in to create their dream home. The builders thought it was hilarious and could not wait to get it finished and hand the apartment over to their clients, fingers crossed within the next few weeks all being well, always provided the young women did not add more to their ever-growing jobs list. The builders were also fitting out an area of the apartment as a joint office so that both could work from home if needed, with an old-fashioned partner's desk for them to share and state-of-the-art technology to enable them to communicate with their offices.

A lot of thought had gone into the renovation works and Lisa and Clara were so excited, neither at all anxious about the prospect of moving in together or buying their first home after such a short period of time together. They knew it was a gamble, with no guarantees, but nevertheless they were both adults and *nothing ventured nothing gained* was their attitude. For each of them it was the first time a relationship had felt so right. They were even prepared to stay in Lisa's rented house, cramped as it was, until everything was perfect, although secretly Lisa was starting to question this now after all Clara's luggage had finally arrived.

Rob and Monica had equally put a lot of thought into their new home and had already decided on most of the furnishings and fabrics, including arranging for the occasional item to be shipped over from Rob's house where they thought it would suit the new property, but there was still a lot to do before it was fully liveable and the keys were safely in their hands, however they were cautiously optimistic that everything would go through without issue.

Monica had always lived in a very traditional home with some of the antique furniture still around from when Ken's parents had lived there, so to be given a free rein by Rob in decorating such a modern and open space was so exciting and refreshing, although to be fair a bit daunting. They were still learning so much about each other, so Monica did not want to take for granted or assume that her style and tastes would be his too, hence she consulted him on most things. After all it was to be his home just as much as hers, even though Rob was buying it for her as his wedding present, wanting to ensure the property was in her name to avoid any complications with his estate should anything happen to him.

Rob felt better than he had in years, and although he knew that he would have to take immunosuppressants for the rest of his life to prevent his body rejecting the new kidney, this was a small price to pay for the second chance he had been given. However, there was always the risk that something could go wrong, so he insisted, knowing that Monica would need security in the event that anything happen to him at any stage. In his mind putting the property in her name was his way of giving her that reassurance.

After Rob's first wife Carrie had died, he had put his estate in order, mainly to avoid all the tax and financial worries that would have been unavoidable should anything have happened to him so suddenly too, but then after all the issues with his health it had seemed important to have everything clear. Anything else would have been a huge burden and an unnecessary worry for Ben and Lucas.

He had recently amended his will to provide for Amanda and his granddaughters too, and now with Monica as his new wife further provisions had been needed. Rob was a wealthy man, and along with his properties in the States, he held a considerable number of shares and investments, so having the clarity about what would happen to that was important to him and his family.

Monica, knowing what Rob's plans were for their future and the financial security she was being offered, and after speaking to her father-in-law Tom, decided to hand the family home to Amanda early. Apart from anything else, she had known from the outset that she wanted something more suitable for her and Rob to have as their UK base; somewhere not only that they could lock up and leave with minimal security risks or maintenance concerns when they travelled, but also somewhere where the memories of Ken did not linger around every corner or in every season as she tended the garden and watched the flowers he had so lovingly nurtured return each year. No, it was time to move on and live her life as Ken had requested, happy with her memories, but eager to make new ones.

Ken had left the house to Amanda anyway in trust under the terms of his will, so it was just a timing issue, and Monica knowing how happy she had always been there raising her family, recognised handing it down to the next generation was the appropriate thing to do. The house was an old Georgian property that was commanding in its beauty and stature in the heart of the village, but it needed attention and maintenance, neither of which she was able to do on her own, and not something she wanted Rob to have to take on.

Amanda was delighted to be given the house, the timing being perfect, and Monica was secretly quite excited to see how she would renovate it and bring it into the twenty-first century. Ken was never one for big renovation projects or fuss when it came to décor, always happy to leave things as they were, with the philosophy *that if it wasn't broken, then why fix it?* He had reluctantly agreed to central heating being installed twenty years earlier and kept on top of the general maintenance, but the rest of the house was quite traditional and retained a lot of its original features. Seeing it with some more modern twists through the eyes of her daughter was something she was looking forward to.

The family house would also give Amanda and Damian some much needed extra space, with its airy rooms and gardens, as well as providing the convenience of being in the centre of the village and close to the school now that Maisie had started in the reception class. There was also plenty of room to create an office for Damian, allowing him the opportunity to spend more time working from home and less time commuting to the city, plus a spare bedroom that could easily be converted into a private space or office for Amanda to work out of, with great light and views over the fields at the rear of the property. She hoped that space would give her the inspiration she needed when designing her new range of Children's leisurewear.

Once Amanda had made her decision about accepting Will's job offer, she had had no regrets at all about leaving teaching or venturing into the relatively unknown world of fashion. The career change meant she had a lot to learn, but in challenging herself she found she was considerably more fulfilled as an individual, getting that much needed buzz from her work she had never previously experienced, of if she had it had been lost in the noise years ago.

Although she missed her pupils and the processes she had employed to nurture their talents, she was now revelling in having her own talents nurtured by the team of professional designers Will had assigned to support and mentor her. She was working with a real eclectic team of people, ranging from the weird and wacky to the straight and conservative, where both extremes were challenging her thinking and creativity immensely.

Working from home had also given her freedom and independence, feeling she had not previously realised she was lacking so badly, plus the ability to balance her life and the lives of her daughters, with all the demands that made on her time with a job she loved.

Her new career, operating in a business world as opposed to academia, also gave her a perspective on life that she had not always appreciated, making her question her ethics on a whole host of topics that previously she had never fully explored; where materials were sourced, how they were manufactured, their costs and the importance of recycling on the environment, with growing pressures on the industry to avoid throw away fashion.

She was learning so much; regularly commuting to the States to meet with Will and the rest of the team was feeding her appetite to be a great designer, as well as giving her frequent opportunities for catching up with Rob and her half-brothers. She was also planning on accompanying one of the senior buyers on a business trip to the Far East and around Singapore to visit suppliers and discuss future requirements, an opportunity she would never have imagined had she remained in teaching.

After they were married, Rob and Monica had discussed splitting their time between the States and England, with their initial plan to spend summers and autumns in New England where the weather and sailing were good, and winters and spring in England, where the weather was milder and the flowers in bloom. Monica always loved springtime and the new life it brought, so being there to see the daffodils she and Amanda had planted bloom around the memorial stone at Ken's grave was important for her. They would act as a constant reminder of that new life and the promise of a brighter future each spring heralded.

Their first Christmas as man and wife though was going to be a proper family affair hosted by Amanda in her new house, with a proper tree and presents galore underneath it. Grandad Tom would be there, along with Ben and Lucas if they could arrange their holidays to get over, although they knew they were welcome anytime. Maisie and Alice, who were completely smitten by their uncles, were delighted to be moving into the new house and after having picked out their own bedrooms had promptly designated one of the spare bedrooms as Uncle Ben's and Uncle Lucas'.

They had all agreed though that summer holidays would be spent in New England where Amanda and Damian had a standing invitation, provided they brought the girls, as neither Rob nor Monica wanted to be parted from their grand-daughters longer than was necessary.

Damian had only been out to America once to visit Rob's home, but had no problem with the idea of holidaying there or even learning to sail, as Lucas was forever telling him how keen he was to teach him and his nieces. Maisie had mastered swimming now and Alice was not far behind her, both taking naturally to the water and hence in Lucas' eyes would make natural sailors.

The more Damian got to know the family, the more he liked everyone and felt comfortable in their company, but the more he appreciated how difficult a time Amanda had had in those initial months. He recognised the pressures she must have felt trying to balance the emotional demands and feelings of losing her dad, against those of finding her biological father, never wanting to let her feelings for him eclipse what she had felt for Ken, but at the same time being drawn towards Rob and what he stood for, knowing that you cannot fight love from whatever direction it hits you.

He now understood more the decisions she had taken about being a living donor, annoyed at himself for how selfish he had been at the time she had first mentioned this. How he had not been there to support her emotionally or physically, falling woefully short on the promises he had made her when they had married. By being a donor, he recognised now she had found a way to make a positive impact on someone's life; replacing the inadequacies she has so obviously felt when Ken had died, knowing all she could do then was look on helplessly. How that helplessness must have played with her mind, and instead of being there for her to unburden herself to, he had not just closed that door, but slammed it shut. Instead focusing all his attentions on his business, as well as allowing himself to be distracted by a meaningless affair.

Importantly he now recognised his many faults throughout all this time, accepting that not only had he not been there to fully support his wife, but that he had almost lost it all and failed her completely into the bargain, risking everything on the back of his fragile male ego. How close he had come to losing everything he perhaps would never know, but being given a second chance was something he would forever remain thankful for and would spend a lifetime protecting.

Chapter 62

As it got late, Amanda walked over to where Damian was standing, wistfully staring at some of the family now dancing as the hotel's resident pianist played. He had a smile on his face and from the look in his eyes his thoughts were in a happy place. She put her arms around him and smiled, grateful that they had rebuilt the intimacy they once had and rekindled the relationship she feared had been lost forever.

'Are you ready to get going?' She asked. It had been a long day and although she did not want to break up the party, she was beginning to feel tired. So far, she had not told anyone other than Damian that she was seven weeks pregnant as it was early days, but more importantly she did not want to detract any of the attention away from the newlyweds. She suspected though that her mum had guessed from a look she gave her earlier when she had passed on the wine at dinner, but she was not ready to confirm it yet. She would tell everyone in the next few weeks when she started to feel a little better, but for now she was ready for her bed.

'I am if you are and I can't tempt you into a quick waltz round the dance floor, but extracting our daughters might be another thing,' he laughed, seeing them both being jigged around by Lucas, one holding each of his hands. They were both like the proverbial Duracell batteries, going on forever, but he was sure as soon as they were in the taxi their eyes would shut.

'I'll pass on that if you don't mind,' Amanda replied, whispering gently, 'I think me and this little bump are ready for our bed.'

Looking around now at the end of what had been a truly wonderful celebration, Amanda saw not just a wedding party, but a family facing a more promising future than anyone would have ever dreamed of just a few short, but eventful months, previously.

For the first time she fully appreciated not just her actions and decisions, but the risks she had taken along the way to get her here. The consequences she had affected had provided second chances not only for her but for those she loved, providing memories to treasure, but just as importantly offering opportunities for many more memories to be created. There were no guarantees that everything would remain rosy in the garden for all concerned, with undoubtably more bumps along the road to be negotiated, but that was for another day and others to worry about.

She smiled to herself on a job well done, and knew that her dad would be smiling down on her from wherever he was. She had carried out his final wishes to the letter, with both her and her mum finding a way to move forward with their lives without ever forgetting the love they had, and would always have, for him.

But for now, it was time for her to put her feet up. Time to go home.

THE END

Printed in Great Britain
by Amazon